Ruthless Scars

JANE BLYTHE

Cover designed by RBA Designs

❀ Created with Vellum

Acknowledgments

I'd like to thank everyone who played a part in bringing this story to life. Particularly my mom who is always there to share her thoughts and opinions with me. My wonderful cover designer Letitia who did an amazing job with this stunning cover. My fabulous editor Lisa for all the hard work she puts into polishing my work. My awesome team, Sophie, Robyn, and Clayr, without your help I'd never be able to run my street team. And my fantastic street team members who help share my books with every share, comment, and like!

And of course a big thank you to all of you, my readers! Without you I wouldn't be living my dreams of sharing the stories in my head with the world!

A big thank you to Jeffrey who was my travel director when I visited Scandinavia and was such a help answering all my questions about the gorgeous town of Geiranger, which was my favorite place we stayed in which is why I decided to incorporate it into a book!

CHAPTER

One

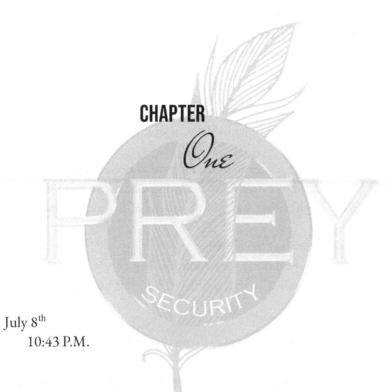

July 8th
10:43 P.M.

Being distracted on a mission was never a good thing.

Especially one that was so personal and had such high stakes.

Still, as hard as he tried Sebastian "Rock" Rockman couldn't seem to keep his head in the game.

It kept wandering.

To a time and place where everything had been perfect.

Until it wasn't.

Until one night that changed everything.

Ruined everything.

One moment of distraction, one grief-fueled encounter, one lie, and everything he loved, everything he wanted, was all gone.

Were there enough lives in the world to save to make up for the one he had taken? Was there any redemption for the pain he had caused the one person he loved more than life itself?

Although he had spent his entire adult life attempting to right his wrongs, assuage his guilt—not for himself, but with the hope that one day he might have earned the right to go to the woman he loved and ask for forgiveness—so far he was yet to find redemption.

Forgiveness wasn't something he deserved or expected, but he craved it more than his next breath.

"Rock. Rock."

His name echoing in his ear drew his attention out of his own head and he blinked and realized that he'd zoned out.

Again.

There was no way his team wouldn't have noticed, and no way they wouldn't know that it was related to the woman he'd loved and lost. No. Not lost. That implied that something outside of his control had taken her from him.

That wasn't what had happened.

Even after what he'd done, he hadn't lost her love, it was only when his guilt led him to tell a lie that destroyed her that he threw away her love.

"Rock."

The fact that there was no chastisement in the voice that called his name only made it worse.

His team was making allowances for him because they knew his head wasn't in a good space lately. Not that it had been for the last fifteen years, but these last couple of days, when he learned that the woman he had been fighting for, the only way he knew how, for fifteen very long years was already right under his nose, he couldn't think of anything else.

Which wasn't acceptable.

Especially when his team needed him to watch their backs.

Like they did right now.

Already, they were one man down since Axel "Axe" Lindon was back at the compound watching over his wife Beth.

Beth who had no memory of who she was.

Beth who had no memory of what had happened to her during the eight months she had been missing before randomly turning back up at the compound almost three months ago.

Beth who was counting on them to get her answers, get her justice, and make sure she felt safe so she could start healing from her ordeal.

Shoving thoughts of Ariel out of his mind, Rock focused his attention on movement close to the tiny, remote shack that was the closest thing to a lead they had been able to come up with.

A shack his team was currently approaching.

Almost half his life had been dedicated to his military career and then his job as the medic on Prey Security's Bravo Team. His entire adult life had been spent climbing into the depths of depravity as first his Delta team and now Bravo Team did what was needed to rid the world of evil, one monster at a time.

He knew a threat when he saw one.

Didn't hesitate to act on his instincts.

"Move out," he ordered into his comms, knowing his team would listen without questioning, their trust in one another implicit.

Focusing on the barely moving target, Rock fired.

There was no need to check to make sure the man he'd shot was dead. Snipers hit what they aimed at.

Instead, he scanned the area, searching for more tangoes. No way did a man like Leonid Baranov send a single person to take care of a problem. The Russian oligarch was wealthy, powerful, and a sick pervert who spent most of his time buying and selling people on the black market. From slaves to work in his home, cooking and cleaning for him, to young women—and, according to some reports, boys as well—to service his deviant sexual needs.

It was Leonid Baranov who had effectively ended Rock and his team's Delta careers almost five years ago when he painted targets on their backs after they managed to get close enough to him to raid one of his properties. In that same raid, they'd found Beth, and it was no coincidence that right around the time Beth was taken for the second time, Leonid disappeared, going completely off radar to the extent that even Prey, with all their resources, was unable to track him.

Only four survivors of Baranov's house of horrors had ever lived to tell what had happened to them. One was Beth, and two others were women Rock and his team had rescued along with Beth. One had been unable to live with what had been done to her and had taken her life not long after being reunited with her family. The other had been given a new name and disappeared.

The fourth was a man.

Taken as a young boy, abused for years, somehow, he had managed to escape and now lived with only one purpose.

Destroying his abuser.

The man—who refused to give them his name—had arranged a meeting with them when they started actively looking for Baranov a few weeks ago after they learned the man had gone off the radar around the same time Beth was kidnapped the second time.

This little hunting shack was where the meeting had been arranged. Somehow, Baranov must have kept tabs on the man who had escaped his clutches. Why he hadn't just recaptured him Rock didn't know. Or maybe it was reaching out to Prey that had put the man back on Baranov's radar.

Whatever the reason, Baranov knew Bravo team was here, and he'd sent in men to take care of the problem.

Problem for Baranov was that Bravo Team was smarter, stronger, quicker, and had all the motivation in the world to destroy him. Beth might be Axe's wife, but she was family to all of them. A baby sister who they would do anything to protect. They'd failed her once, it wouldn't happen again.

There.

Right by the shack, someone attempted to follow Gabriel "Tank" Dawson and Patrick "Trick" Kramer.

Rock aimed, adjusted for the slight breeze and fired.

The man dropped.

Although he scanned the area carefully, he couldn't find any more targets, so he eased himself up. "Got them both," he told his team. "One was coming from the cabin, doubt our guy is still alive in there."

"Only one way to find out," Mason "Scorpion" Markson said.

On the way down to join his team by the shack, Rock stopped to check on the two men he'd taken out. Not to ensure they were dead, the bullets he'd fired between their eyes had taken care of that, but he wanted confirmation they were Baranov's men.

The brands seared into the left palms of both men marked them as Baranov's.

"They were his," he said as he joined his team.

There were no heat signatures in the shack, which meant that either the man they'd come to meet was already dead or that he'd never been here in the first place.

"Set up?" Rafe "Panther" Neal asked.

There was no way to know if their guy had lured them into a trap. But his gut said no.

"I don't think so," Tank said. "You read his messages, he had one purpose in life, and it was bringing down Leonid Baranov. Don't think you can fake that kind of hatred."

Although they knew no one was in there—at least no one alive—his team was a cautious lot, and they entered the shack vigilantly. As expected, they found a body lying in the middle of the room. What they didn't expect was the computer equipment lining every wall and stacked into every available space.

"This wasn't just a meeting point, this was his home base," Panther said, awe in his tone as the tech geek turned in a slow circle, taking in all the equipment.

"Why ask us here? He was taking a huge risk," Scorpion said.

"Don't think we'll get any answers." Rock knelt beside the body. The man had been horribly tortured, his body a mess of blood, open festering wounds, and obviously broken bones.

"They were here for him, not us," Trick said. "If they were here for us, Baranov would have sent more than two men."

"So how did they find him? And why did they kill him now? Seems like too big a coincidence that he gets murdered just days after reaching out to us," Rock said.

"Any chance it's not him?" Tank asked.

Since he was closest, Rock reached out and unzipped the man's pants. As much as he didn't want to touch the guy's penis it was the only way to confirm.

Pulling it out of the dead man's boxers, he located the brand, burned into the man's flesh, right where Baranov marked his victims.

"It's him. This means someone knew where he was all along, and someone wanted to keep him from talking, but not kill us. How does that fit into Baranov's plans when we already know he has us marked for death?" Rock asked no one in particular because their one chance of getting some answers lay dead at his feet.

∼

July 9th
   6:52 P.M.

Ariel Emerson laughed at the text message that popped up on her phone. Leave it to her best friend to be able to cheer her up after a bad day.

Every day she was more and more grateful that she'd said yes when her colleague Tallulah "Tillie" Russel had reached out and asked for help.

All of her introvert, protect herself from pain at all costs instincts had screamed at her to decline, but in good conscience, she couldn't.

Now she was so glad she hadn't.

Tillie wasn't like other people. She was a little on the shy side herself, although you'd never know it if you heard the story of how she had refused to give in to a mafia boss trying to threaten her into backing down after she followed through on a report of abuse. Tillie had been prepared to give up everything, including her life, for the sake of the crime lord's six-year-old son.

Had come perilously close to losing her life.

While still recovering from the gunshot wound that had almost killed her, and balancing rebuilding her new life with the man she had fallen in love with, Tillie never missed an opportunity to reach out. Just a simple check-in from someone who cared about her meant more to Ariel than her new best friend could ever know.

Since they both loved books—were a teensy bit obsessed with them you might even say—Tillie had sent her a meme about ever-growing and never conquered to-be-read lists. It was just the laugh she needed after a rough day.

Being a social worker might be her calling, and she did love her job, and loved that she could make a difference in children's lives, but that didn't make it an easy job. Seeing the horrors that parents inflicted on their own offspring was always horrendous, and there were lots of days Ariel was sure she couldn't look at another damaged little soul, but no matter how bad it got or how hard it was, she would never walk away.

It was her penance.

Fifteen years was a long time to ruminate over the past, and she knew now that she was responsible for what had happened. If, by helping children when she could, it was possible to somehow even out the scales, then she would do it.

Besides, without the job she never would have met Tillie—or her boyfriend Tank who had become like a big brother to Ariel—and she really did like knowing she was helping kids who otherwise might lose their lives in the hell they were stuck in.

Just as her mood started to dip, her phone buzzed with another text. Another meme, this one about romance, their favorite genre, and another laugh chased away her grief before it could really dig its claws into her.

Whoever said time healed all wounds was a liar.

Typing out a quick reply, Ariel realized she was glad she had come tonight. She hadn't wanted to, hadn't wanted to deal with the noise at the bar or the guys who would inevitably hit on her, but her bestie had insisted it was what she needed. While she hadn't been so sure, cozy PJs, chocolate, and one of her favorite author's books were her usual go-to when she'd had a bad day and what she'd rather be doing right now, at least she'd get in a few laughs.

Maybe Tillie was right, and taking her mind off the mess one of her cases had turned into was for the best.

Feeling eyes on her, Ariel shifted uncomfortably. The last thing she wanted was to pick up a guy tonight. Okay, so it had been over a year since she'd last had a boyfriend, but dating was difficult for her. She couldn't trust, open herself up, or allow herself to be vulnerable with them.

Been there, done that, had the scars on her heart to prove it.

How much longer till you get here?

> Fifteen minutes tops

She sighed. Another fifteen minutes?

It wasn't like she was annoyed with Tillie. The woman was still recovering from her injuries, and Tank didn't like her to leave the safety of the compound where they lived very often. Not because the man was controlling—although he was definitely all alpha—but because the memories of how close he'd come to losing her were still too raw.

Knowing Tillie was coming to hang out with her, even though she was still supposed to be taking it easy and the noisy, bustling bar was not an easy place to do that, meant a lot to her. Their friendship was still brand new, and she wasn't quite used to having someone in her corner like that.

Still, maybe tonight just wasn't the right night for hanging out.

Truth was, Ariel just didn't think she could sit here for another fifteen minutes on her own.

> How about a raincheck?

> Don't you dare bail on me!

Her brow furrowed.

Something suddenly felt a little off.

Why was it so important to Tillie that they catch up tonight? Now that she thought of it, her friend had been acting a little weird for the last few days.

Was she just being paranoid or was something else going on?

> Tell me you're not leaving

> Why can't we just catch up some other time?

She watched as the dots danced, waiting to see what her friend would say. Someone was still watching her—after being mocked and bullied her entire senior year of high school, she knew what it felt like to be watched—but now she was more worried that this fledgling friendship with Tillie was already hanging in the balance.

> I need to talk to you about something

> Need to do it in person

That did not sound good.

Paranoia or not, it was never a good thing when someone said they needed to talk to you.

> Please trust me

> I'm your friend and I promise what I need to

> talk to you about is because I'm your friend

> I know how you are but you're my friend— best friend

> and I'm looking out for you

> Trust me, Ariel

> Please

Thing was, despite her paranoia and inability to let anyone get too close to her, she *did* trust Tillie.

At least enough to stay until Tillie got there to see what her friend needed to talk to her about.

> I'll be here when you get here

> Thank you! <3

Despite the trepidation sitting like a rock in her stomach, Ariel smiled at her friend's enthusiasm. Tillie had proven herself to be a loyal friend. Whatever she wanted to talk about couldn't be all that bad.

That smile faded as she realized that whoever was staring at her had yet to shift their gaze from her back.

Drawing up her courage, Ariel turned, intending to tell the man politely she wasn't interested, but instead, when she turned around all the air left her lungs in a rush.

The world narrowed down until it contained only one thing.

Him.

The man she had loved, the man she had been convinced she was going to spend her life with.

The man who had crushed her so thoroughly she still wasn't over it fifteen years later.

Tears blurred her vision.

Pure instinct took over, and as her fight or flight reflex kicked in, Ariel snatched up her purse and fled.

Outside, she stopped to drag in a few breaths, trying to feed her starving lungs.

How could he be here?

Was it a coincidence he'd turned up at a bar she rarely frequented right at the same time she happened to be there?

Did it have anything to do with what Tillie wanted to talk to her about?

No. It couldn't. She'd told Tillie a little about her past, but how would her friend even know Sebastian Rockman?

> Not feeling well
>
> Have to go home

After she quickly typed out the text to her friend, she turned off her phone. Knowing Tillie, her friend would know something else was going on. Later, she'd explain everything, but now she just needed to get home as far away from Sebastian as she could get.

Just as she shoved her cell phone into her purse something moved behind her.

Before she even knew what had happened, a bag was thrown over her head, and she was being pulled backward by at least two sets of hands.

Shock immobilized her for what felt like an eternity before common sense returned, and she began to fight against the hands that she already knew weren't just dragging her away from the bar, but away from life.

She wasn't stupid.

She knew that she was being taken for a reason, and that reason didn't include letting her live.

"Ariel!"

The man who had destroyed her heart screaming her name was the last thing she heard before something pierced her neck and blackness stole her away.

CHAPTER

Two

July 9th
7:07 P.M.

Coward.

He should have made his move sooner.

Now it was too late.

She was gone.

Snatched right in front of him.

Damn. Rock didn't even have a weapon on him to do something to try to get her back and stop the abduction from happening.

Hadn't thought he needed one.

This op had been all about making the first move in winning back the woman he should have made his sole goal in life to protect. Why would he need a weapon for that? At least the shooting kind, hell, he'd take the stabbing kind. Anything that would have stopped that van from speeding away with his Ariel inside.

He shouldn't have come.

Knowing that constricted the strand of barbed wire that seemed to have tangled itself around his heart.

This was his fault.

She'd run because she'd seen him. Because she hated him. Because she couldn't even stand to be in the same room as him.

Why hadn't he listened?

Because he was an idiot.

A selfish idiot.

Hadn't he learned anything in the last fifteen years?

Had it all been a waste?

All that time trying to redeem himself, earn back his self-respect, become a man worthy of a woman like Ariel, wanting to prove to her that he was a better man now, one who cared about others and not just himself, all a waste. Because when it boiled down to it, he hadn't even been able to wait until Ariel had been warned that their paths were about to cross before he went to see her.

Fifteen years of living without her had been hell, and he hadn't been able to hold off a single second longer.

His selfishness had likely signed Ariel's death warrant.

Ariel.

Sweet, shy, beautiful Ariel.

Thick black locks that cascaded down her back all the way to her backside. The softest milky white skin he'd ever had the pleasure of touching. Huge golden-brown eyes framed by long black lashes. She was like an even more stunning version of Snow White. With the way her eyes seemed to glow like golden orbs, he'd always thought she really could have stepped out of the pages of a fairytale.

Now she was gone.

Rock stood staring in horror at the now empty street where the white van had long since disappeared around the corner.

He's chased after it, of course, but he'd failed to catch up with it.

Seemed all he did when it came to Ariel was fail.

"I called it in," Trick said, running up beside him. The words were meant to be comforting but they offered none.

There was no one else to blame for this other than himself.

If he had waited until Tank and Tillie got here, given Tillie time to prepare Ariel for the news that the man who had crushed her so thoroughly was right under her nose.

It was pure fate, no other way to describe it, that a random case assigned to Prey had led Tank to Tillie, a woman who happened to work for social services with Ariel. That the two women were friends, had since become best friends, could have worked in his favor. Could have given him a way to spend time with Ariel without her feeling pressured to forgive him.

But he'd thrown away that chance.

"Rock?"

Tillie's panicked voice was like a needle digging its way through his skin, between his ribs, and into his chest.

The barbed wire wrapped tighter around his heart.

This wasn't just about him and Ariel. Tillie had been working hard to earn Ariel's trust and be a good friend to her. The woman had a heart of gold and was always putting other's needs before her own, and she'd felt trapped between her loyalty to her best friend, especially as they were just building the foundations of a friendship, and the fact that he was a teammate of the man she was in love with.

When Tillie had told him point blank she was prioritizing Ariel's feelings and needs, he had respected the hell out of her. Been glad that Ariel was finally letting in another friend. Ever since Tillie had confessed that she knew about his past and that Ariel worked alongside her as a social worker, he'd been begging her to talk to Ariel on his behalf.

He'd pushed so hard that Tillie had finally caved and set up tonight's meeting in a neutral location.

All he'd had to do was wait until Tillie talked to Ariel before approaching, but he'd just had to position himself where he could watch his Snow White. Of course, he should have known that she would realize she was being watched.

"What happened? Where's Ariel?" Tillie asked as she and Tank all but ran down the alley toward him.

Raking his fingers through his dark hair, Rock had to force himself to meet the woman's gaze. "Ariel was just kidnapped."

"She was what?" Tillie asked, her blue eyes widening in horrified shock.

"Cops are on the way, and we got the license plate," Trick said for him because honestly, Rock didn't know what to say or what to do in this moment.

Years of military training had flown out the window when it was his woman who had been snatched off the streets. Fear did crazy things to a person, and while he had long since learned how to control the fear for his own life and safety there was no training, no preparation, no way to control the fear of knowing the most important person in your world had just been abducted.

No doubt sometime in the next few hours, Ariel would wake up and realize the magnitude of her situation. He had seen her stop struggling when one of the kidnappers jabbed her with a syringe, so he knew she had passed out. In his mind, he could see it playing out like a horror movie he couldn't shut off. She would wake to darkness, disoriented with her hands and feet bound, she'd scream and cry, beg for help, and then she'd fight.

His Snow White was a fighter, that was what he had to hold onto.

"I'm sorry," he whispered, not quite sure who he was talking to. Ariel who was long since gone, Tillie who would hate him more than she already did when she learned he was the reason Ariel had run out here, or himself for being the selfish, pathetic loser he'd been as a teenager and once again hurting the woman he had always loved.

"You didn't wait, did you?" Tillie asked, her small body shaking with a combination of anger and fear.

"Easy, pixie," Tank murmured, slipping an arm around Tillie's waist, whether to support her or restrain her, Rock wasn't quite sure.

"I knew when she sent that message saying she was sick and leaving something was wrong. You went in there, you didn't wait for me to talk to her first, you had to go and ambush her." Tillie's voice rose with each word she flung at him. Every one of those words squarely hit its mark.

"We'll find her," Tank said, tightening his hold on Tillie but focusing his gaze on Rock, and he knew the words were for both their benefit.

"I told you to wait," Tillie continued as though Tank hadn't spoken, voice high-pitched, tears rolling down her cheeks in a steady stream. "This is your fault. I hope she never forgives you." Wrenching herself free from Tank's hold with a strength that belied her barely five-foot-tall frame, and the fact that not even three months ago she'd been shot in the chest and barely survived, her hand cracked against his cheek. The blow, although not particularly hard, stung with an intensity he would feel for a lifetime.

When Tank reached for her, Tillie collapsed against him, sobbing. Gathering her up, Tank shot him a look of apology as he turned to carry Tillie back down the alley.

"She'll forgive you, man," Trick said, clapping a hand on his shoulder. "Whatever happened between you and your girl it's been clear as long as I've known you that you love her and are prepared to do whatever it takes to win her back."

His friend was wrong.

It was Tillie who was correct.

This was all—both now and what had happened in the past—his fault, and he didn't deserve Ariel's forgiveness.

There was no redemption for a man like him, not enough good deeds existed to erase the bad ones he'd committed.

Thing was, he did believe he and his team could find Ariel, that would be the comparatively easy part. The hard part—the impossible part—would be convincing her to forgive him for the unforgivable things he'd done and give him a chance to prove that he could be part of her life and bring her joy instead of pain.

Once upon a time, the two of them had been inseparable. That they would spend their lives together was already a foregone conclusion. Sure, there had been obstacles—all great love stories had them—but Rock had known that Ariel was it for him the moment he had first laid eyes on her.

Now, she had one more reason to hate him, and he feared he'd never get a happy ending with the woman he loved.

Their story wasn't a fairytale, it was a Shakespearean tragedy, and he was the villain.

~

July 10th
12:16 A.M.

. . .

Cold.

She was so cold.

That was the first thing that drew Ariel out of the darkness that cloaked her mind and into reality.

Thankfully, reality took a few moments to settle in and if it were possible she would have clung to those seconds of confusion and refused to let them go.

But life didn't work that way.

Seconds continued to tick by even though sometimes you just wanted to stop them for a while so you could enjoy the good times while they lasted.

Problem was, sometimes you didn't realize that those good times wouldn't last forever.

As a teenager, she had thought she had it all. Parents who while often absent and wrapped up in their own lives, loved her and showered her with everything she asked for. From toys and clothes, to her own horse and riding lessons, to dance classes and a figure skating coach, to vacations all over the world crossing off places on most people's bucket lists. Two best friends who were always by her side. Kayla who laughed with her, teased her, whispered secrets, helped her conquer algebra, and was always there when she needed her, and Sebastian, the man she'd been in love with since before she even really understood what it meant to love someone.

Then one second changed everything, and all that she had slipped through her fingers and was gone.

For so long she had felt alone and isolated, cut off from the life she'd lived before, only now did Ariel realize how lucky she had been. While definitely abandoned by everyone who had been in her life before, she had still had a life. She'd gone to college, gotten a job doing something important that she was good at and enjoyed, had the little house she'd bought with her trust fund, and had the freedoms to do what she wanted when she wanted.

Now as reality seeped in, she knew she was no longer that lucky.

Against her will, her eyes sprung open. As much as Ariel wanted to hide in the darkness a little longer before she had to face facts, she knew she couldn't. Hiding was cowardly. How many times had she told herself that over the years?

Too many to count.

Did that lesson ever truly sink in?

Nope.

Cowardly or not, she spent most of her time hiding either at work or at home. If you didn't let anyone else into your life, then you couldn't be hurt. Home was quiet and peaceful, a respite from her job and the only place she could truly let go and just be. Work was chaotic and busy, but it gave her time outside her head to focus on other people's problems instead of her own pain.

Now she had neither.

No peace.

No quiet.

Nothing to occupy her mind so she could hide from reality.

Reality was here, all around her.

It filled her limbs with a weird kind of cottony feeling like they were both heavy and light all at the same time. Her head similarly suffered from the cotton effect, and underneath it she could feel a vicious headache just waiting for the lingering foggy feelings of the drugs she'd been given to fade so it could truly make itself known.

Cold air swirled across her skin and brought with it the realization that she had been stripped of her clothes, left in nothing but her underwear.

Had she been ...?

No.

Couldn't go there.

Not now, not yet, not ever.

Concrete beneath her feet, concrete walls on all sides, no windows, and a single set of stairs leading to what she assumed was a locked door meant she had to be in a basement. The damp chill confirmed it, as did the stale, musty odor.

Her arms were yanked above her head, bound at the wrists she hung from the ceiling, her feet a good foot off the floor.

The pain in her wrists and shoulders was nothing compared to the terror she felt.

She was helpless.

Completely and utterly helpless.

Tears threatened, but she didn't let them fall. She hadn't cried since the day the man she loved had shattered her heart. That day she had learned tears didn't change anything. Begging didn't change anything. The truth didn't change anything.

Sebastian had been one of her best friends, he'd been the man she wanted to spend her life with, the man she loved. She'd given him her virginity, given him her heart, and he'd thrown it all back in her face in the cruelest way possible.

It was such a long time ago, half a lifetime, yet it still hurt as though it were yesterday. Although Ariel pretended otherwise, she wasn't over him.

Never would be.

Out of sight didn't mean out of mind.

If only life were that easy.

He'd been there at the bar, watching her, following her when she ran. He'd called her name as the bag had been thrown over her head and she'd been dragged away. Ariel knew that even though he hated her, he would try to find her. Last she'd heard—although she did her best not to be kept updated by her parents on anyone from her past, but especially Sebastian —he worked for some security company after leaving the military.

Sebastian might look for her, but he'd never find her.

Voices.

Someone was coming.

"I see Sleeping Beauty is awake," a mean-looking man snarled as he came down the stairs.

Being called Sleeping Beauty reminded her that Sebastian used to call her Snow White. As a girl, the name had always made her smile, it made her feel special, wanted, cared for and about, and she had deluded herself into thinking he was the handsome prince who was going to carry her off on a white horse and give her the fairytale life of her dreams.

Instead, he'd become the villain in her story.

"She's a little thin, and her breasts aren't much," another man said, staring at her with no expression on his face like he was merely discussing the weather. This man scared her more than the other one. While the other was ugly with several scars marring his face, and obvious lust lurking in his muddy brown eyes, he looked like a thug. From the black T-shirt that stretched over beefy muscles to his thick hands curled into fists, he was the epitome of the "bad guy".

But the other one was dressed in a dark gray suit, with his hair neatly combed and a pair of glasses perched on the end of his nose, he didn't look like a threat. But the empty expression, dead eyes, and slightly disinterested tone told her he was the more dangerous of the two.

"She's gorgeous," the thug said. "The hair, those eyes, not a single blemish on her skin, and she's uptight. The uptight ones don't sleep around much, bet she's tight." He pressed one of his meaty hands low against her stomach, his fingertips just millimeters from the apex of her thighs. When she instinctively pressed her legs together in what would be a futile attempt to stop him from touching her any lower should he try to, he grinned and chuckled. "She'll bring us a small fortune, guaranteed."

Nausea swelled in her stomach.

Ariel was going to be sick.

They hadn't just kidnapped her to rape and murder her.

They intended to sell her.

No, no, no, no, no.

This couldn't be happening.

What had she done to deserve this?

Why did the universe hate her so much?

For once couldn't it just cut her a break?

Was this her punishment for the crimes Sebastian had accused her of? At first, she hadn't believed them, had known he was wrong, that she hadn't done what he accused her of, but over time those words had seeped into her brain and taken up residence there. Now she believed herself to be the uncaring, selfish, vile woman he claimed she was.

A woman who had to pay for what she'd done.

A woman who would soon pay in pain and blood for her sins.

Ariel wanted to beg them to have mercy, to let her go, and was willing to promise that she wouldn't go to the cops, anything in exchange for her freedom, but she already knew that men like this had no mercy inside them.

Still, a small plea tumbled from her lips as her body began to shake and the tears she'd tried to hold back fell free. "P-please," she stammered.

The suit merely frowned at her like she was an annoying inconvenience, but the thug grinned, his fingers digging into the tender flesh on her stomach. "Oh, you'll beg all right. Beg and plead, scream for mercy, but you'll learn. You're just a piece of meat here, Sleeping Beauty. No one cares about you beyond what we'll get for selling you."

No one cared about her full stop.

Alone.

Like she'd always been.

Destined to suffer unimaginable horrors until the Grim Reaper finally came for her soul.

Before she knew what she was doing, she was sending a small plea out into the universe. Sebastian, find me, please.

CHAPTER Three

July 10th
  4:36 A.M.

There was no worse hell on earth than knowing someone you loved was suffering.

There was no denying the fact that he had messed up in a major way with Ariel, Rock knew that, he had known it since the moment the words came out of his mouth.

But there had been no way to take them back, no way to make it right, although he'd spent half his life trying to become a man worthy of Ariel. He'd had to live with the consequences of his actions, as had Ariel.

His stupid, selfish, grief-stricken, guilty sixteen-year-old self hadn't realized the ramifications of what he was doing. All he'd cared about was attempting to alleviate the crushing weight of pain he felt knowing he had taken a life, and then on top of that, ruined what should have been a special moment between him and Ariel.

So instead of acting like a real man, he'd lashed out and ruined the best thing to have ever happened to him.

"How you doing?" Scorpion asked as the lights suddenly flashed on and his team entered the room.

After giving statements to the cops, he and his team had driven back to the compound where they lived a little over an hour outside the city. The seventy-acre plot, hidden deep in the woods, was divided up between himself and his teammates. They each had ten acres to call their own, and the other ten was used as a communal space. They had a training facility out here, along with a couple of buildings, including the one with a ton of computer equipment and a couple of conference rooms where they ran intel and planned out ops.

Unable to go to his own place where his cabin was a virtual shrine to Ariel and the childhood and adolescence they had shared, Rock had come here instead. The quiet and dark had helped him center his mind again and find a way to compartmentalize the terror still threaded around his heart, so he could do what he knew how to do.

Ariel was counting on him.

Letting her down again was not an option.

"Holding it together," he answered. That was about as much as he could hope for right now and all that really mattered. No one expected him to be in top condition, and it wasn't like Prey was going to sideline him.

Prey Security was a world-renowned, billion-dollar security firm that did everything from private security to black ops missions for the government. Owned and run by the six Oswald siblings, the oldest sibling and founder of the company former SEAL Eagle was married to a woman who had come to work for Prey under false pretenses. Eagle and Olivia were happily married and parents to three-year-old Luna and six-month-old Apollo, and given that they had met through Prey, same as a few of the other Oswald siblings, Eagle could hardly implement a don't mix work and pleasure policy without looking like a hypocrite.

Eagle himself had worked the op when Olivia had been kidnapped, despite having long since retired from fieldwork, and several of his siblings, the guys from Alpha Team, and Tank had all been involved when the women in their lives had found themselves in danger. So Rock wasn't worried about someone trying to remove him from this op, what he was afraid of was somehow messing it up because he couldn't keep his fears for Ariel under control.

Won't let you down again, Snow White.

Praying that was a vow he could keep, he watched as his team took seats at the large conference table. Even Axe was there, and for that, Rock was extremely grateful. Since Beth had turned back up here on the compound almost twelve weeks ago, the man had barely left her side. Not that his constant presence had helped Beth regain her memories. Still, they all understood that right now Axe's priority was his wife.

"I'm sorry about Tallulah," Tank said as he took the seat beside him. "She was out of line, but she's worried about Ariel and blaming herself. She thinks if she had chosen a different place to meet tonight it wouldn't have happened."

Knowing Tillie was beating herself up over Ariel's abduction only added to his guilt.

It wasn't her fault, the blame rested squarely on his shoulders and his alone.

He'd been supposed to wait out of sight until Tillie had told Ariel that he was one of Tank's teammates. Rock wasn't quite sure how he had envisioned their first meeting going in more than a decade, but it hadn't been like it did.

Of course, he hadn't thought Ariel would smile and throw herself into his arms or anything even remotely like that. But he had thought that maybe she would be willing to give him a chance to apologize to her.

Naïve of him, most definitely a case of wishful thinking, but he'd thought about her nearly every second of the last fifteen years, and while there was pain involved because he knew how badly he'd hurt her, most of those seconds had been spent remembering the good times. It wasn't the same for Ariel, all her memories of the good times they had shared would have been tainted by what he'd done.

"There's no need to apologize," he told Tank. "Tillie has been stuck in the middle of this thing between me and Ariel since she figured out I'm the man from Ariel's past who hurt her. She was doing me a massive favor by offering to talk to Ariel, telling her I work with you, and setting up the meeting. And she's right. This is my fault."

"No way you could have known what would happen," Panther reminded him.

Didn't matter.

Lack of clairvoyance skills was no excuse.

He *should* have known that Ariel would freak at the sight of him. If he were her, the first thing he would have done if he showed up was turn tail and run. While, sure, he couldn't have known that she would have been snatched off the street right before his eyes, any number of things could have happened to her if she went running outside a bar at night distracted by her emotions.

"Doesn't change the fact this is on me," he said firmly. His team didn't know the story of what had happened to him and Ariel when they were sixteen. It wasn't the kind of thing you shared, and only two people knew the truth. Him and Ariel. Only he'd made damn sure he got in first and spread his lies as far as he could.

Painting the shy, quiet girl as the villain when he was the popular star quarterback had been easier than it should have. And while he had tracked down every single student and teacher who had been at the school at the time to tell them the truth, in the end, that didn't undo the damage he had caused.

Right now, though, this wasn't about the past.

The past was irrelevant while Ariel was being held prisoner, it was something that would be dealt with when he got her back.

When, not if, because allowing if into the equation would render him completely useless.

"Tell me we have something," he pleaded. If they were going to get her back they needed a break, something to start from.

"We do." Panther shot him an encouraging smile as he opened his laptop, tapped away on the keyboard, and then turned it around.

On the screen was an image of a white van with the same license plate as the one used in Ariel's abduction.

Hope surged inside him.

"You found them?" Rock asked.

"The van," Panther clarified. "It was reported stolen early yesterday morning. It was a florist van used by a local company that primarily deals in weddings and funerals. There was a logo on the side. It had been painted over."

"So, whoever took Ariel has the skills to spray a vehicle or knows someone who does," he said. Anything, however small, could be the key to finding her. "Where was the van found?"

"By the park, a couple of hours after you saw it, it had been torched," Panther replied.

"So, no forensics?" While forensics would have been helpful, he was confident in his and his team's ability to track down whoever had kidnapped his woman without them.

"Nothing in the van, but when I knew where it was found I started searching CCTV footage to try to track its path. I found they stopped at a drive-through only fifteen minutes after they abducted Ariel. I got a nice clean image of the driver." Panther tapped on the keyboard, and a moment later, the picture of the van disappeared and was replaced by an image of a mean-looking man. The man had several scars on his face and a crooked nose indicating it had been broken at some point.

Anger flooded his system. This was the man who had kidnapped Ariel. The man who had dared to harm a hair on her head.

A man who would die a long, slow, painful death as soon as Rock found him.

"You got a name?" he asked Bravo Team's tech guru.

Panther's smile held the same controlled rage and protective energy he felt emanating from every man in the room. Bravo Team was a family, and nobody messed with them. Ariel was his, which meant she was important to all of them, and whoever this man was he had no idea what he had messed with by kidnapping Ariel.

"Oh, brother, I got more than a name," Panther told him. "I have a list of all his previous convictions, all his contacts, and all his known addresses."

That tiny flicker of hope that had sprung to life inside him when he learned the van used in the abduction had been found now surged into a fiery inferno. An inferno that would burn down a path to his woman and take out anything that had harmed her in the process.

Hold on, baby, I'm coming.

~

July 10th
    5:49 P.M.

Was it getting colder in here or was it her imagination?

Ariel was sure it was her imagination, but whether real or imagined, the effect on her body was the same.

She couldn't stop shaking.

That would be annoying enough anyway, but left chained to the ceiling, dangling by her wrists with her feet a foot off the floor, it was so much worse. The whole-body tremors kept sending her swinging wildly about. That sent pain flaring through her already aching arms and shoulders.

Her entire body was one great, big throbbing mess, and they hadn't even hurt her.

Yet.

There wasn't a doubt in her mind that it was coming.

Just like there wasn't a doubt in her mind that she would cave under whatever pressure they put on her.

She wasn't strong. Maybe she was a survivor. She'd managed to make it through the horrors of her junior year of high school and then being shunned her entire senior year, and she'd rebuilt her life all alone with no support. But Ariel didn't think any of that made her strong. She had simply done what she had to do to survive.

But this ...

This was on a whole new level of hell she had known at the back of her mind existed but which always felt so foreign and remote. Everyone knew that human trafficking was a thing. You heard about it on the news or read a post on social media. You saw the posters of a missing kid or woman and wondered if they had fallen victim to the atrocities of the underworld, but it didn't touch you.

Until it did.

Now here she was, kidnapped, tied up, waiting to be sold, terrified about what her future held and how she was possibly going to survive it.

Wondering if it was even worth trying to survive.

Surely death was preferable to whatever was coming.

Not that she knew exactly what was coming.

How exactly did you go about selling a person? Obviously, she knew she wasn't going to be shoved in a cardboard box and mailed to someone. But how was she going to be bought? She'd heard of auctions. Was that what was going to happen to her? Was she going to be paraded across the stage in some showroom and people would bid on her?

This time it was a tremor of fear and not cold that had her body swinging wildly.

Ariel cried out as pain shrieked across her back between her shoulder blades. The pain was getting worse by the second, and even though she was positive she couldn't endure another moment of it she had no choice but to.

Nobody here cared that she was in pain.

Nobody was coming to take her down until they were good and ready.

And she had no idea when that would be. Surely it had already been hours since she was abducted. Already she'd had to pee, although she had held on for as long as she could, nature was nature and eventually her bladder had given up on her, emptying the contents into her panties and down her legs. Since the basement was so cold, having the wet panties on lowered her body temperature further, and added to her torment.

Her stomach had been grumbling for a while. She'd skipped lunch the day she was kidnapped because she'd been caught up in a case that had spun further out of control than she had realized, and then she'd been waiting for Tillie and Tank to arrive before ordering dinner. While the gnawing hunger pains were the least of her worries right now, they, too, added to her torment.

The combination of hunger, cold, and fear was exhausting but she dared not close her eyes and sleep. Even as she knew sleep would give her a respite from her current situation, it also left her even more vulnerable than she already was.

It wasn't just having to survive the hunger and cold now, it was the glimpses of her future she was sure they gave her that made it so much worse.

Working child protection cases, she had seen the horrors children had been subjected to. Starved, beaten, raped, tortured, she knew what evil was out there even if she had never personally experienced it.

Was that her future?

How did you make someone become a sex slave?

She had no desire to be forced to pleasure some sick pervert who thought being rich entitled him to treat other people like property instead of fellow human beings.

Still, sex trafficking couldn't be a thing if the slaves couldn't be coerced into obeying.

How exactly were they going to coerce her?

Ariel had heard of sex slaves being trained, but what did that mean? Wasn't like there was a real school for that. Threats would obviously be involved, as well as punishments. And not the kind of go to your room that has a TV, a laptop, and your cell phone kind of punishments she got as a kid on the rare occasion when she acted up.

These punishments would be physical. Beatings she was sure, maybe they'd use a whip or burn her.

Break her bones.

Pull out her fingernails.

And what else would they do?

She was going to be a sex slave. Rape wasn't even in question. It was going to happen. And not just vaginal rape. They'd touch her ... back there as well. Probably put their things in her mouth. Damn, she hated that.

Hated sex.

How could you like something when after your first time, you'd been accused of being a sick and cold-hearted whore who had used her best friend's death to get sex from a man who didn't see her as anything other than a friend? That was totally enough to scar you for life. So, while sure, she'd had sex in the years since high school, she had hated every second of it.

Men could tell too.

Any relationship she'd ever tried had ended shortly after she allowed that relationship to become physical.

A shrill, near hysterical laugh filled the room, and it took Ariel far longer than it should have to realize the sound had come from herself.

Guess she didn't have to worry about being a sex slave ruining sex for her, that was a positive. Right?

All of a sudden, she couldn't catch her breath.

It seemed to elude her, air dancing right by her mouth and nose but refusing to enter her lungs.

She couldn't do this.

She couldn't.

She couldn't.

It was too much.

Impossible.

She wanted to go home.

Wanted to be inside her sweet, charming little cottage with its soothing blue walls and floaty white curtains. With the huge white couch that was kind of impractical given her propensity to be a little clumsy, but which she had fallen in love with on sight. It—like her bed —was scattered with dozens of brightly colored pillows, splashes of color in her boring, lonely world.

If she were at home, she could be lying in her huge jacuzzi tub, with the bubbles and the heat soothing her tight muscles, helping her relax, a book in her hands as she lost herself in another world.

How she wished right now she could lose herself in another world.

Anything but this reality.

When the door to the basement opened, Ariel let out an ear-piercing shriek. What was the point of pretending she was strong when she wasn't? She wasn't some tough warrior girl, she was just boring old Ariel who was scared out of her mind and needed someone to come and save her because she sure as hell couldn't save herself from this situation.

As the thug stalked toward her, her stupid body forgot that it was tied up and tried desperately to run away from what it knew was a threat, causing her to start swinging wildly out of control.

The pain tearing through her shoulders was nothing compared to the fear running rampant inside her. It brought with it its own kind of pain as her chest constricted tightly, and her head roared with a headache.

She probably would have spun forever if thug man hadn't wrapped an arm around her chest and pinned her against his own.

"I love it when they scream," he whispered against her ear. The feel of his hot breath against her skin made her gag, and she was suddenly grateful her stomach was empty.

Now that he had her still, he released her, and the next thing she knew, something large and round was being shoved between her teeth and secured at the back of her head. A ball gag. She'd heard of them but never seen one, certainly never worn one. To each their own, but that kind of thing had never interested her.

Not that it mattered.

She didn't matter here.

All these hours she had been praying to be let down, but when thug man lifted her off the metal hook that the ropes binding her wrists had been hooked on, she wondered why she'd ever thought it was a good idea.

Agony tore through her arms as the deadened limbs were lowered and then the ropes cut. It felt like a thousand tiny knives stabbing into her skin over and over again until it was hard to think of anything else.

The pain kept her distracted and she was set on the floor, her wrists now bound in front of her with new ropes tied over the torn skin, her ankles likewise bound.

Then she was picked up and shoved inside a metal crate like one would use for a dog. As the cage was locked shut with a padlock, Ariel found one tiny, silver lining in the hellish world her life had become. She'd always been a fainter, been embarrassed by it numerous times. But now, as a hazy blackness descended, she jumped happily into its embrace, thankful for anything that would take her out of this new reality even if for just a few moments.

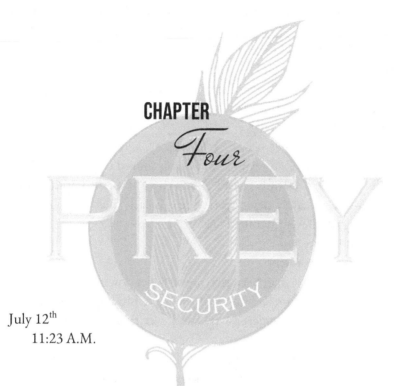

CHAPTER
Four

July 12th
11:23 A.M.

Two days ago, he'd been so full of hope.

Two days ago, it had all seemed so easy.

Two days ago, Ariel had felt so close, well within his grasp.

Now it felt like there was an entire universe between them.

That hope had long since extinguished, leaving Rock empty inside. Nothing had gone right so far. Having a list of all of Dan Johnson's associates and addresses hadn't helped them at all so far.

Sure, they had tracked down several of the man's contacts, but no matter how much they threatened them with being charged as accomplices in Ariel's abduction, none of them had cracked. Every single one of them maintained they had no idea where Dan was, what he was doing, or who he was doing it with. To make it worse, every single one of them had also produced a verifiable alibi for the time of the kidnapping, meaning they couldn't even bring one of them in on suspicion of being involved to tighten the screws a little.

While Prey worked well with law enforcement, and Eagle was a well-known and well-respected man with contacts everywhere, that didn't mean he and Bravo Team had free reign to do whatever they wanted, they weren't above the law. So as much as he would love to beat answers out of Dan Johnson's associates, he couldn't without risking charges being filed against him and his team because no way would they let him take the fall on his own.

If it were only his own freedom hanging in the balance, he might go for it anyway, but Panther had an eight-year-old son, and Tank had Tillie who was already blaming herself for Ariel's abduction. Besides, if he was in prison, who would look for Ariel?

Prey would never give up on her, Rock knew that, but they also wouldn't search for her with the same intensity that he would.

Nobody would.

Because nobody loved her like he did.

Which meant he had no choice but to follow the trail of bread-crumbs and pray he got to her in time.

Each passing hour made Ariel's abduction seem more real, and Rock was coming to several realizations.

First, it was time he made a call to Ariel's parents to tell them what had happened. Her picture had been all over the news the last two days, but according to his parents, hers were currently out of the country on a round-the-world cruise to celebrate her mother's retirement.

Second, it was time to tell his team what had gone down with Ariel.

They deserved to know the truth.

Deserved to know he was willing to sacrifice anything to get her back alive.

They might be a team, but Rock didn't expect them to make those same sacrifices. He needed them to know that he was prepared to go off the grid if need be, do whatever it took to find out where Ariel was being held, and deal with the consequences later.

As if on cue, the door to his cabin opened and his team walked in. Although it was almost midday, he had the blinds drawn and it was dark inside, not that anybody bothered to turn on a light, which he was thankful for. It was easier to tell this story in the dark.

The guys took seats in his living room, but nobody spoke, giving him time to pull himself together.

Grateful as he was, there was never a good time to tell someone your greatest shame.

Knowing Tank likely already knew didn't help.

If anything, it made it worse.

For a long moment, he stared into the fire flickering in the fireplace. The summer day was too warm for a fire, but Ariel loved them, and right now, he needed to feel closer to her any way he could. Personally, he hated the smoky smell of a fireplace, but when he'd built this place it had seemed only natural to add the things Ariel would like to it.

Unlike the rest of the guys' cabins, this one wasn't charming and rustic. Rock had gone with a more modern interior. The interior walls were all painted a crisp white, with the back wall almost entirely made up of glass. The view over the edge of a cliff down to the forest below was breathtaking, and the moment he'd seen this spot, he could hear echoing inside his head Ariel's gasp, her eyes bright and shiny as she stared at the sparkling water lined by tall fir trees. She'd tell him that she could spend every spare second of the day staring at it, and so he did. Whenever he was here, he sat right in this spot, between the fireplace and the windows overlooking the view.

Because somehow he couldn't seem to get it through his head that the future he dreamed of with Ariel by his side was never going to become a reality.

His house sat empty and lonely with only himself and a head full of memories of the past, and images of a future that was never happening.

Now the white couches he'd picked because they were what Ariel would choose were filled with his teammates. To break up the white, there were bright splashes of color, paintings on the wall, the toaster and kettle in the kitchen, the frames for photos of him and Ariel in their youth.

The whole place was like some sick sort of mausoleum to a future he had killed.

A future he wanted to revive so desperately it hurt.

"Anything?" he asked Panther. He knew the man was constantly running every search he could think of to find them another lead.

"Nothing new. We know she was in the basement of the abandoned house next door to Dan Johnson's former in-laws, but I can't get a lead on where she was taken after that."

Although Panther's voice was apologetic it gave Rock no comfort.

There had been nothing new in the two days since they had raided that house and found her discarded clothing. They'd likely missed her by mere hours.

"I won't stop looking," Panther assured him.

Rock nodded. "I'll do whatever it takes to get her back. I won't give up on her. Ever. No matter how long it takes me to find her." The rest of his life if that's what it took, even if that meant quitting Prey.

"We're right there with you," Tank promised.

He eyed the other man. "I assume you know. About Ariel and me. I'm guessing Tillie told you when she figured it out."

Tank shook his head. "All I knew was that Ariel was the woman from your past you're hung up on. And I only found that out the day she was taken. I knew something was going on after I saw Tallulah freak over your tattoos, but she wouldn't tell me what. When she told me she said that Ariel was her best friend and deserved her loyalty. Rock, she also said that while she hated the guy you were back then, the boy who hurt Ariel, you're not that guy anymore. She thinks you're a good man."

"She thinks I'm to blame for Ariel's abduction and she's not wrong."

"That's her fear talking."

"Your woman has too big a heart, she should hate me. Ariel does, and I deserve every ounce of that hate." Now or never, best to get it over with. "We were best friends growing up, the two of us and a girl called Kayla. We did everything together. Inseparable. We were all different, I was a jock, Ariel was a geek, and Kayla was the class clown, but we were the best of friends. I loved Kayla as a friend, but Ariel ..."

With her it had been different.

Even his preteen self had known that.

"I knew I was in love with her from the beginning. Knew she felt the same way. But neither of us did anything about it. Guess we were both scared about how it would impact our friendship with Kayla. Which was stupid because she would have been thrilled for both of us. One night, we were out hanging around, not doing much of anything. As we were driving back home, we hit a deer. I was driving. I walked away with a single scratch." Rock touched a finger to the barely noticeable white line on his temple. "Ariel broke her collarbone where the seatbelt caught her. Kayla had taken her seatbelt off because she was joking around as always. She went through the windshield. Died instantly."

Memories of that night ran through his head on a loop. There was no off switch.

The pain in his head.

His racing heart.

Ariel's hysterical screams.

And silence from Kayla.

"I was the driver, I blamed myself. Ariel blamed herself because she and Kayla were being silly, which is why Kayla wasn't buckled in. We didn't see each other until the funeral, and after we snuck away. Without the barrier of Kayla between us we had sex. First time for both of us. It was ... perfect. But in the morning, when I realized that Kayla was dead because of me I was smothered by guilt. I lashed out and said horrible things. Told Ariel that she used her best friend's death to get me to have sex with her because it was the only way she could get me. I spread that rumor through the school, anything to divert the attention away from me and the fact that I'd killed someone. I deserve Ariel's hatred. Tillie's too. All of yours. What I did was despicable, and I've spent the rest of my life trying to become a man that is worthy of Ariel's love and forgiveness even though I deserve neither. I will find her, no matter what I have to do to make it happen because if it's the last thing I do, I will apologize to her in person."

～

July 15th
　8:11 P.M.

She hadn't known it was going to be like this.

When she'd been brought to this new place—another basement because apparently human traffickers had no imagination—and no one had laid a hand on her other than to remove the gag and ropes and shift her into another cage, Ariel had thought this was going to be easy. Expecting beatings and rapes, being left alone in a cage sounded about as good as she could have hoped for, and she had begun to think that she could actually do this.

Sebastian might be a horrible person, but he wasn't so horrible that he wouldn't have been looking for her. The cops, too. Her abduction had been public, there was every chance her picture and story had been blasted across every news channel in the country.

Surely that would make buying her risky for someone who would have to stay under the radar if they didn't want to wind up in prison.

All she had to do was hold on until the cops came for her.

Locked in a crate and left alone was something she could handle.

At least that's what she had thought.

Because she'd been stupidly naïve.

These people weren't amateurs, they knew what they were doing, and likely making her think she could do this was part of their plan.

No longer did she think this was going to be easy.

It wasn't.

Not even close.

Desperately, she pressed her hands tighter against her ears like that was going to actually make a difference.

Hours—days maybe she wasn't sure—of the music being blasted at full volume had her ears aching. There was a difference between loud music and loud music. This horrendous, pulsing, screaming sound that seemed to reverberate through her body with a relentlessness that drove her insane—as it was intended to—couldn't really be classified as music.

It was torture.

Plain and simple.

Just like the plate of food sitting on a small table just out of reach from her cage.

It wasn't just awful "hostage" food either, no slice of stale bread and glass of dirty water. Nope. This was a full meal. A full hot meal. It was changed out every so often and replaced with something that looked even better.

Or maybe it was just that she got even hungrier.

At first, Ariel had thought that dealing with hunger was a piece of cake. Obviously, she'd known nothing about true hunger. While not millionaires or anything, her family had been very well off when she was growing up. Well off enough to cater to her every whim even if what she had wanted the most was time with her parents. Never once had she gone to bed hungry. Never once had she gone to school without a lunch packed by the housekeeper or money to buy something.

Never.

While as a social worker she didn't make nearly enough as her two surgeon parents, she made enough to cover her bills. While eating out was a bit of a luxury, Ariel never cared because she preferred hanging out at home and cooking anyway. And with only one person to feed, she always bought what she felt like eating and not just what she could afford on her weekly trips to the grocery store.

True hunger was indescribable.

It wasn't just about feeling hungry. Yes, her stomach was cramping so badly she was curled up into a ball on the rough, cold concrete with an arm wrapped around her middle, but there was so much more to it. Her head pounded, her limbs felt shaky and much too heavy to move, and she had that foggy feeling that made it so very hard to concentrate.

Her cage had its own water supply. If you could call a rusty faucet embedded in the concrete of the back wall of her cage a water supply. It dripped constantly, there was no tap to turn it off and on. It tasted bad, but it was all she had to drink. It wasn't much, it was literally just a drip, but it was enough to stave off dehydration and to wash herself after she used the filthy bucket in the corner.

Between the hunger, the cold, and the complete lack of sleep, Ariel knew she was hanging on by a single thread.

A thread that was already badly frayed and dangerously close to snapping.

The point of course.

They were trying to break her.

Knowing that didn't really do her any good.

She wasn't some well-trained warrior. She wasn't a cop, or in the military. She was just a simple woman who worked as a social worker, well acquainted with the horrors of the world, but not in an up close and personal way like this.

What chance did she have of outlasting the monsters who had taken her?

None.

Not a single one.

She would break. That was already a foregone conclusion. What exactly was she holding out for?

Help wasn't really coming, that was just a lie she whispered to herself in her dark prison so she could make it through the next few seconds. But she knew it was a lie and it was quickly losing any comfort it had given her those first few hours.

Knowing that Sebastian could have survived this torture and anything else anyone threw at him was like rubbing salt in the wounds.

Why did he always have to be so good at everything?

Everything came so easily for him. Star quarterback, straight-A student, popular, funny, and a full scholarship awaiting him to pretty much any college he chose to attend. As a child, she'd thought he hung the moon in the sky, she'd been so hopelessly in love with him, but after Kayla's death she'd begun to resent him and his perfectness.

It wasn't fair.

She hadn't blamed him for Kayla's death just because he'd been driving, nobody had. Not even Kayla herself would have. Kayla was bright and loud, full of energy and life, and losing her had been a huge blow, especially since she knew she had been egging Kayla on to play that stupid game, which was why her friend had taken off her seatbelt.

But she'd needed Sebastian. They'd needed each other.

At least that's what she'd thought.

Obviously, she couldn't have been more wrong.

Another tearing cramp ripped through her stomach, and she moaned, the sound swallowed up by the screaming music.

What she wouldn't give for a big bowl full of cheesy pasta.

Mmm.

Ariel could picture it in her mind. The stringy cheese stretching as she piled up as much as she could fit on her fork. It would taste so good, all hot and cheesy, so delicious.

Dry as her mouth was, it salivated at the thought.

Movement caught her attention, and she saw the thug walk into the room, a steamy bowl held in his hands.

As though he'd reached right into her mind and read her thoughts, Ariel caught a whiff of cheese, and when he set the bowl down on the table, she saw that it was indeed a bowl filled to the brim with cheesy pasta.

Pure instinct had her shifting, crawling toward the door to her cage.

That was when she knew.

She had lost.

He had won.

The thug knew it, too, because he grinned, and a second later, the room went blessedly silent.

Relief swamped her and she almost collapsed back onto the hard concrete floor, but her brain was focused on only one thing.

Food.

Need food.

That thought propelled her as she dragged herself to the door and curled her shaking fingers around the bars.

When the thug unlocked the door, she fell forward along with it, landing in a heap at his feet.

Even his hand tangling in her hair and dragging her to her feet couldn't pull her mind from its single-track focus.

Food.

Please.

Ariel wasn't aware she had whispered the word aloud until the thug spoke.

"What would you be willing to do for a taste?"

"Anything." The word fell from her lips without conscious thought, and although she hated herself for it, for a chance at eating and for the music to stay off she was prepared to do whatever he asked of her.

Unbuckling his pants, the man dropped into the chair beside the table. Although her terrified glance landed briefly on his long length protruding from beneath his boxers, it quickly returned to the food.

How desperately she craved it.

All consumingly.

She needed it.

Her tongue traced along her bottom lip, already tasting the food even though none had gone into her mouth.

The thug chuckled like her whole situation amused him. "You get me off you get half the bowl. You get me off, and you let me get you off, and it's all yours."

Of course, the logical side of her brain told her not to do it. This was the first step in becoming the slave he wanted her to be. If she took it there would be no going back. Worse, Ariel would know that she had participated in her own downfall.

But the food ...

And the quiet ...

Could she say no and go back into that cage knowing the unrelenting music would start back up and the bowl of pasta would sit there silently taunting her?

No.

She couldn't.

Call her weak, call her pathetic, call her whatever you wanted but she was so hungry, and her ears hurt so badly.

Slowly she nodded her head.

Triumph lit the man's muddy brown eyes, and he nodded to his length as he picked up the fork with one hand. "Stand before me, legs spread."

Doing as he told her, self-loathing consumed her as she reached out and took his erection into her hand. When his free hand went between her legs, she squeezed her eyes shut.

When the first mouthful of pasta hit her tongue, it no longer had the same flavor she'd been dreaming about. It tasted like cardboard, it tasted like failure, it tasted like pain and suffering and humiliation.

It tasted like her future.

CHAPTER

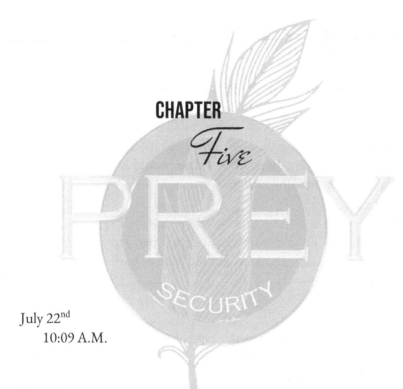

Five

July 22nd
   10:09 A.M.

Tomorrow night would mark two weeks since Ariel had been abducted right in front of him.

Two weeks of agonizing every second over where she was and what was happening to her.

Two weeks of chasing down leads, getting his hopes up every time only to have them dashed when they didn't pan out.

Dan Johnson had gone to ground. None of his contacts would say where he was, if they even knew, and while it was clear he had help staying off the radar so far, they hadn't been able to find where Ariel had been taken after she'd left that first house.

Knowing that she was out there, that she needed him, that he was failing her over and over again with the rising of the sun each morning and the setting of it each evening, was like being trapped in his own version of Groundhog Day.

Only his version was filled with blood, pain, and suffering.

Because while Ariel was the one living through it, he was right there with her in his imagination. Rock had worked enough human trafficking ops both in Delta and with Prey to know how those people treated their victims. He'd rescued enough victims to know that even if they were removed from that hell it stayed with them forever.

Even if he was able to find and rescue Ariel, the girl he had once known would no longer exist.

Scrubbing his fingers down his face, Rock surveyed the mess surrounding him. He was sitting on his bedroom floor, papers spread out on every available space. They littered the floor, covered his bed, they lined the top of both the dresser and the armoire. There was everything Panther had been able to gather on Dan Johnson. When they weren't out chasing down a lead, he was in here going over and over the documents, searching for something they had missed.

Scattered amongst the paperwork were photos.

Every photo that had ever been taken of him and Ariel together had now been printed and was sitting in his room. It was the only way he could feel close to her, and every time he picked one up, he silently begged her to hold on, tried to convince her that he was coming for her.

Of course, his team had refused to back away even knowing the truth of how badly he had messed up.

Excuses were just that. He could say he'd only been a kid back then, that he was grieving one of his best friends, and he was dealing with a heavy ball of guilt knowing he was the driver and therefore responsible for Kayla's death. But truth was, none of it excused the way he'd treated Ariel.

He deserved all the suffering in the world for what he'd done, but Ariel didn't deserve any of it.

She deserved happiness and peace. She should be sitting in her office right now, saving another child's life, showing them someone cared about them, that they were important, that they deserved a safe and stable home and life. She should be safe and living her own stable life, not in the hands of monsters who cared nothing about her.

If it were possible, he'd trade places with her in a heartbeat.

But life didn't work that way.

Rock was forced to go on knowing what was happening to the woman he loved but was powerless to stop it. Even in sleep, there was no respite. Ariel's suffering merely played itself out in his dreams like it did in his mind when he was awake.

No respite for her, no respite for him, and a huge chasm between them he was desperately searching for a way to cross.

The sound of his front door opening and closing barely registered. If it wasn't for the hope that it was Panther with another lead for them to look into, he wouldn't care which of his teammates it was and why they were there.

And they were always there.

One of them came several times a day bringing with them food they forced him to eat. Eating was the last thing he wanted to waste time on, but their arguments that the only way he was of any use to Ariel was if he took care of himself was a sound one and so he did it. Didn't matter that the food had no taste or that it sat like a rock in his stomach, he ate because he had to, because the only thing that mattered was finding Ariel.

"R-Rock?"

The tentative voice caught him by surprise, and he looked up to find Tillie standing in the doorway. She moved nervously from foot to foot, her hands twisted together in front of her. With the dark circles under her eyes, her pale complexion, and the messy bun her long blonde locks were twisted into, it was obvious she was doing no better than he was.

While he didn't hold her accusations against her—agreed with her assessment that he was to blame for what had happened—he was emotionally tapped out right now. He had nothing to give her, nothing to offer her to help ease her fears when his own were slowly dragging him down into a deep pit of despair.

"What do you want, Tillie?" he asked. There was no anger in his tone, it was flat, as empty as his heart, but she flinched at it, nonetheless.

"I ... I shouldn't have ... I was wrong ... I'm sorry," she stammered.

When her eyes filled with tears something broke inside him. He might as well be sixteen all over again, standing in his bedroom after waking up to find Ariel tangled in his arms, the realization of what he'd done crashing down around him. His tone that morning hadn't been flat and empty it had been angry. His mouth had hurled out horrible words and even as he'd said them, watched as Ariel's big golden eyes filled with tears like Tillie's turquoise ones just had, he'd known that damage was irreparable.

It was insane to expect Ariel to give him a second chance.

Insane to believe he could save enough lives to make up for taking Kayla's.

Insane to hope he could become a man worthy of Ariel's love and earn her forgiveness.

The utter hopelessness of it all burned through his system, scalding his insides, and that barbed wire that wrapped around his heart tightened to the point where he had to rub his chest in an attempt to ease it.

A small sob came from Tillie, and the next thing he knew she was throwing herself into his arms.

"I'm sorry," she said through her tears, her wet face pressed against his neck.

His arms wrapped around her, and he held onto her, trying to imagine it was Ariel instead. "You were right."

"No. I was wrong. It's my fault."

Rock shook his head and tightened his hold. "You asked me to wait until you talked to her and broke the news. I couldn't stay away. Being that close to her and not being able to see her, I couldn't do it. She ran because she saw me."

"I handled the whole thing wrong. I should have told her as soon as I saw your tattoo and put two and two together. I shouldn't have told you that I work with Ariel until I had told her you were one of Tank's teammates. I got in the middle of something I shouldn't have and look how it all turned out." Tillie pulled back so she could look up at him. "I'm so sorry. Can you ever forgive me for getting the woman you love kidnapped?"

"Oh, blondie." He crushed her to him in a fierce hug. "None of that is your fault. This is all on me. I'm the one who messed things up with Ariel in the first place, and I'm the one who asked you to set up a meeting. If I wasn't such a coward, I would have gone to face Ariel before now. But I couldn't handle the thought of her rejecting me. I deserved it, but if I went to her, apologized, told her how hard I've tried to become a man worthy of her, and she still sent me away, I would have to accept it was truly over between us. As long as I kept my distance there was still hope. I was selfish—again—and because of that, Ariel got hurt. Again."

As much as he'd loved there to be a way to place the blame on something else, he couldn't. It would be a lie.

And even if there was someone else to place the blame on, it certainly wasn't this big-hearted woman.

"Trust me, blondie. This is not your fault. At all. You were doing me a favor. Trying to be a good friend to Ariel and me at the same time when our best interests didn't align. And you were trying to be a good girlfriend to Tank and help out his teammate. You are good, sweet, and kind, and you care so much about others you get yourself in trouble. If I were even half the person you are, Ariel and I would have been married right after we graduated, we'd probably have kids by now, we'd be together, a family, happy. Our lives would all be drastically different."

Tillie's expression turned earnest. "It's not too late for you to be all those things. I know you guys. You do whatever it takes to get the job done, I'm proof of that. You'll find Ariel, and when you do, she'll have all of us there to support her as she recovers. I know you regret what happened, and I know you've tried to become better to make up for it. I believe that Ariel will find it in her heart to forgive you. Then you can both have the future you still want."

Believing that would be far too easy if he let himself.

But Rock was done living in a dream world.

Saving Ariel's life was more important than anything else. Then, if she needed him to walk away so she could heal, he'd do it.

Because he was done being selfish.

July 26th
   9:53 P.M.

Turned out, being sold was nothing like she had thought it would be.

There was no auction with a man in a tux on a microphone and a parade of girls—herself included—being walked across a stage as men in the audience put in bids.

In fact, there was no auction at all.

Her being sold turned out to be a quiet affair with no one present but the thug, the man in the suit, and the man who had bought her.

A few days—at least she was guessing it was days although trapped in the basement with no glimpse of the outside world there was no way to tell time—after she broke that first time, she was given a bath in luke-warm water, had her hair and makeup done, was dressed up, and photographed. The session seemed to last forever, her outfit was changed at least a dozen times, and she was positioned in all manner of sexually suggestive poses. By the end of it, she was both exhausted and demoralized, but she was beginning to learn how to numb both her mind and her body.

Surely that was the key to her survival.

The only key.

If she couldn't remove her body from the situation, she had to remove her mind.

Block everything out.

That was her mantra.

Pretend it wasn't happening, pretend she was somewhere else, pretend this wasn't her life.

It might not be real, but who cared?

It was better than the alternative.

Better than letting sick, perverted men play with her like she really was nothing but a sex toy. These last ... however many days she'd been here ... she'd been made to perform with her mouth and hands. Failure to give whoever stuck their thing in her face an orgasm resulted in punishments, and these men were experts in inflicting pain without leaving marks that might make their merchandise—her—less valuable.

Been forced to let them touch her in all manner of ways as well. Toys, hands, mouths, they'd all been used on her, sometimes to make her come, other times to leave her hanging until, despite the fact she hated what they were doing, she was begging to be given a release.

Just how they wanted it.

Messing with her mind was an effective tool.

All it took was loud music and a lack of food to create that first crack.

That crack had long since grown into a gaping fissure as the realization that she wasn't walking away from this alive finally sank in. This was her life now, and she had to find a way to make peace with it.

Why make things harder on herself than they had to be?

If they were willing to feed her, she was going to eat, if the option was to be tortured by the loud music or have blissful silence, she was choosing silence. If she could avoid being hurt then why shouldn't she?

Even if it made her weak it wasn't like she had all sorts of options.

Also it didn't mean she hadn't earned herself dozens of punishments. Ariel still hesitated when she was told to do something. Just because she didn't want to be punished didn't mean she liked anything about what was happening to her. When those men made her come there was no pleasure in it. The opposite in fact. It stole a piece of her each time.

She hated it here.

Hated them.

Spent many an hour daydreaming about how wonderful it would be to have the tables turned so she could torture them mercilessly.

Each time she wasn't quick enough to blindly follow an order she was punished. Anything from them using pressure points to inflict unimaginable pain, to being locked in a box that was more like a coffin, to being strapped to a machine that kept her hovering on the edge of orgasm for hours without bringing her any release, to being made to come over and over again until she was sobbing and begging them to stop.

Now the only known in her world was gone.

Awful as it was, Ariel had come to understand what was expected of her here. She knew the rules, knew she was nothing, knew what would happen for any infraction, and knew what to expect.

But now she had been sold.

The future was huge and daunting.

What was the man who had bought her like? Was he better or worse than the men who had been here training her? Did he like to inflict pain? Images of some of the outfits she'd been dressed in entered her mind. Was he going to treat her like an infant? A pet? Was he someone she could pretend to make a connection with and then use it to escape?

Just what kind of monster was he?

She was yet to get a glimpse of him. A couple of hours ago, one of the men had come to her cage to collect her. She'd been thoroughly bathed, her hair washed and styled until it gleamed like the night sky. For the first time since the photography session, she had been dressed in clothes. It felt weird to have the soft material against her skin. As much as she hated walking around naked, she'd become accustomed to it and the humiliation she'd felt those first few days had faded.

After being washed and dressed, she'd been left alone in a tiny, dark room. There had been a chair for her to sit on and so she was sitting here, waiting to see just how bad her future would be.

Waiting was almost unbearable.

How badly she wanted to fidget, but apparently fidgeting was against the rules for a sex slave. She wasn't supposed to do anything to draw attention to herself, she existed merely to cater to the whims of someone with more money than her who had paid for the privilege of owning her.

Still, as the door opened and a shaft of light fell over her, Ariel flinched and pressed back into the wooden chair as though it might possess some kind of ability to save her from her fate.

Of course, it did not, and so she watched as two men entered the room. One was the guy in the suit from that very first day. While she didn't see him often, he appeared to be the one in charge.

The other was her new owner.

Master.

She was supposed to call whoever bought her, master. When she was given permission to speak that was.

"She's even more stunning in person," a new man said as he stepped into the room behind suit man.

The first thing Ariel thought when she saw him was that he looked so completely and utterly normal. He was dressed in jeans, with sneakers on his feet and a T-shirt that showed off a lean body. While he couldn't quite be called handsome, his mouth was a little too big for his face, and his nose a little too small, there was something compelling about him. A thick head of golden-brown hair offset some of the disproportionate facial features, and his irises were half blue and half brown giving him a very unique look. Add in some killer dimples and she was sure this man didn't lack attention from women.

Maybe he wouldn't be as bad as she had been fearing.

"The money has cleared our account, so she's all yours," suit man said, managing to somehow look both professional and bored at the same time. "Do you have specific requirements on how you wish her to be transported?"

"Very specific," her new master said with a smile. He had a slight accent, but she couldn't place it, not that it mattered. Wherever he took her, she wouldn't be leaving. Opening the backpack he'd been wearing, the man removed two sets of padded leather cuffs, a ball gag like the one she'd been made to wear when she was transported from the first house to this one, and what looked like some sort of chastity belt with a toy attached to it. "It's a long journey home and I want her anticipating exactly what's going to happen when we get there."

Horror overtook common sense and Ariel whimpered.

Thinking there was anything human about this man just because he looked normal only proved that she was still much too naïve considering her circumstances.

At the small sound she'd made, her master's eyes narrowed. Moving faster than she thought a person could move, he had her off the chair, shoved up against the wall, and his hand around her neck pinning her in place. "I don't permit sounds unless I've asked you to make one," he growled.

Terrified that even a nod of her head in acquiescence would set him off, Ariel just hung there, fighting her natural instinct to claw at the hand cutting off her air supply.

Apparently, that pleased him because as quickly as he'd lost his temper he seemed to regain it. Setting her on her feet, he grabbed the hem of her dress and yanked it off, tossing it aside. With quick, efficient movements, he nudged her legs apart, slid the toy inside her, and then locked the chastity belt into place. Wrists were bound behind her, then she was shoved back into the chair and her ankles were also cuffed.

The man lifted her with ease, reminding her how uneven their positions were.

He had all the power.

She had none.

Rather than panic as she was lifted and placed inside a suitcase, the ball gag fitted before it was zipped up, it was more an empty kind of exhaustion that filled her.

Tell someone something often enough and they come to believe it.

She had come to believe the words Sebastian had hurled at her the morning after Kayla's funeral. And she had come to believe what she'd been told here.

She was nothing.

Just a toy.

No worth.

Sinking into the depths of her own mind, Ariel barely noticed when the toy inside her began to vibrate. Being nothing was infinitely easier than being a sex slave.

CHAPTER Six

July 29th
2:35 P.M.

Another week had come and gone.

That made three now.

So much for finding Ariel being the easy part.

When they'd gotten that image of her abductor so quickly, IDed him, and gotten so much intel on him, Rock had allowed himself to believe that he could find Ariel before she was hurt. Before the darkness of the world got a fingerhold inside her soul.

Before it was too late.

Raking his fingers through his short-cropped dark hair, Rock cursed his own stupidity. His own uselessness. His own failures. He should have done more that night. Now he feared Ariel was gone forever.

Actually, it was getting more likely by the second that she really was lost to him.

Still, he clung to hope that he would find her and knew he would never stop looking. But what good was looking if he couldn't find her and bring her home?

Three weeks.

Twenty days since she had been snatched off the streets right in front of him. He had stupidly—arrogantly—believed he'd be able to find her. That he'd ride in on his white horse and become her savior, that in saving her life he'd finally have his chance at winning her heart back.

Stupid.

Stupid, stupid, stupid.

Ariel could be gone forever, and once again, her pain was his fault.

Panic threatened to drown him, but he shoved it down. Panic never got you anywhere, that had become his mantra these last three weeks. Every time he felt it choking him, tightening that stranglehold it had on his heart, he reminded himself that keeping a clear head was Ariel's best chance.

Her only chance.

"Rock." He looked up from his laptop to see Panther standing in his bedroom grinning at him.

Hope fluttered in his chest. Likely he was jumping to conclusions, once again allowing himself the deluded belief that Ariel could be found, even though he knew most trafficking victims were not, but he couldn't seem to help himself.

There was actual light in his teammate's dark eyes.

"Yeah?" he asked cautiously, refusing to let anything fan that flicker of hope until he had more information to go on.

"I have good news and bad news," Panther announced.

That hope dimmed.

All but disappeared.

"Yeah?" he asked again, this time with no undercurrent of hope. Good news was one thing, but bad news could easily outweigh any good.

"I think I might have a lead on who bought Ariel."

This time, there was nothing he could do to stop hope from flaring inside him with the force of a tornado. What could possibly be bad news after that?

A lead on who had bought Ariel was everything they needed. It basically gave them a map to follow right to her location.

There was no bad news that could outweigh that, it was more than he could have hoped for.

It was everything he needed.

Still, if Panther said there was bad news coming, he had to brace for it.

"And?"

Panther's grin faded, replaced by a troubled frown. "And we've heard of the man before."

While they didn't exclusively work human trafficking cases, didn't even mostly work trafficking ops, he and his team had worked enough of them to know several major players. After the op that cost them their Delta careers, they all had a personal interest in bringing down traffickers, so it wasn't uncommon for them to look into things on their own time even if it wasn't connected to a case for Prey.

Right now, there was one name topping his list, the only one he could think of that would have that look on his friend's face.

Bad news.

No matter how good the good news was, there was always bad news that could overshadow it.

Rock should have known better than to forget that for a second.

If the man he was thinking of was the one who had bought Ariel, then winning her heart back wouldn't be his biggest problem. Wouldn't even be one of his top ten problems. Because there might be nothing left of the woman he loved but an empty shell of a person after the man who bought her was through with her.

"The others are waiting for us in the conference room," Panther informed him.

With great trepidation, Rock closed his laptop and set it on the bed, then pushed to his feet. Neither spoke as they walked downstairs and stepped out into the bright summer afternoon.

The heat that immediately engulfed them served as a swift reminder of where Ariel might be right this second.

That thought was enough to steal any warmth the sun offered, dousing him instead in an icy cold chill.

Since there was nothing to say to fix this, he followed Panther as they crossed through the woods to the large main building on their shared acres of land. By the time they got there, the other four guys on their team were already there waiting for them.

On all four faces there was a combination of unwavering support and understanding empathy. Obviously, Panther had given them the news before coming to fetch him.

Instead of reassuring him that his team had his back so thoroughly, it only increased the sense of dread growing inside him.

If the man he was thinking of did have Ariel then getting her back wouldn't be easy.

Not in the least.

Refusing to meet any of their gazes, he dropped into a chair at the far end of the table from where the others were seated. No one called him on it, and he was glad, he needed a little physical space right now when he was so close to spinning out of control.

One more thing added to the weight he was carrying and he'd snap.

"So, as we know, Dan Johnson was responsible for Ariel's abduction. The van was stolen, nothing to link the owners, and the house where she was first taken didn't yield any forensics besides confirmation that Ariel had been there. I've been looking into anyone associated with Johnson but everything ran into dead end after dead end," Panther said.

It was hard not to hurry his friend, but he knew Panther's mind ran in a very linear manner, he liked to run through things from beginning to end. It was what made him so good at what he did, it helped him to see patterns and tiny details that would otherwise be missed.

"After running through the life of everyone associated with him, I widened the net and found something. We already knew Johnson's been in and out of prison mostly on assault charges before doing time for kidnapping. One victim managed to escape and claimed Johnson talked about selling her. I realized a few people in his circle have the same parole officer. Seemed like a long shot, but I started looking into him. Cory Paxton."

"He the missing link?" Trick asked.

"Oh yeah." Panther's grin was triumphant. "Once I started looking into him it was like finding a treasure trove. I was able to find a dark website linked to Paxton. Human trafficking site. Ariel passed through the site." Panther paused and looked at him. "You sure you want to see this?"

Did he?

No.

Would he?

Yes.

Because whatever it took, he was getting her back, no shortcuts, he couldn't risk missing something.

At his nod, Panther flicked a switch and images of Ariel dressed in a range of different sexually provocative outfits in equally provocative poses appeared on the large screen hanging on the wall.

That wasn't what he focused on though.

His focus went right to her eyes, her vacant expression. It was like she was already gone even as he was looking right at her.

"Who bought her?" Rock asked tightly. Just because he had an idea, it didn't mean he was willing to accept it. Yet. Not until he heard the words.

"We don't know his identity, but we've come across him before, he's friends with Baranov. We know him only as Mr. Freeze."

At Panther's words, Rock felt the bottom dip out of his world.

No.

Not that anyone who would have bought Ariel would be the kind of person he would want around his woman, around any woman, but Mr. Freeze was an internationally known serial killer and rapist with going on two dozen bodies to his name.

Known for keeping his victims for months at a time, the man had a fascination with ice that had given him his name. Several of his victims had been found with ice burns to their back, chest, and extremities, and in some cases mild to severe frostbite. As of right now, no one knew where the man lived or what country he was from, but it was assumed he was wealthy because his victims quite literally spread across the globe.

Linked together by the state their bodies had been in when they were found, all the women—all aged in their twenties and thirties—all with dark hair and pale complexions, just like Ariel, had been scrubbed with bleach inside and out. From under their nails to their eyeballs, to bleach being poured down their throats in case they had inhaled any fibers that could lead back to him, Mr. Freeze took forensic countermeasures to the extreme.

And it had paid off.

There were no leads despite him being wanted by several countries and Interpol.

This was the man who had Ariel.

According to the timeline Panther had on display, she had been with him for several days now.

What hell had Mr. Freeze put her through in that time?

September 4th
6:16 A.M.

Guess she couldn't have picked a better person to buy her.

Or a better plan of surviving.

Numb.

It had become more than her motto of survival, it had become her entire life.

Ariel was numb from the time she awoke in the morning until she went to sleep at night. Actually, sleep was kind of too strong a word for the hazy, foggy state of mind that qualified as sleep these days.

Good thing she didn't have to be up and focused for work because she was more zombie than human these days.

A shrill, borderline hysterical laugh filled the small space, and as soon as it bounced around, sounding much too loud for her ears, fear instantly consumed her.

A noise.

She'd made a noise.

Frantically, she looked about to see if he was here somewhere, watching her. He liked to watch her. Pretend he wasn't there while secretly observing her inside her freezer-like cell. Ariel knew this because those first few days she'd been here she had made the mistake of attempting to give herself verbal pep talks, and then singing to herself to try to pass the interminable hours spent tied up in this room.

Punishments.

That's what she'd gotten because, apparently, her master had a real thing about her not talking unless she was given express permission.

Which he never did.

Nope, he liked her to be silent. No matter what he did to her.

It was not an easy feat when submerged in an ice bath. Pure instinct would have you gasping in those first seconds when that freezing water touched your skin. Still, she'd learned pretty quickly to control the impulse.

Anything to avoid a punishment.

That first time he'd caught her talking aloud to herself in what she thought was the privacy of her own prison—stupid of her really, she was a possession to her master, of course she didn't have the luxury of privacy—he'd taken her outside and stuck her hand in a pile of snow until her skin turned blue and she was sure she was going to get frostbite.

Ice and ropes.

The man was obsessed with both.

Ariel liked neither.

Not that it mattered of course.

As much as she hated hanging in this cold room, it was preferable to be in here alone than when he came for her.

Just like back at the place she'd been trained, there were no windows in this room so figuring out the passing of the days was difficult. Honestly, she could have been here a week, a month, or a year. It all blended together into one long, hellish nightmare.

Shibari, a Japanese form of tying someone up with ropes, was obviously his passion. Ariel had heard about it only because she'd worked a case last year with two little boys who had been tied up and raped by their father and his friends. When caught, the father had tried to claim he was simply an artist and the boys were his canvas.

That excuse hadn't flown with her or the judge.

He was currently serving a prison sentence, and last she heard, his cellmates didn't take too kindly to the pedophile.

Although it was supposed to be an erotic form of bondage between two willing partners, her owner didn't care whether or not she liked it.

And she did not like it.

No offense to anyone who did enjoy the practice, you could be into whatever you chose so long as you were actually into it, but the positions he tied her in were painful, and he left her tied up for hours, making her limbs numb and heavy. Excruciating pins and needles were bad enough, but her skin was also littered with rope burns. The worst were around her wrists, those wounds from that very first day had never fully had a chance to heal, but there were new burns added to the collection every single day.

What she hated most about being tied up, was that her owner used it as an excuse to feed her and to help her use the bathroom.

There was something horrifyingly intimate about having someone help you with things you'd been doing on your own since you were a toddler. And the way he spoke to her, in that crooning tone you usually used when talking to a baby or a pet, it totally creeped her out.

With nothing to do but hang—literally—around, Ariel had had a lot of time to think.

About the past, about the future, about herself, about Sebastian.

All those thoughts wound up circling back around to him. He had been the center of her world for so long it was hard not to think about him at a time like this.

What had he been doing there at the bar that night?

That question continued to haunt her.

Had he been there for her or was it a coincidence? And if it wasn't a coincidence how had Tillie been involved?

It hurt to know that all this time she had allowed herself to make another friend, something she had been too afraid to do after Kayla's death, only to wind up being betrayed. It felt like the whole thing with the funeral, losing their virginity, and Sebastian all over again.

Maybe it should hurt less. She was older now, not a teenage girl, and she hadn't known Tillie very long, plus she should have learned her lesson about trusting people, but it did hurt.

Given her current situation, it seemed a silly thing to worry about a boy who hurt her when they were both sixteen, and a friend she'd had for all of a couple of months, but just because you kept piling hurt on didn't mean that you couldn't still feel each wound.

At the tell-tale sound of the door being unlocked all thoughts of Sebastian and her old life fled from her mind.

Her master was back.

Seemed like he'd only just left.

Despite her best efforts to remain numb, panic set in like it always did.

Blocking it out to the best of her ability didn't mean she wasn't painfully aware of everything done to her.

Some things sunk down too deep to ever get rid of.

"Good morning, my ice queen," he said in a cheerfully breezy voice as he walked into the room.

As always, he didn't seem fazed by the cold dressed in his customary jeans and a T-shirt. Ariel had always heard that the cold made a man's penis kind of shrink, but if that was true then it definitely wasn't the case for this man. Already his length stood to attention, jutting out like a sword ready to pierce her.

Since speaking was forbidden, she merely hung there, watching him. He didn't seem to mind her watching him, on the contrary, he seemed to enjoy it.

"You're such a good little ice queen." He said it as though it were a compliment and tweaked one of her nipples as he walked over to the freezer.

Inside it was a large slab of ice that was kept permanently frozen, by now she already knew the drill. He came, picked up her bound body, and carried her into the freezer. Although she knew it was colder in there, her body was so used to being cold it hardly noticed the difference.

Her skin prickled as it rested against the ice, and now her body began to shake as the cold penetrated. Her owner fiddled with the ropes, retying them so she was bound to the block of ice spreadeagled.

Then he went to the freezer again.

This was the part she hated the most.

The ropes were for his amusement, his enjoyment, but the ice seemed to be related to some sort of crazy delusion she had yet to figure out. It was like he thought she was infected by some sort of virus that he would contract if he didn't neutralize it first. His way of neutralizing it seemed to be the ice.

Her eyes tracked his movements as he retrieved the phallic-shaped block of ice.

As he moved so he stood by her feet his eyes glittered with lust. The man might be kind of insane, but that didn't mean he didn't absolutely know that what he was doing was wrong.

He just didn't care.

It was what got him off. Knowing she was his helpless victim, that he could do to her whatever he wanted, that there was no way for her to stop him.

Moving slowly, he placed the frozen ice block penis between her legs and shoved it inside her.

It took every ounce of control she had not to cry out at the intrusion. Being put in an ice bath was one thing but having that ice inside your body was a whole new level of cold hell you couldn't explain.

But worse was to come.

Rotating the ice bed she was tied to, he went back to the freezer to retrieve the second ice block, this one in the shape of a plug.

The only way to hold in her moan of pain and sharp sting of cold as this one was inserted into her backside was to bite on her tongue hard enough she tasted blood.

Tears of humiliation burned the backs of her eyes, and since she was facing the floor and not her captor, she allowed a couple of tears to slip free.

There was no worse feeling in the world than knowing you were partly responsible for your own pain and humiliation.

She really was worth nothing.

CHAPTER

Seven

September 10th
  8:44 P.M.

So close but not quite there yet.

Not that Rock was giving up.

It had been a whirlwind of a couple of months, but each day seemed to bring with it a new discovery on what had happened to Ariel and where she was being held.

They weren't there quite yet, but they were getting closer.

He could feel it.

Not much longer, honey. Hold on for me. Don't give up now. I'm coming, I won't give up until I find you.

Every few hours he stopped and uttered those words, silently pleading that they find their way through the universe and to Ariel. He could only imagine how terrified and alone she felt, that was maybe the worst part of it. For so long, she'd isolated herself from others, his fault he knew that, and now she was going through the worst thing a person could endure and she had no one to turn to, no one to comfort her.

Knowing that made him want to rip his own fingernails off just to distract himself from the pain in his chest. Which was why he only allowed himself a few minutes every couple of hours to think about Ariel, the rest of the time he had to block her out to function.

There would be time later to focus on what Ariel had lived through.

Not much longer, Snow White, I swear to you I'm close.

Dragging in a breath of chilled air, he shoved down the tangled mess of emotions that would swamp him if he let them. They were getting close, and he wasn't going to mess things up now.

"You got anything?" he asked as he headed back inside the small cabin high in the fjells—mountains—of Norway. They'd been tracking Dan Johnson and his parole officer Cory Paxton, who had gone off the grid shortly before Panther was able to link him to the illegal activities of Dan and several of his other parolees.

It hadn't been a smooth path getting here. They'd bounced across the globe moving from one breadcrumb to another, but he didn't care how many times he had to get on a plane and fly somewhere else as long as that brought him closer to his goal.

To his woman.

To his heart.

His life.

His everything.

"Might," Panther answered. His fingers were flying across the keyboard almost faster than the speed of light. The man didn't like to be interrupted while he was tugging at a string, so he didn't move his attention from his screen as he continued to tap away, working his magic.

Magic Rock was counting on working.

Tank was on the phone, likely to Tillie, while Trick and Scorpion played cards at the kitchen table. While he had insisted that he wanted to come along, Rock had been equally insistent that Axe stay home with Beth.

With all that was going on with Ariel, Rock knew what was most important in life. It was the people you loved. Not the stuff, not what you did, not what you worked for, not where you lived, although there was nothing wrong with any of those things, but it was the people that really made you alive. Right now, Beth needed Axe. Whether she remembered her husband or not, Axe would move heaven and earth for her. Her best chance of getting her memories back was spending time with the man who loved her.

When he got Ariel back, he was going to ask Eagle if he could take some time off. Time he intended to dedicate to helping Ariel process what she'd been through and begin her journey of healing, a journey that would take a lifetime, but he would be there through all of it. He wasn't giving up on her or giving up on a chance at getting her back. Almost losing her made him realize how stupid he'd been to let his fear keep him away for so long.

At first, he'd just needed to become a man he could respect so he might earn Ariel's respect back. It was why he'd given up scholarships, decided against playing pro football, and hadn't followed his brothers into the family business. The military seemed like a good place to go when you wanted to save lives on a major scale to make up for the one you had taken.

But as the years ticked by, the distance between him and Ariel seemed to grow, and the more it grew the more afraid he got of her rejection.

Deserved as it would be, it would crush him.

So he'd stayed away.

Been selfish. Prioritized his own needs over Ariel's. He shouldn't have let so many years slip by, years he could never get back, years where he knew neither of them were happy. Although he hadn't seen her between graduation and the night at the bar, he'd kept tabs on her. Pumped his parents mercilessly for information on her and how she was doing.

Selfish as it was, each time he heard that a relationship of hers had ended, he'd felt sweeping relief.

Knowing she was dating was a whole new type of hell, and he'd been torn between wanting her to be happy, and praying that she only found happiness with him.

"Got it," Panther announced, drawing all their attention.

"Got what?" he asked.

"I think I found them," Panther replied.

His heart rate accelerated. "Found Ariel?"

"Maybe. I think I found where Cory Paxton has been staying. No guarantees that Mr. Freeze is there, too, but it's closer than we've been so far," Panther explained.

Rock would take it.

"Let's go," he said, already reaching for his pack.

"You don't even know where we're going," Tank said with a small laugh.

"Don't care. What do we need? A plane? Car? We walking?" he asked, anxious to get moving. So long as he was doing something constructive, he was able to keep his emotions under control, it was only on those down times that he struggled.

"Just a car for this one," Panther told them. "Looks like our guy is only a few miles away."

Perfect.

Energy and optimism flooded his system, making him feel antsy. If they really were this close to finding Ariel, she could be in his arms by the end of the day. The thought was both reassuring and terrifying. What state would she be in when they found her?

It wasn't just her physical condition he was worried about, it was her psychological one.

"We should call Piper," he said as they all gathered their weapons and prepared to move out and hopefully track down Cory Paxton. Piper Hamilton-Eden was Prey's on-staff psychiatrist, and had recently married Antonio "Arrow" Eden, a member of Alpha Team. Not only was the woman a fabulous psychiatrist, but she had been through an ordeal similar to what Ariel was going through now, only thankfully she hadn't been in her stalker's clutches for this long. If anyone could help Ariel through this, it was her.

"She's on standby," Tank assured him.

"We should also have a doctor on standby," he added. Although he was the team's medic and could take care of any immediate needs she might have, he wasn't a doctor, and he would feel better once she had been properly checked out.

"We have one," Tank said again. He appreciated his team stepping up to make sure everything was in order while his mind wasn't quite where it needed to be.

They piled into two vehicles. Panther programmed the GPS with the coordinates of where Cory Paxton was staying, and they took off.

There was tension in the car, the kind of protective energy that filled him with warmth and a little optimism. His team knew the truth about how badly he'd messed up with Ariel, and yet they hadn't turned their backs on him, that meant more to him than he could express. These men weren't just his teammates, weren't just his friends, they were every bit as much his brothers as the two men who shared his DNA. They were there for both him and Ariel, and that was the only reason he knew they could get through what lay ahead.

Less than thirty minutes later, they approached a remote cabin surrounded by trees that would hide their approach.

As they all climbed out of the vehicle. This time when a rush of fear for Ariel hit him, Rock didn't bother trying to shove it right back down. He let it burn through his system, let it add fuel to the fire flaming inside him. There was a whole lot of anger inside him, and he was just looking for an outlet for it.

Hopefully, he'd found one.

Like the well-oiled machine that they were, Bravo team descended on the cabin. The idiot inside didn't even know they were there until it was too late. If there was any doubt about the parole officer's guilt in the human smuggling operation that had taken Ariel, it was erased when they found the man red-handed browsing through a stack of photos of other women dressed in the same outfits Ariel had been.

The look on his face when they broke down his door was priceless.

The hunter had become the hunted.

Rock was the predator and Cory Paxton was the prey.

He pounced.

That first hit unleashed a beast inside him and every bit of fear and anger he felt over Ariel's abduction came out as he pounded on one of the men who was responsible for daring to hurt the woman he loved.

There was only one reason he didn't beat the man to death and that wasn't because he wanted to show mercy. It was because there was only one way he was going to get the answers he needed as to the name of the man who had bought Ariel and where he was currently keeping her, and that was through this pathetic excuse for a human being.

~

September 12th
    10:52 P.M.

Ariel shivered in the cold, dark room.

What she wouldn't give for a moment of warmth.

A single one would be enough.

Just to have something warm snuggled around her, a nice cozy blanket or quilt, maybe a nice soft mattress to lie on too.

It sounded like heaven.

Not a bath or a shower though.

No more water. She was so sick of being around it that she didn't even want a nice hot bubble bath, and she usually loved sitting surrounded by the fluffy bubbles. She'd spent too many hours and days being spent tied to blocks of ice. She'd be happy if she never had to get wet again in her life.

Still, the cold had its advantages.

Each day she took another step closer to becoming completely numb.

Another day or so and she'd be there.

Say goodbye to the horrors she was living, and just slip away into a peaceful void of nothingness.

As a little girl, she'd always been afraid of death. Ever since she was the one who found her grandmother's dead body in their guest room when she was six. No one had been able to properly answer her questions about dying, and the answers she had been given, that Grandma was old, that she was sick, that she'd just gone to sleep and never woken up, had terrified her.

For years, she had hated her birthday because she was getting older, and older meant death. No one had explained to her exactly how old old was. And any time she got even the simplest of colds she was almost in a panic, worried she was about to die. Don't even get her started on the phobia of sleep that had taken her years to overcome, because she had been so scared she'd be like her

Grandma and go to sleep one night and not wake up in the morning.

Ironically, it had been Sebastian who had helped her overcome her fears of death, back when he was her everything. He'd told her that death was a part of life, it could come for you any time, no matter how old you were or whether you were sick or healthy, and the only way to beat it was to live the life you had to the fullest. No holding back, no barriers, no worrying about what others thought. Be the very best you it was possible to be and live every second of your life.

Those words had stuck with her for a long time.

Comforted her during the darkest days after Kayla's death and Sebastian's rejection.

They held no comfort here though, not in this Godforsaken place.

How long had it been since she was taken?

Long enough for her to have given up hope. At first, she was so sure that Sebastian would find her, come for her, it seemed like the very least he could do after all the pain he'd caused her when they were teenagers. But with each new day that hope died a little more.

Until now it had run dry.

There was nothing left.

Nothing to hold onto.

Coldness, darkness, and pain were her three constant companions, and spending all day every day with them she lost a little piece of herself each time she woke to find she was still trapped in hell.

Now she just wanted to die.

Anything to end the suffering.

Death was no longer the nightmare it used to be.

Comfort.

That's what it represented now.

A blissful place where there was no pain, no fear, no regrets. Nothing but silence and peace.

Sounded like heaven.

The usual clunk of the lock told her the door was about to open.

He was back.

Already.

Felt like he had only just left, but really, it could have been days since she last saw him. Time meant nothing here in this place.

Even if she wanted to fight him, she had nothing left to give. Weak from lack of movement, and always being tied up, from not being fed enough to fuel her body, she didn't have it in her to fight him. Her mind was weakening, too, fracturing off and hiding away in that quiet, peaceful little corner where it didn't have to focus on what was happening to her body.

Two figures stepped through the door.

Two?

Had he brought a friend with him?

Usually, it was just him, here to play with his ice and his ropes. Why did he bring someone with him?

Ariel would have whimpered in fear despite the lessons she had learned to keep silent at all costs if it didn't take more energy than she had.

How was she supposed to deal with two men?

A crack appeared in her mind. Not like a crack in the sidewalk but a crack in the universe that led her to another place. Feeling like Alice in Wonderland she moved toward it. Peeked through. On the other side was a velvety, soft blackness. It slid over her skin like silk when she took a tentative step through the crack.

As she moved further into the darkness everything else slipped away.

Leaving behind this world was easy even if it meant disappearing into nothingness.

Wasn't she already nothing?

She had nothing else to lose, nothing to live for, slipping away into the blackness was for the best.

A hard voice muttered a curse. "It's going to take us too long to cut her out of all those ropes."

She froze.

Turned away from the blackness.

That voice.

Could it ...?

No.

Of course not.

He was never going to find her.

"Ariel, sweetheart, can you hear me?"

That was Sebastian's voice, and when a gentle hand cupped her chin, she could have sworn that was his touch. Her eyes were open, and when she blinked, the shadowy outline of Sebastian's face came into view.

How?

Hallucination?

The hand holding her chin had a small shake, nudging the peaceful crack out of her reach.

Ariel moaned her disappointment.

Whether Sebastian was real or a figment of her fractured mind she didn't care. It was already too late. She didn't want to be saved she just wanted to be gone.

"That's right, honey, come back to me."

No.

She wanted to leave.

For once couldn't she make her own choices about herself and her life?

A small spark of anger lit inside her.

"Come on, Snow White, snap out of it."

Warm hands caressed her chilled skin, moving briskly as they stroked up and down her arms. Was it her imagination or were the ropes binding her loosening?

Inside her mind, the crack that had just moments ago offered her the refuge she longed for shimmered and disappeared, leaving her trapped here.

Trapped.

That was exactly how she felt.

Was it too much to ask for just a moment of freedom?

"Baby, please." The broken tone of Sebastian's voice startled her enough that she blinked again and a little of the numbness that cloaked her faded.

"Sebastian?" Her voice was a croak. Since she wasn't allowed to speak, her throat was dry from lack of use. Still, he seemed to hear her because he touched his lips to her forehead and held them there. Ariel felt something wet drip onto her chilled skin. Tears? Was Sebastian crying?

Why?

Why would he care enough about her to cry over her?

"I'm here, baby. I'm so sorry it took me so long to find you." His voice had so much emotion that it left her more confused than ever.

Arms lifted her, took her weight, and cradled her as a man she had never seen before continued to cut at the ropes until she was free. Ariel sagged in Sebastian's hold, her deadened limbs not strong enough to do anything, and she braced herself for the coming rush of agonizing pins and needles.

It came as it always did, and since she had been conditioned to not make a sound, she pressed her lips together and let her scream of pain turn inward rather than outward.

As though he knew exactly how she was feeling, Sebastian's arms tightened around her and he pressed another kiss to her forehead.

"Let's get you out of here, sweetheart," Sebastian said softly, his lips touching a kiss to her temple like he couldn't get enough of kissing her.

This was all wrong.

Was it real?

Was she really being rescued?

It all felt so surreal.

Ariel honestly wasn't sure what was happening. While she might have missed her chance to check out of this world, she wasn't really completely in it either. More existing on some sort of alternate plane. Too much had happened to her, and if she really was being rescued, she had no idea how she was supposed to survive the aftermath and live like a normal person.

Because she no longer was a normal person.

Sebastian carried her out of her prison, but just as he started up a flight of stairs someone started shooting at them.

CHAPTER
Eight

September 12th
11:30 P.M.

Fear like no other crept down Rock's spine.

After nine weeks of hunting for Ariel, having lead after lead fall through, slowly piecing together a puzzle that was a lot more terrifying than he'd originally thought, when he and Scorpion had walked into that room, and he'd seen her with his own two eyes, he'd thought it was over.

She was alive, she was safe in his arms, and he would do whatever it took to help her heal and earn her trust back.

Now, with her seconds away from being out of her prison they were being shot at.

Throwing himself and Ariel to the floor, Rock rolled slightly so his body took the brunt of the fall, then quickly rolled again so that he was covering her, using his own body as a shield to protect her from the worst of it if a bullet should hit them.

There was only one person who could be shooting at them.

A man who would pay for his sins with his life.

A bullet whizzed by close enough that he felt it skim across his cheek before slamming into the floor an inch from his head, sending shards of concrete into his face.

Trusting Scorpion to have his and Ariel's backs, Rock tightened his hold on her, curling his body closer around hers until he had her completely surrounded. The sting from the concrete barely registered as the man who had bought Ariel continued to shoot at them.

Beating answers out of Cory Paxton hadn't taken all that long considering the man's taunts that they couldn't make him talk. All that proved was how the parole officer didn't understand that his op was personal to him.

Violence might be part of his job, but it wasn't something Rock enjoyed.

Until Cory Paxton.

Knowing that the now former parole officer had been running an underground human trafficking ring for going on three years now, using the men he was supposed to be supervising to do it, made it easy.

Knowing the man was responsible for Ariel being taken made it even easier.

While he'd held out a short while, it turned out that Paxton wasn't as much a fan of being on the receiving end of the same kind of pain the women he sold had to endure. In the end, he had given them the name of the man who had bought Ariel.

Riley Maddox.

An innocuous-sounding name for an innocuous-looking man.

Turned out, the worldwide infamous serial killer wasn't a billionaire, he was just a pilot who flew other billionaires around the world. Using either blackmail to secure those billionaires' assistance in disposing of his victims or bribing them with some time with his victims before he killed them, he was able to use both his job and his clients to place his victims' bodies around the world while hiding out in the fjells of Norway.

When they'd tracked down the man's remote cabin, he hadn't been there. While the rest of the team were waiting in the main cabin, Rock and Scorpion had searched the property for any other buildings. Finding the tiny shack with a staircase leading underground, he had known even before they saw her that this was where Ariel was being held captive.

Now, he pressed her against the cold concrete, terrified she was going to get hit by a stray bullet. She was so still, so quiet. Too still, too quiet. Had she been hit? Or were her injuries too severe and she was slowly dying?

No.

He wouldn't accept that.

Couldn't.

Already he'd spent far too long without her in his life. Put off explaining what he should have told her a decade ago because he was afraid it wouldn't do any good. That what he'd done was unforgivable and he was just deluding himself.

No more being a coward.

All he'd wanted these last fifteen years was to become a man worthy of Ariel's respect, but he'd gone about it all the wrong way. It wasn't about saving lives, it wasn't about eliminating evil, there was no way to balance out Kayla's death, not even if he lived to be a thousand. The only way to become a man worthy of Ariel was to fight for her.

Bullets continued to fly. One struck the concrete right beside where Ariel's head was tucked under his chin.

Red rage clouded his vision. What Rock wouldn't give to kill this man with his bare hands. Still, dead was dead and in the end, Ariel was all that really mattered to him.

While he might not have any official training, Riley Maddox obviously wasn't about to let his prize possession go without a fight. It was the fact that he had so little training that was making him almost more dangerous. His shots were wild, unfocused, and unpredictable.

Scorpion stood between him and Ariel, and Rock trusted him to take out one of the world's most notorious serial killers, his only job was to protect Ariel.

Something he'd failed at too many times to count.

Suddenly everything fell silent.

Was Riley Maddox dead?

No way was he moving so much as a millimeter until he had confirmation that there was no longer a threat in the room.

"He's dead," Scorpion called out.

Cautiously, he lifted his head. "We're clear?" he confirmed. When it came to Ariel's life there was no such thing as being too careful.

"We're clear. Let's check your girl out and then get her out of here."

That sounded perfect. Carefully, he lifted his body off Ariel, and shifted so he was on his knees beside her. Since they hadn't had Maddox in custody they needed to move quickly, do a straight extraction, and then check her out. There hadn't been time to cover Ariel's naked body or for him to do more than a very preliminary check of her vitals to see if there was anything life-threatening that had to be attended to before they could move her.

Now he was almost afraid to probe deeper.

Afraid of what he would find.

Ariel would live, but she wouldn't be the same woman he'd once known.

There would be scars, if not physical then definitely psychological, and Rock had no idea how to help her heal those wounds. No mission had ever scared him more than what he was facing right now.

Keeping his voice soft and soothing, he picked up her wrist to check her pulse. "Hey, Snow White, I'm just going to take your vitals."

There was no response as he took her pulse, then her blood pressure, and listened to her heart and lungs with a stethoscope. While there was nothing to be overly concerned about, they were weaker than he would have liked. And she hadn't opened her eyes yet.

For as long as he lived, he would never get the image of Ariel, tied into what had to be a painful position, hanging from the ceiling of what felt like a refrigerator. It wasn't just seeing her naked body strung up like that, it was the look in her eyes.

Vacant.

Like she was already gone.

Fighting back tears, he stroked the backs of his knuckles across one cold cheek. "Okay, honey, I'm going to check you for injuries now." Given what she'd been through the last thing he wanted to do was just start touching her without warning. Although since she didn't so much as flinch at his words, he guessed the warning was unnecessary.

While there were scratches and burns from the ropes being tied around her, she had no broken bones and no larger wounds that he could find. Once he'd finished running his hands over her limbs, he took the blanket Scorpion offered and draped it over her.

"How is she?"

"When we get her to the hotel, I'll set up an IV and give her fluids and antibiotics. She's not great, but she doesn't need a hospital. Still want the doctor to check her out though." There was blood on the inside of her thighs as well as on her backside. Didn't have to have an imagination to figure out where it had come from. Having a female doctor do an internal exam would let them know if there was internal bleeding they needed to be concerned about.

As he scooped Ariel into his arms and stood, dark lashes fluttered against cheeks that were far too pale. As far back as when they were little kids, he'd called her Snow White, but never before had she looked so very much like snow.

It took a moment as though she had no strength left in her body, but when her eyes opened, they were bottomless golden-brown pools of pain.

"Sebastian?" she croaked.

His name on her lips was everything he'd wanted for so long. But not like this. He'd expected to hear it in anger, maybe one day once again in love, but not so weak it was a mere hint of a sound.

"Shh, baby, you've done your part, you held on and didn't give up, now you just rest and let me take care of you." He touched his lips to her forehead and held them there for a long moment, unable to break contact with her.

Without protest, Ariel closed her eyes again and rested her head against his shoulder. Holding her felt every bit as good as he'd been dreaming, but he was far from getting the one thing he wanted the most in the world. Ariel's heart. They both had a long, uphill battle ahead of them.

~

September 13th
   2:29 A.M.

. . .

Numbness continued to unfurl throughout her body, slowly drawing her back toward the crack.

Ariel went willingly.

It wasn't until warmth blanketed her that she felt something resembling peace, and maybe a smidgen of security.

Time lost all meaning.

There was no cold, no pain, she felt like she was floating on a cloud.

Not that she trusted the feeling.

How many times had she dreamed she was safe, warm, and free from pain only to wake back up in that cold underground hell?

Too many to count.

"Come on, sweetheart, it's time to wake up now."

A voice had been telling her that often, but she hadn't had the strength to do as it asked.

Didn't even want to do as it asked.

It was so much better here inside her mind. Nothing could touch her in here. It was a safe place to curl up and hide.

"Right now, Snow White," the voice said, this time an obvious order.

Somehow, it worked and her eyes popped open at the command. She found a face hovering above hers. Short dark hair, gray eyes, a face she'd daydreamed about as a kid. A face that had haunted her over the years.

Her white knight.

Her destroyer.

Her savior.

Sebastian had become both the hero and the villain of her story, and she wasn't sure how to feel about that.

Actually, she was. And she didn't like it. Not one little bit.

"Hey, honey." A hand reached out as though to touch her, but seemed to think better of it and pulled back at the last second. "Are you in pain? Do you need more drugs?" Sebastian asked, concern evident in both his face and tone.

While she mostly understood that concern, he wasn't a monster after all, and she wasn't so numb that she didn't know that what she'd been through was horrific, it still seemed extreme. It wasn't like the concern you had for a stranger or even a person from your past. It felt ... personal.

But there was nothing personal left between them.

Just some old memories that were more bitter than sweet for her.

Her mouth opened to answer his question, but somehow no sound came out.

Talking wasn't permitted.

As though he knew exactly what she was thinking, Sebastian shifted and perched on the edge of the bed beside her. He was careful not to touch her and she appreciated that more than she could express.

"You're safe now, Ariel. Free. No one is going to hurt you. Whatever he told you you were and were not allowed to do doesn't apply anymore. No one is going to hurt you again. Ever. If they even try they'll have to go through me first."

The words were spoken with such an impassioned tone that any rebuttal was surprised right out of her mind.

Safe.

That word was so foreign to her. Right now, she couldn't even fathom what it would be like not to be hurt.

Pain had been such a large part of her world since she'd been taken that it didn't seem like she could ever be free of it.

What exactly did Sebastian mean when he said that anyone who tried to hurt her again would have to go through him?

Wasn't like he was going to be part of her life, so how did he expect to enforce that?

Did it even matter?

She might still be alive, might even be free, but she didn't feel free. She was still trapped in a prison, it was just a different kind of prison now.

"Do you need more painkillers?" Sebastian asked.

Knowing she was allowed to speak at will now, that there would be no punishments, didn't wipe away what had been instilled in her. For days, weeks, months, however long she had been in that freezing underground room, she had known that speaking meant punishment.

How was she just supposed to accept that she wasn't a prisoner any longer?

"I-I'm okay," she croaked, her voice feeling weird and scratchy in her throat, and she couldn't stop a tremble of fear as her conditioned body braced itself for coming pain. To distract herself, Ariel looked around to find herself in a small room that reminded her of a hotel room. She was on a bed, bundled in blankets, with an IV ran from the back of one hand. She was clean, dry, and warm.

Really, she was a whole lot better than okay.

The curtains were drawn so she couldn't see out and had no idea where she was, which filled her with anxiety. Ariel was sick of being moved around like an inanimate object with no thoughts, feelings, or needs of her own to be considered.

"Where are we?" The question came out as a squeak as her pulse spiked. She needed to know where she was, she needed even some basic control over herself and what happened to her.

"Somewhere safe. We'll stay here for a few days until you're strong enough to travel, then we're going home."

Home.

After what she'd been through, it had seemed like a dream that would never come true.

Only like dreams often were, in the cold light of day it didn't seem as wonderful as it had when it was just inside your head.

What did home look like now?

Could she go back to her cute little house? To her job?

Could she go back to living life like a normal person?

Truth was, she was far from normal. She couldn't even speak without crushing fear that she was about to be punished for it. There was no way she could be a successful social worker. No way she could take on anyone else's problems when her own smothered her. Without a job she would have no way to support herself, and her parents wouldn't be interested in taking her in, they had always been more worried about their own lives than her.

"Ariel, we're going to need to talk about what happened," Sebastian said, his voice so impossibly gentle it brought tears to her eyes.

No.

She couldn't talk about that.

Not with anyone but especially not with Sebastian.

What would he think of her if he knew she had taken the first step that precipitated her demise? Already he thought that she was nothing but a whore. If he knew that she had willingly allowed a man to touch her, give her an orgasm, and given him one as well, just for a bowl of pasta then he would despise her.

Wildly she shook her head.

No.

No way was she talking about what those men had done to her.

Never.

Those were secrets she would carry with her to her grave.

Besides, it wasn't like talking about it was going to change anything. It couldn't undo what had been done, couldn't take it back.

"You need to talk about it, sweetheart," Sebastian continued like she wasn't on the verge of a complete and utter meltdown. "You can't keep that kind of stuff inside because it will destroy you from the inside out if you let it. If you can't talk to me then we have a doctor who's waiting outside to check you out and a psychiatrist that works with me and my team flying in."

What help could the psychiatrist possibly give her?

Wasn't like they would know anything about what Ariel had endured. All the doctor would likely do was pump her full of drugs and sedate her into oblivion.

Would that really be such a bad thing?

It could help her find her way back to her peaceful crack.

"I have a lot I need to say to you, Ariel." This time when he reached toward her, he didn't pull back.

Unable to tear her gaze away from his fingers as they moved closer, she watched as they trembled, surprising her, and when they touched her cheek, although she flinched, she was even more surprised to find that she didn't pull away.

Being touched was the last thing she wanted, and being touched by Sebastian was even worse, and yet she couldn't move no matter how much she wanted. Like he'd put her in some sort of trance.

"A lot to make up for," he continued, his voice smooth as silk and washing over her with a wave of calm.

No.

Be strong.

Remember how much he hurt you before.

Remember how he left you utterly broken.

Don't fall for this. It's not real. Just an act. He's just caught up in the emotions of saving your life. He doesn't love you. Never did.

Despite the pep talk she gave herself, Ariel could feel herself weakening, succumbing to his charms.

"I've spent the last fifteen years trying to become a man worthy of you, of your love, your heart, your trust. I'm ready to fight for you, Ariel. Fight for us."

If he'd said those words to her before she'd been abducted they might have meant something, but now the woman he claimed he wanted to fight for no longer existed. She'd died weeks ago and all that was left was this shell of a person.

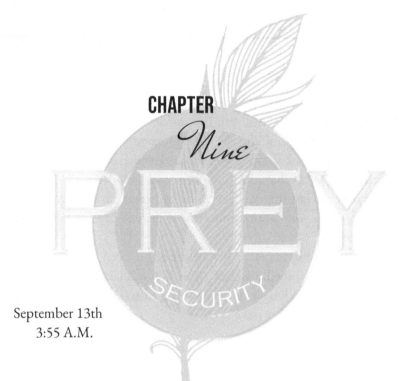

CHAPTER
Nine

September 13th
3:55 A.M.

"How's she doing?" Scorpion asked as he opened the door.

"She's alive," Rock replied as he stepped around his friend and into the hotel room next door to where he'd just left Ariel with the doctor.

Just because she had no life-threatening injuries and she had finally woken up, it didn't mean she was anywhere close to being what anyone could call okay. It was her eyes, they scared the hell out of him. They were so vacant, so empty. The woman he'd loved for most of his life wasn't inside there.

Where was she?

And how did he get her back?

He had no idea how to reach her. It was like the Ariel he'd known and loved since they were kids had been lost during her ordeal.

He wanted her back. So badly it hurt. He literally had an ache in his chest that was only getting worse. Finding Ariel, getting her back, holding her again, he'd thought it would make everything better, but it hadn't. She felt as far away from him now, even though she was right next door, as she had when he had no idea where she was or who had taken her.

"She'll get there," Trick assured him, but the words didn't come anywhere close to providing any assurance.

Would she?

Was it possible to survive what Ariel had and still be able to live anything close to a normal life?

"She needs you, man. Don't give up on her," Panther said. "You being there will get through to her eventually, you just have to give it time."

Time.

Already he'd wasted more time than he should have. Time he could never get back, and to know that there might never be a chance for there to be a future for them cut deep.

Doubt raged inside him. Was he the best person to help her through this or was he doing more harm than good by shoving himself on her, inserting himself into her life whether she liked it or not?

Did that make him no better than Riley Maddox? Than Cory Paxton? Than Dan Johnston? Was he just another person taking over, removing her control over herself and her life?

"Just be there because she knows you're there," Scorpion told him. "In the car, even when she was out, she kept herself curled into you like you were her safe haven."

She had?

He had been too busy checking and rechecking her vitals, needing the reassurance that she was alive, that she hadn't left him, to notice anything else.

The knowledge that even in unconsciousness she had sought him out for security bolstered his confidence a little. Maybe things weren't completely hopeless.

"There's no worse feeling in the world than knowing you're hurting someone you love," Tank said softly. Despite her forgiveness and the fact that they were a couple now, Rock knew that Tank hadn't yet forgiven himself for using Tillie and lying to her about it.

Same way he felt about how he'd hurt Ariel.

Even if she forgave him, he would never be able to forgive himself for being so heartless and cruel.

"There really isn't," he agreed. "I'm so scared that I'm making everything worse by being here. I have to be the last thing she needs right now, the last person she wants around her." As badly as he wanted to fight for them, if Ariel told him that to heal and recover she needed him not to be around, then he would leave.

For now.

Give her some space, but he wasn't ever walking away from her again.

When the door to the hotel room opened all five of their heads turned to see the doctor walk through it.

Doing his best not to pounce on the unsuspecting woman, Rock strode over to her. "How is she?"

"All things considered, she's doing very well. She's stable, the fluids and antibiotics are helping. I rechecked and recleaned all her wounds. None of them look serious and all are healing well. The ones around her wrists in particular are deep and will take a while to heal. They'll leave scars behind, but there is no infection in them. She's weak and after weeks of inactivity her muscles have atrophied, but with some gentle physical therapy, it shouldn't take her long to get back into shape."

"Did she consent to the internal exam?" he asked. As much as he hated the need for one, he couldn't live in denial. Ariel had been kidnapped by human traffickers, sold as a sex slave, there was no chance she hadn't been raped. And even if he wanted to pretend that he'd gotten to her before that happened, he'd seen the blood.

The doctor gave an almost imperceptible wince. "She did. There's some bruising and a little bit of tearing, but she'll heal, and will be able to have sex again once she does."

The if she even wants to ever have sex again hung unsaid in the air.

It didn't need to be said, they all knew that Ariel wasn't just going to magically get over the trauma she had endured.

"I understand you have a psychiatrist on the way in?" the doctor asked.

"Arriving tomorrow morning," he confirmed.

"Good. She doesn't need a hospital, and there's nothing more I can do for her. Keep her comfortable, let her get plenty of rest, don't push her to do more than she's ready for, but also encourage her to try to get out and move about. It's a beautiful place here, peaceful, even with the cruise ships in. Make sure she knows she's not alone, that she has a support system. She was asking for you," the doctor told him.

Surprise rendered him silent for a moment.

Ariel actually wanted him in the room with her?

No way was he letting that opportunity pass by.

Without another word, Rock hurried out of the room and into the one beside it. Ariel was still in the bed, right where he'd left her, but the doctor had opened the curtains and sunlight streamed into the room. The view from the hotel was stunning, looking right out into the fjord. With the snow-capped fjells surrounding the tiny town of Geiranger, it was a gorgeous place. The doctor was right, there was an air of peacefulness, and he prayed it helped Ariel find some measure of peace.

Her head turned and she watched him walk toward her. Since she made no move to shrink away as he came closer, he stretched out beside Ariel on the bed, sitting so he was propped against the headboard. Carefully—tentatively—he reached for her, pulling her into his arms. She came, not willingly, more like she was a rag doll being moved, but at least she didn't fight him.

Small steps.

This wasn't a sprint it was a marathon. Rock had always known it would take time, a lot of it, to earn back Ariel's trust, and that was before this major roadblock had been thrown up between them.

If he wanted to get her back, he had to prove to her that he was never going to hurt her again, that he was somebody she could trust. That was going to take time.

Lots of time.

"I'm here, sweetheart," he whispered as he touched his lips to her forehead. "Don't give up, baby. Please."

"It's too late," Ariel murmured. When she lifted her head off his shoulder he watched as tears flooded her eyes. Tears he would do anything to take away.

This was hell.

Why couldn't there be some sort of magical words to use to take away all of her pain and make it his own?

"No," he said firmly. "I won't believe that. You survived nine weeks of hell, you are not giving up now. I won't let you."

A small smile tipped her lips up for a moment, and from the look in her eyes it surprised her as much as it surprised him.

It faded far too soon, replaced by a worried frown. "What if he comes back?"

"The man who bought you? He can't. He's dead, honey." Although he believed that Riley Maddox had gotten off far too easy considering what he'd done to Ariel and the number of innocent women he had bought, tortured, and murdered, the important thing was he was dead. Ariel wouldn't have to deal with the added trauma of a trial, which he hoped would help her on her journey of healing.

"No. I meant Arthur Gomez. He wants to get rid of me, when he finds out I'm alive and free he'll come back."

Rock felt his blood turn to ice at her words.

They had assumed Ariel had been snatched at random, but what she'd just told him meant she had been targeted on purpose.

Because someone wanted to get her out of the way.

Which meant his sweet Snow White wasn't safe.

∽

September 14th
11:03 A.M.

Was it possible to just let go and let yourself die?

Ariel wondered that as she lay in the bed with Sebastian's arms around her. Although her body was slowly getting stronger, her mind was getting weaker.

All the time she'd been held captive, all she had wanted was to live, to go home, to be rescued, but now that she was, she found she didn't know how to live anymore.

How did you process what she'd been through?

Right now, it felt like there would never be a light at the end of the tunnel.

What scared her the most was that she didn't even care.

Slipping away into nothingness didn't seem so bad at all. It was definitely the easier of the two options. Living meant having to fight. Not just once or twice, but every second of every day. Maybe that would change at some point, but right now, it was so overwhelming she just didn't even want to try.

Dying might mean giving up but it also meant being free.

Completely free.

That was such a tempting thought that it made her not even want to give fighting a chance.

After all, what was she really fighting for?

To go back to her lonely life, where all she really had was her job and one friend who she was pretty positive knew who Sebastian was and had been trying to set up a meeting between her and the man who came dangerously close to destroying her the night she was abducted.

That didn't seem as appealing as it had when she was tied up and hanging from the ceiling in her owner's underground room.

It would be so easy to just ... let go.

Stop eating—wasn't like she had an appetite anyway—stop drinking, just lie here in bed and ...

Sooner or later it would be over.

"I'm not letting you go, Ariel," Sebastian vowed as though he was somehow privy to her private thoughts. "I'm fighting for you, for us. Fighting for you like I should have done sooner."

How could she believe that?

Why would he want to fight for something he'd already had but thrown away?

There was a part of her that wanted to believe Sebastian. Right now, she felt all alone even if Sebastian had barely left her side, it would be nice to think there would be someone there, someone who would never leave. All her childhood dreams had revolved about the man sitting beside her. How could there not be part of her that would love to see those dreams come to fruition?

But Sebastian had hurt her.

Badly.

Even if he was telling her the truth, and he did want to be with her, too much time had passed. And she just didn't have the energy to deal with Sebastian and their complicated past. What she'd been through was too awful to deal with and occupied every ounce of energy she had.

"You're just going to give up, Ariel? That's not the girl I remember. The girl I remember was tough enough to survive anything. The girl I remember would do anything for anyone, she had the sweetest heart and the sunniest personality. The girl I remember had more strength than any other person I knew."

"The girl you remember doesn't exist anymore." Maybe she never had.

When had she ever been strong?

Not when she'd used Kayla's death to sleep with Sebastian. Not when she'd been heartbroken and never healed or moved on from Sebastian's betrayal. Not when she'd willingly handed over her body to be abused.

Not ever.

She wasn't strong.

In fact, she was the very definition of weak.

"No. I don't believe that. You don't either, stop lying to yourself."

A spark of anger flickered to life inside her.

How dare he tell her she didn't know her own mind.

She was so sick of people acting like she wasn't an autonomous person with her own thoughts and feelings. Her own wants and needs. So sick of everyone expecting her to take what they gave her and accept it.

From her parents expecting her to be happy with the scraps of attention they threw her way when they weren't too busy with their jobs. To Sebastian who didn't make a move on her until the most inopportune time then threw it in her face. To the men who bought her and thought she would cave to their will simply because they were bigger and stronger than her.

No more.

"I'm not a liar," she snapped.

Instead of contradicting her or getting angry with her, Sebastian grinned down at her. "There's my girl, I knew she was still in there. And no, baby, you're not a liar. What you've been through is horrific, and I know it will leave scars, but trust me, sweetheart, if anyone can get through this, it's you. I believe that. I believe in you."

Sebastian believed in her?

Why did that seem so unbelievable?

And why did it bring to life a glimmer of hope?

The time when he was the center of her whole world was long since passed. It ended when he'd shattered her world. Now he was back, and he seemed to want her. He'd said several times that he was going to fight for her, earn her trust back, but she still didn't really know what that meant or whether these so-called feelings he had were because of her or just because he felt sorry for her.

Could she put her faith in him?

It seemed like too big of an ask, yet ... her heart begged her to take the chance. Let Sebastian take care of her, carry a little of her load.

But what if he wound up hurting her again?

There was no if.

He would.

She couldn't believe this sudden change of heart of his. Still ...

"You believe in me?" she asked softly.

"Always, baby. Always. I never gave up on you, I was just trying to become the man you deserved."

She had no idea what he meant by that.

And she was too afraid to ask.

Allowing Sebastian to take over, take care of her, and make all her problems go away seemed like taking a step backward—or at least staying right where she was—rather than taking a step forward.

Make it or break it time.

Ariel had to decide. Was she going to crumble into a thousand pieces, pieces too small to ever be put back together, give up and fade away until she really did become numb and disappeared into nothingness, or was she going to fight with everything she had to forge some kind of life?

Weak or strong?

What was she?

Problem was, even if she did want to be strong, be a survivor, she had no idea how to do it.

A knock on the door drew her attention, and Sebastian's arms tightened around her, his lips pressed to her temple. "I wish we had all the time in the world to get you strong, sweetheart, but we don't. I don't want to push you too hard when you have so much going on, but I can't walk away either. I'll prove to you how much you mean to me. I'll prove to you that I'll never hurt you again. Whatever it takes."

With that, he stood and walked to the door.

Ariel stared after him, still not really comprehending what was going on here.

Sebastian wanted her?

She meant something to him? He had a funny way of showing it. Ripping out her heart, humiliating her, insulting her, turning the whole school against her, and then disappearing for fifteen years.

Yeah, she totally could believe she meant something to him. Insert eye roll.

"Ariel, this is Piper. Piper, Ariel." Sebastian made the introductions, and she looked past him to see a petite brunette standing there. The woman was dressed in a pretty pale pink sundress, a diamond sparkled from her left hand, and she had a small baby bump.

A jolt of longing hit her hard.

For years she had resigned herself to spending the rest of her life alone. No husband, no kids, and no family of her own. Just her.

Maybe she hadn't done as good a job of convincing herself she didn't want any of that as she'd thought. Her gaze drifted back to Sebastian. Or maybe it was this man playing games with her head and her heart.

"Hi, Ariel." The smile Piper gave her was sincere and she felt an instantaneous connection. Which made absolutely no sense. She struggled to connect to people, the taunts of the kids from her school always echoed in her ears, reminding her of Kayla's death and that no one could really be trusted.

"Umm, hi," she returned, suddenly self-conscious and all too aware of the fact that she must look a mess. Unwashed, with tangled hair, gaunt, and much too pale, she looked more zombie than human and felt it too.

The last thing she wanted to be doing right now was meeting someone new. Especially someone as beautiful and put together as the woman standing before her. What could this woman possibly know about what Ariel had just lived through?

"Piper is the psychiatrist for Prey Security, where I work," Sebastian told her.

It was on the tip of her tongue to say she didn't need help, but of course, that would be ridiculous. Of course she did. She was drowning here and in desperate need of someone to throw her a life ring.

Instead of Sebastian reassuring her, the woman moved around him, closing the distance between them. "I know what you're going through, Ariel, because I went through something similar. I know what it's like to want to simply cease to exist because it's just too hard to figure out a way to go on."

Piper had just echoed her every fear. Maybe there was hope for her yet.

Or maybe, like always, the rug would be pulled out from underneath her, and she'd wind up in a worse position than she was already in.

CHAPTER Ten

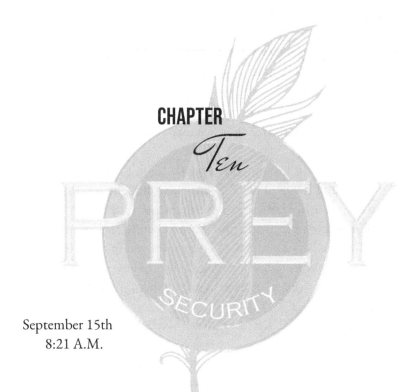

September 15th
   8:21 A.M.

Ariel actually looked better.

After spending some time with Piper the day before, she seemed to have found something to hold onto.

Wasn't like Rock was kidding himself, she was a long way from being anywhere close to okay, but at least it felt like she wasn't so far away from him she was out of reach. At least she was trying, and that was all he could really ask of her.

Although they had things they needed to discuss, both personal and professional, he had pulled back on the questions he needed to ask to give her time to breathe, and pull herself together. There was no doubt that Piper was a miracle worker because Ariel had actually gotten out of bed. She'd avoided the shower but had something to eat and even read for a while. When he'd offered her something to help her sleep, she surprised him by accepting without argument and had slept right through.

This morning she had gotten herself up and dressed and was now sitting out on the balcony staring out at the fjord before them. Since they'd gotten up early, they'd been able to look out at the view without the cruise ship there to spoil it.

It was beautiful here, and even though the population grew by about a hundred times in the peak of summer with all the tourists, it was a sweet little town, and with fall approaching things were calming down. Rock had never heard of this place before they'd decided to spend a few days here, only because it was fairly close to where Ariel had been held, but he was glad they had. This was the perfect place for Ariel to begin her journey of healing. If any place could help her start on the road to recovery, it was this little town of Geiranger.

Her mesmerized gaze was locked on the water, but he sensed she was finally starting to believe she was safe. Rebuilding her life wouldn't be easy, but he knew she could do this, and he would be beside her every step of the way.

"Good morning," Piper said as she came breezing through the door, her husband Arrow right behind her. In their arms they carried plates piled with pancakes. "Who's hungry? Arrow spoke to the kitchen and they made us pancakes we could bring to the room."

"Pancakes are Ariel's favorite," he said as he went to take the plate from Piper's hands. "When we were kids, we used to have so much fun trying out different things in them. White chocolate chips with mango are her favorite."

"White chocolate chips and mangoes?" Arrow made a face. "You're crazy," he told Ariel who was watching them with a smile.

"Hey, don't knock it till you try it," she said, and he felt his heart lurch at this moment of normalcy. "I'll cook you some, I know you'll ... oh ... I don't ... just because Piper ... I know we're not friends ... I just ..."

"Will make me some when we get home," Arrow said firmly.

"Ariel, what happens or doesn't happen between you and Rock, you will always have a family at Prey," Piper told her. "That's how we are, and you're a part of us now. And don't listen to Antonio, I think white chocolate chips and mango sound like they would be amazing in pancakes. So does the little one," she said as she rested a hand on her small baby bump.

"Uh-oh. Another pregnancy craving," Arrow teased. "Better hope the hotel has mangoes."

"You try being pregnant and see how you deal with it." Piper swatted at her husband's shoulder.

Rock watched Ariel watch the couple as they bantered and teased one another. There was a wistfulness to her expression along with longing, and when her gaze shifted to him, he didn't bother to hide that he'd been watching her. He wanted her to know that he was all in, that he had nothing to hide and was desperately in love with her and hoping for a second chance.

Instead of quickly looking away, Ariel stared back at him, her expression turning thoughtful. So far, she hadn't given him any indication of whether or not she could forgive him or give him a second chance. Of course, he understood why, she had bigger things to deal with than him, and he hoped her silence meant she was at least thinking about letting him in.

"I'm ready," Ariel announced suddenly. Standing, she came back into the hotel room, closing the door behind her and taking one of the two armchairs. He had intended to give her a little longer before pressing her for answers about the revelation she'd made, but if she was ready then they'd do this now. Maybe having an opportunity to be involved in her own case would help her find a measure of control he knew had been lacking in her life since she had been abducted.

"Do you want us to go?" Piper asked, indicating herself and Arrow.

"No, stay, please," Ariel answered.

When Arrow looked to him to see if he minded them staying, Rock nodded his head. Whatever made this easier for Ariel, that was all he cared about. If she needed Piper to stay, he was happy to have the psychiatrist there. Both Arrow and Piper worked for Prey, and this was a Prey case so it wasn't like they were going to hear anything they shouldn't. Yes, whatever they learned would be turned over to the cops, but Prey would also be working this.

Piper was right, Ariel was part of the Prey family now. Sooner or later, she would figure out that meant she had just acquired a few dozen overly protective big brothers and a whole bunch of sisters who would support her with everything they had to give.

"I'm proud of you, honey," he said as he returned his gaze to Ariel. "You got this."

She nodded somewhat uncertainly, but there was fierce determination in her pretty golden-brown eyes. "Arthur Gomez was accused of hitting his daughter. I was assigned the case. It should have been open and shut, there were independent witnesses, the girl had bruises all over, and an untreated broken arm. He tried to bribe me, offered me an insane amount of cash to keep my mouth shut, but there was no way I was going to do that."

"No way," he echoed. His Snow White was pure to her core. There was no way she would turn her back on a child in need, not for anything, and certainly not for money.

"The girl told me she'd had a sister. A sister her dad sold. No one believed me or the girl. Arthur tried to use that, say that his daughter had psychological problems and had been harming herself. That the co-worker who saw him hit the girl didn't realize he was really trying to stop her from hurting herself. He was lying, I know that little girl was telling the truth." Her imploring eyes moved between them begging them to believe her.

"No one is doubting you, Ariel," Rock assured her. She was smart, and intuitive, and if she believed the little girl was telling her the truth then he believed her.

"You do? Without even talking to the girl?"

"If you believe her, then we believe you."

"Cops couldn't find any evidence of this sister. I don't know how he did it, Sebastian. Somehow, he kept that girl locked in the house away from everyone, for over a decade. Without proof of the sister's existence, the whole case would be dropped. I was the only thing keeping it alive, I would never have stopped fighting for that girl."

No, she wouldn't.

Which meant she was a threat to a man like Arthur Gomez.

"Do you know for a fact Arthur was involved in your abduction?" he asked.

"I ... no," Ariel said softly. "Not proof, but I know it was him. He sold his daughter, and he thought selling me was the perfect way to get rid of me. I thought I heard him once, right at the beginning, but ... I don't know. Maybe I'm just trying to make sense out of a senseless thing." Her voice grew distant, her eyes seemed to look through him. "After I thought I heard him, they moved me to a different location. It was ... they did terrible things to me there ... things I didn't even know people did to one another. It was my fault, I became exactly what they wanted me to become."

Screw giving her space, no way was he going to let her think even for one second that she deserved what had happened to her. Moving closer, he perched on the edge of her chair and took her hands, pressing them between his and rubbing them, wishing he could wipe away everything she'd been through. "I'm so sorry, sweetheart. I hate that you went through that. I hate it so much, but listen to me carefully, Ariel. It. Was. Not. Your. Fault. I don't care what you did. I don't care if you had to let them do things to you to keep yourself alive."

"But—"

"No. No buts."

"Don't look at me," Piper said with a laugh when Ariel looked at her. "I'm not going to agree with you. You survived. That means you did everything you were supposed to do."

"I'd never disagree with my wife," Arrow added, smiling warmly at Ariel.

Ariel's brows dipped, her forehead furrowed, there was surprise in her eyes now. "You meant it."

"Meant what, honey?"

"When you said that you believed in me, that you've never given up on me."

He wanted to shout his relief and joy, he'd finally made the first crack in her armor. Rock wanted to drag her onto his lap and kiss her, but she was in no way ready for that kind of intimacy. Instead, he settled for squeezing the hands he still held. The hands she still let him hold.

"We will figure this out, Snow White, I promise you that. We'll get justice for that little girl, and for you, that is a vow I won't break. I won't ever lie to you again or hurt you on purpose. Do you think you can find a way to forgive me and give me a second chance?"

∾

September 15th
    1:19 P.M.

Could she forgive him?

Sebastian's question had been spinning around and around inside her head for hours, and she was no closer to coming up with any sort of answer. Even now, as they strolled along the small street outside the hotel, the sunlight glinting off the clear water of the fjord, and the tree-filled fjells surrounding them, they weren't enough to steal her attention.

Ariel honestly wasn't sure whether or not it was possible for her to forgive him and give him a second chance. He'd shattered her heart, embarrassed her, shunned her, and then walked away like she was nothing.

But they had been young at the time, only in high school, and grieving and guilt-ridden on top of that.

Maybe maturity had helped him realize how badly he'd hurt her, how wrong what he'd done was. Because young, grieving, and guilty wasn't an excuse for hurting someone you supposedly cared about.

Everything he was saying was what she had dreamed about hearing for so many years. It was hard not to believe those words. He'd come looking for her, too, there must have been a reason, and he'd fought to find her while she was trapped in Hell. He'd saved her life.

If he hadn't been so determined to find her, she would still be in Hell.

Sixteen-year-old Ariel would forgive him because she was a people pleaser, but thirty-year-old Ariel knew that when you tried too hard to please people all that happened was that those people wound up walking all over you.

"I ... don't know," she whispered, giving him the only thing she could right now. Her honesty.

While he didn't say it, she could feel Sebastian's disappointment, knowing exactly what she was talking about despite her answering hours after him asking.

Still to his credit, his smile was gentle as he looked down at her, and he reached out and took her hand, lacing their fingers together.

"It's okay, Snow White, I understand."

He might, but she still felt the need to explain. "It's not about forgiving. I can forgive. Life is too short to hold onto grudges. You hurt me, but I actually believe you when you say you regret it. And you're the reason I'm alive right now, and free. It's just I don't know about the second chance ... right now, I don't have the mental energy to deal with anything other than surviving."

If she'd expected him to be annoyed with her, to pity her, or reaffirm her fears that she was weak, he did none of those things.

Instead, he stopped walking, tugged her toward him, and wrapped his arms around her, lifting her feet right off the ground as he buried his face against her neck and held it there. Then he feathered a kiss to her temple.

"I am always proud of you, honey. Always. I know I messed up. I know I hurt you deeply. I've spent the last fifteen years trying to find a way I can be worthy of you, and now I know the way to do that was just to be here. Beside you. Always beside you, Snow White. I want to be here for you while you deal with everything you've been through. I want to listen if you need to talk, dry your tears after you've cried, and make you laugh if you need cheering up. I want to be your friend again. Do you think we could just start there?"

Maybe that was something she could do.

Friendship. No pressure for more.

For so long she'd wanted her two best friends back, but it had felt like it was impossible. Kayla was gone and Sebastian may as well be.

But now Sebastian was back, and every time he spoke, he sounded so sincere that she couldn't not believe what he was saying, even if she'd thought he had broken her trust beyond repair.

Now was the time when she needed as much support as she could get and people kept offering it to her, no strings attached. Piper and Arrow, Sebastian's teammates, none of them knew her, and yet they had all promised her that anything she needed, all she had to do was ask, and they'd do it.

Sebastian had been a tower of strength for her these last few days.

He'd been there, he had been honest but not pushy about what he wanted. He was attentive, he knew what she needed before she did, and his presence offered a comfort she knew she couldn't find anywhere else.

"I think I'd like for us to be friends again," she said. Having her best friend back felt both wonderful and weird.

The relief and joy on Sebastian's face about stole her breath. Wow, he was good-looking when he smiled like that. It would be a lie to say that she wasn't attracted to Sebastian, she always would be. It would also be a lie to say that she wasn't scared that she would wind up wanting more than she had to give.

"I can't promise more though," she quickly added.

"I'll take friendship for now," he told her.

That was what worried her.

What if for now lasted forever?

Was she setting herself up for disaster by even agreeing to friendship?

When he realized she might not have it in her to give him what he wanted, would he just throw her away again?

"What if I can't ever give you more? What if I'm not capable of it? What if I can't trust ever again? What if I can't love ever again? What if I can't ever have sex again?" While Ariel couldn't say sex was high—or even on—her list of priorities right now, it was about the fact that she had to accept she might never be a normal woman again. Even before being abducted, sold, and raped she hadn't liked sex all that much, now the very idea of it brought her out in a cold sweat.

Realizing she'd asked that last question loud enough that the other tourists around them had stopped and were looking at her, Ariel blushed, her eyes filled with tears.

This was so humiliating.

Bringing it up to Sebastian was bad enough, but strangers hearing her made it that much worse.

Taking her hand, Sebastian guided her away, slightly off the street and in between two buildings. One of his hands cupped her cheek, his fingers gentle as they caressed her temple. "Snow White, I don't want to be with you to have sex with you, I want to be with you because I'm madly in love with you. I want to spend the rest of my life with you whether we have a sex life or not."

"Sure," Ariel scoffed. A man who looked like Sebastian did, who had a drool-worthy body like he did, who was smart, sensitive, and literally saved lives for a living, didn't give up sex. Not for anyone. "A man like you needs sex."

His gaze was direct, face serious. "A man like me? You mean one who is so in love with one woman he can't see straight. That it doesn't matter if it's fifteen years or fifteen seconds without seeing her it all feels like an eternity. A man who has only ever wanted one woman, and no one else can even come close. No one else matters."

Ariel's mouth dropped open. Was he saying what she thought he was saying?

"You mean you've never been ...?"

"With another woman? Never wanted to. I ruined what should have been the most special night of our lives because I blamed myself for Kayla's death, and it felt like I'd used it to finally have all of you."

"That's what you accused me of doing." Like it was just yesterday pain lanced through her chest.

His deep gray eyes filled with as much pain as she felt. "I made the biggest mistake of my life lashing out at you like that. I couldn't deal with the guilt I felt so I tried to shove it away. Onto you. I don't deserve your forgiveness, Ariel, I know that. I don't deserve the second chance I asked for or even your friendship. But it's only ever been you for me. I've spent the last fifteen years trying to become a man who was worthy of you. There haven't been any other women, I didn't have time for other women, or care about them."

So, he'd only ever had sex the one time they'd both lost their virginity.

Because of her.

Because he loved her.

More tears welled in her eyes. "I've ... there have been ... I'm ..."

Silencing her with a finger to her lips, he leaned down and kissed her forehead. "You've been with other men, that's okay. I mean, I hate it, makes me want to track them down and rip their hearts out for touching you, even if they were good men who treated you well. Were they?"

"Good men?"

"Yeah."

Ariel nodded. "They treated me well, but ... they weren't you."

A smile wiped away a little of the grief in his eyes. "Good. I'm glad they treated you like you deserved. I'm also glad they didn't make you feel the same way I do."

So was she.

The future was uncertain. She didn't know what it held for her and Sebastian, but she knew right now she needed to focus on healing, to figure out a way to recover and rebuild from the horrific ordeal she'd just lived through.

"I promise you won't regret giving me a chance to prove I can be your friend again," Sebastian vowed, then lifted her hands and touched a kiss to the back of each.

"What happens next?" With them? With her? With the man who wanted her to disappear?

"Now we give you a few days to recoup before we travel home. Then me and my team figure out a way to nail Arthur Gomez. Then once he's not a threat to you, I figure out a way to fix what I broke between us."

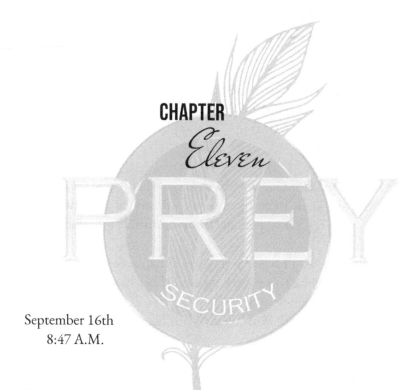

CHAPTER
Eleven

September 16th
8:47 A.M.

"Where are we going?" Ariel asked.

Rock had to hand it to her, she was an absolute trooper. It hadn't been a good night. Even with the help of the sedative he'd given her to help her sleep, she'd tossed and turned most of the night.

Nightmares had plagued her. Waking her hadn't helped, playing her favorite music hadn't helped, keeping the TV on so she knew she was someplace safe hadn't helped either. In the end, the only thing he'd been able to do that had actually worked was sliding into the bed beside her and holding her in his arms.

Although that had helped, by the time he'd resorted to that— holding off on doing it earlier because he hadn't wanted her to feel like he was taking advantage of the situation or do anything that would wind up being counterproductive—it had been five in the morning. Neither of them might have gotten much sleep because there was no way he could sleep while he knew Ariel was suffering, but they'd both had a great morning.

Deciding they needed to get out, get some fresh air, and go further than the tiny main shopping street, he'd planned a little day out for all of them. After working relentlessly for nine weeks searching for Ariel, plus another ten months before that trying to find Beth, and then who had abducted her, his whole team needed a break.

"Somewhere fun," he told her, taking her hand and entwining their fingers.

"That doesn't tell me anything," she grumbled.

"Was that an eye roll?" he teased.

A small smile curled up one side of her mouth. "No. I don't do eye rolls, you must have me confused with Tillie, she's the eye roller." As though realizing what she'd said, her half-smile faded. "Did she know?"

"Tillie? About who I was?" he asked. Rock had known this would come up sooner or later, but he'd hoped not until they were back home, and Ariel could see and talk to Tillie herself to see how much her friend cared about her.

"Yeah. I told her about you, about our past, not long after she got out of the hospital. She's why you were at the bar that night, wasn't she? She was going to tell me that you were on Tank's team and set up a meeting."

Lying might be easier, it might spare Ariel's feelings, but not in the long run. Besides, he didn't want any lies between them, and he'd do whatever it took to patch up Ariel's friendship with Tillie if it needed the help. "She saw my tattoo and figured it out."

"Your tattoo?"

Since he'd thought about her every day of the last fifteen years, it was easy to forget that she hadn't really been part of his life. "Your birthday and mine in Roman numerals on my chest and a butterfly. She put two and two together and realized I was the man from your past. She didn't tell me you used to work with her until a couple of days before she set up the meeting. She was really protective of you. She cares about you a lot and takes her job as your best friend seriously."

"I wish she'd told me right away."

"I know. She does too. She blames herself for what happened to you, blames me too."

Ariel's brows crinkled in that cute way they did when she thought someone was being ridiculous. "It's not either of your fault. It's Arthur Gomez's."

"Are you going to be okay? You and Tillie?" Since Tank and Tillie were together, and there was no way he was walking away from Ariel, even if all they ever had was friendship, he needed her in his life, so if Ariel wasn't able to forgive Tillie, it would make things a little awkward.

She drew in a deep breath and exhaled slowly. "Yeah. She has a good heart. She was trying to balance being both of our friends and do the right thing. Besides, she's the only best friend I have."

"Hey, what am I?" he teased.

"You're ... you." She said it so seriously that something shifted inside him. It wasn't too late to have a chance at the future he'd always wanted, he just had to be patient, supportive, and prove to her that he could be the man she needed.

"And you're you." He framed her face with his hands, wanting so badly to kiss her, but fearful of doing anything that would hinder her recovery. Despite her fighting with everything she had to make it through this storm, Ariel was still emotionally and psychologically fragile. No way she couldn't be after going through that. Rock didn't see it as a weakness, her strength shone through, but she had barely set her first foot on the path of recovery. It was going to be a long road, and he wanted to walk it with her, not knock her off balance.

Still, the way she looked up at him, the way her gaze shifted from his eyes to his lips and back again. It was obvious that she was still attracted to him, and he knew deep down she still loved him every bit as much as he loved her. But this wasn't just about love. It was about trust, and he'd decimated hers. No wonder she was wary of giving him an inroad into her life again, especially when she was going through so much.

"Hey, lovebirds," Trick called out, smirking when Rock threw him a glare. "If you guys don't get a move on, we won't get done everything we planned today."

"I still don't know what we planned." Ariel huffed.

"First stop is some beautiful waterfalls not far from the hotel," he told her. There was a fine line between surprising her and making her feel out of control, and from the almost imperceptible hint of alarm in her tone, he knew it was time to clue her in on the day's plans.

Rock felt rather than saw Ariel relax a little. "Sounds nice."

"Then we're going to drive up to Dalsnibba. It's one of the mountains up there." He waved a hand at the mountains surrounding the valley.

"Fjell," Ariel corrected with a grin.

"Cheeky." Tweaking her hair like he used to do when they were little kids earned him a scowl. "We get amazing views down to the entire valley. Then, we're going to do and drive the Trollstigen."

"What's the Trollstigen?" Ariel asked.

"It's a road made up of eleven hairpin bends that wind their way up the steep mountain—fjell—sides of the Romsdalen Valley," he explained. "Before we drive down the road, we thought we'd have a picnic up top and look down at the views. There are two great viewing platforms we can walk to."

"Sounds like a great day, and I love picnics."

"I might have forgotten to mention, I packed salmon for the picnic."

Ariel's eyes lit up, shining like two glowing golden orbs. "Salmon is my favorite. And Norwegian salmon is the best."

As he laced their fingers together, and they followed the others as they headed for the start of the trail, about a five-minute walk from their hotel, Rock couldn't wipe the smile off his face. Everything was going to work out between him and Ariel, he could feel it. All he had to do was prove to her that he was in this for the long haul, and that he'd never let her down again.

From the way she kept sneaking glances at him as they walked through the majestic forest, he knew she felt it too. Something that couldn't be put into words, a bond that might fray and stretch but could never be broken.

It was the kind of fairytale love that didn't make sense, but was all the more beautiful for its strength, uniqueness, and ability to overcome anything.

Did he think winning Ariel's trust was going to be easy?

No way.

But he did believe it was possible.

"Oh, wow," Ariel breathed in quiet delight when they reached the collection of falls that streamed down the side of the fjells. "It's so beautiful."

"It is," he agreed.

When she saw he was looking at her and not the waterfalls, she blushed. "I meant the waterfall."

"I know what you meant. I just happen to think this view is more beautiful." Brushing a lock of hair off her cheek, he tucked it behind her ear. "Know what your most beautiful feature is?"

Her blush deepened. "My eyes. You told me that a million times when we were kids."

"I used to think that," he agreed. "Because your eyes were a window to your warm, kind, generous soul. While I still think your eyes are gorgeous, and your soul sweeter than sugar, your most beautiful feature is your strength. You survived what would crush most people, and you're still here, finding beauty in nature. There are going to be days when you doubt that strength, doubt its power, but when you do, I'll be right there to remind you."

Ariel's blush deepened, and when she averted her gaze, he gently took her chin between his thumb and forefinger and tilted her head up until she was looking at him.

"Whether you can ever see me as more than a friend or not, I am going to spend the rest of my life loving you. I'm yours forever, Ariel. No matter what. By your side is the only place in the universe I want to be."

~

September 16th
    2:32 P.M.

"I'm afraid to look." Ariel scrunched her eyes closed as they took the first bend. It wasn't that she was afraid of heights ... well, not exactly. She didn't mind being up high, it was just the fear of falling that made her stomach feel like it had taken up permanent residence on a merry-go-round.

"This is the best bit, the best view," Sebastian told her.

"Yeah, but we're up so high. What if the car goes over the edge?" From up here, and with all the rocks they'd hit on the way down, it would be certain death.

"You insulting me there, Ariel?" Scorpion asked from the driver's seat. She'd learned that the man had been the other one she'd heard when Sebastian had found her in the underground prison. Since she'd spent the last couple of days with Bravo team, getting to know them, she'd found they were all similar to Sebastian and Tank. Protective, confident, and a family. A family who liked to tease one another. A family they were trying to include her in.

Tears stung her eyes, and she was a little embarrassed to cry again in front of all these tough guys. Knowing it was because her emotions had all been thrown into disarray with everything she had lived through these last several weeks, didn't make it any easier.

Balancing on a mental tightrope never was.

One wobble, one gentle gust of wind, one misstep and she'd fall.

Not a small fall, but plummet into oblivion just like their car would if it went over the side of the mountain.

"Not insulting. I believe you guys are all superheroes, but even superheroes go over the edge of the road sometimes," she said.

"Come on, Snow White, take a peek. If you can look at the view from the top, you can watch as we go down," Sebastian said, his fingers tightened around hers.

"When we were up there, we weren't going to fall," she protested. "Mr. Maniac Driver here wasn't trying to make us go over the edge by driving so fast."

Scorpion laughed. "We're barely moving. In fact, we're going to have to stop to let this bus take the turn."

"Come on, Ariel, do it, just take a peek. I promise you won't regret it," Sebastian urged.

Regret.

Of course, there were lots of regrets in her life. The usual ones that most people had, and then more serious ones related to her abduction.

This was such a tiny thing in the scale of regrets and issues she had facing her right now, but it might be something she really would regret.

With the struggles ahead of her, did she want to add to it? Even with something so small?

If she could survive being repeatedly raped and tortured, she could surely take a peek out the car as they drove down this amazing road.

"You won't let go of my hand, right?" she asked. It was silly to need to hold onto Sebastian's hand when all they were doing was driving on a road, but right now, everything, no matter how small, seemed so much bigger. Another product of her ordeal. Another thing she'd have to get used to moving forward, but she wasn't going to give up.

At least she hoped she wasn't.

But there would probably be days when she did feel like giving up. It wasn't possible to stay here in Norway forever. Being here was like being in a little bubble. They might be physically closer to where she had been held prisoner here than she would be back home, but somehow this place just brought her a sense of peace she knew would disappear as soon as she left.

These moments had to be enjoyed while they lasted.

Because once she got home, she was pretty sure the full force of her trauma was going to come crashing down upon her.

"Never letting go of you, Ariel."

With Sebastian's comforting presence, Ariel forced her eyes to open as they started driving again.

Her breath left in a whoosh. The view was stunning, so much better than it had been from up the top. Up top, they'd been looking down on the view, but here they were part of it. Part of nature. Part of the trees and the rocks, part of the fresh air, part of this amazing road that did indeed look like a Troll's ladder just like the name meant.

Transfixed, she barely blinked as they wound their way around one hairpin bend to the next until they finally reached the valley floor.

Scorpion parked, and the other car carrying the rest of Sebastian's team pulled in behind them. They all piled out, and Ariel looked up at the road they'd just taken. It looked crazy enough from down here, but nothing compared to driving it.

"Glad you opened your eyes?" Sebastian asked as he moved in behind her, wrapping his arms around her waist, and urging her to rest back against him.

It was easier than she would have thought if you'd asked her just a couple of months ago, even a couple of days ago. It was even easier than it maybe should be because while she believed Sebastian when he told her he loved her. It was harder to believe that he wouldn't wind up hurting her all over again.

Time, more than either of them wanted, was the only solution.

But today, this moment, wasn't about the past, and it wasn't about the future. That was why this place had filled her with a sort of magic she was afraid would disappear as soon as they stepped onto the plane, because here it was only about the present. Nothing existed but being here, surrounded by steep, rocky mountains, the lush valley spread out around them, and a few snowy peaks.

Tranquility.

This place was the absolute definition of peace, and she didn't want to leave.

"So glad I opened my eyes," she said softly, letting go of the burden her anger toward Sebastian had been as she sunk into his embrace. There would always be a lingering scar, his words that day had cut deep, but she was ready to move forward. Truly forgive and move on. That didn't mean jumping into a relationship with him, but it did mean allowing him to be part of her life again.

These moments—where everything was as close to perfect as it could be—were what she would hold onto when the bad days came.

They were coming.

She could feel it, building like a storm inside her. All she could do was try to be as prepared as she could for when the hurricane hit.

"Glad enough that you want to climb up with us?"

"Climb up?" she squeaked, pulling out of Sebastian's arms so she could stare up at him in horror. "You're going to climb up?" It had been bad enough in the car. There was no way Ariel could imagine climbing those rocky cliffs that were as close to vertical as they could be without actually being vertical.

"Sure," Sebastian said cheerfully. "They've even got ropes there for us to use. And we brought along our gear."

"By gear, you mean like wings?" she asked. There was no way

anyone could climb out of this place, not even these guys, and they were former military men. It was just impossible, she was sure of it.

All the guys laughed like she was a comedian. Only Piper swatted her husband's shoulder and nodded in agreement.

"I'm with her. No way you guys can climb this without wings or wheels," Piper said.

"Oh, you of little faith," Arrow told his wife. "What are you going to do when this little one wants to build a treehouse? Or go indoor rock climbing? Or ride his bike down a big hill as fast as he can?"

Planting her hands on her hips, Piper shot her husband a withering glare. "First of all, Antonio, we don't know if it's a boy. It could be a girl who loves playing dress-ups, having tea parties, and coloring. Second of all ..." Piper sighed, and then grinned. "Boy or girl, it's going to want to follow its daddy around like he hangs the stars in the sky, and I'm going to have to get used to having a daredevil."

"Just so you know, angel, I will gladly dress up in fairy wings, sip tea at a stuffed animal tea party, and color like I'm a world-famous artist." Arrow kissed his wife, and all the guys gave exaggerated awws.

"So, you going to climb with us, Snow White?"

"Not even if I had wings." No way on Earth was she going to attempt to climb this mountain. Not even if this whole valley was on fire, and climbing out was the only way. Heights was one thing, but falling off a mountain was quite another.

"You don't need wings to fly," Sebastian told her. "All you need is faith."

Those words stuck with her. Ariel was still thinking about them hours later after watching the guys climb out of the valley and drive back to the hotel. Was faith enough for her to fly, or was she already destined to crash and burn?

CHAPTER

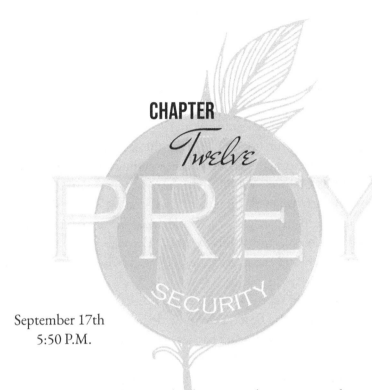

Twelve

September 17th
5:50 P.M.

He could feel the change in her happening but was powerless to stop it.

Rock hated being powerless like this. It had to be the worst feeling in the world.

If they didn't need to get back home to start working on finding proof that Arthur Gomez had a daughter he had sold, he would have been tempted to stay in Norway for as long as Ariel needed.

But they couldn't. Coming home was something that had to be done eventually, may as well just get it over with. Ariel couldn't live in a bubble forever. Prolonging popping it and returning to the real world was only going to do more harm in the long run. The only way to even have a chance at dealing with what Ariel had lived through and going on to live a normal life was to face it.

Running never helped.

It only ever made things worse.

If anyone knew that more intimately than he did, he'd like to meet them. He'd wasted fifteen years he could have spent with the love of his life, and now their future was uncertain. Sure as he was that he could win back Ariel's trust there were no guarantees.

Right now, the only guarantee he could see was that they were on shaky ground. Him, Ariel, and them as a couple. There was no stable place to plant their feet as they navigated this new world that neither of them was really prepared for.

"Hey, where are we?" Ariel suddenly asked.

He'd been waiting for her to clue into the fact that they hadn't headed into the city to her apartment. Since getting off the plane an hour ago, all she'd done was sit slumped in the passenger seat of his car.

Other than their original discussion after landing where she had wanted to take a cab to her place, and he'd asked her if she'd left her mind behind in Norway, they hadn't spoken. His joke had drawn the last smile out of her, and the more they'd driven the more anxious she had become.

Like she always did when she was nervous, Ariel's left leg bounced up and down to an erratic beat, and she twirled a lock of hair around her finger. The fingers on her other hand were constantly on the move, tapping against each other or her leg, curling into a fist and then uncurling again.

The constant motion was making him nervous as well.

"We're going to my place," he answered with a whole lot more calm than he felt. With Ariel's anxiety bleeding off onto him, it was a wonder he could speak calmly at all.

"Your place? I thought you were taking me home!" There was an edge to her tone, but he wasn't sure if it was because she was angry that he was bringing her here without discussing it first, or because she was actually afraid to go home alone but didn't want to admit it.

If he were her, he knew he wouldn't be looking forward to being alone. She'd spent weeks alone, tied up and locked in a small, cold, windowless room. What she needed right now was people around her.

Balancing this tightrope wasn't easy, but this wasn't something he was prepared to compromise on. If Ariel was dead set against staying at his place, he'd stay at hers. If she refused to let him stay inside her house, he'd stay in his car on the street outside it.

Bottom line was, he couldn't leave her alone right now.

"I thought you might enjoy the peace out here," he said. Long Island was a nice place to live but it was the suburbs, people everywhere. Out here was pure, untouched nature. Trees, birds, wildlife, streams, and fresh air. It wasn't Norway, but it was a whole lot closer than her home would be, even if they were only a couple of hours away from it.

"You can't just make decisions for me, Sebastian," she snapped, and while he didn't enjoy making her angry, seeing the spark of fire in her eyes was infinitely preferable to the empty desolation.

"Wasn't trying to make decisions for you, just doing what I thought was best for you."

"That's not your place. We're not together."

While true, the words were like painful needles stabbing across every inch of his body. "No, we're not together, but we're friends, and nobody on this earth loves you more than I do. I'm sorry if I made you feel like I was taking your control away from you, that wasn't my intention, but I'm worried about you. There is a man out there who wants you gone enough to pay someone to kidnap and sell you. A man ruthless enough to sell his own daughter. I won't leave your safety to chance."

Maybe it was playing unfair to bring up the threat that was still hanging over her head, but Rock was prepared to do whatever it took to make sure he kept Ariel close. Call him selfish, call him an over-the-top alpha male, call him any name you wanted, but his woman was hurting, she was in danger, and losing her again was not an option.

Like a deflated balloon, Ariel sagged in her seat, the fight draining out of her. Almost. "Well, I can't argue with that, I guess. Still, you should have talked to me first. I was kidnapped, Sebastian. Locked in a cage, made to do things I didn't want to do, bought by a lunatic, I had zero control over my life. Zero. I can't ... I need to make my own decisions ... okay?"

"Are you asking me if it's okay or telling me it's okay?" he asked, glancing over at her.

"I'm ... telling you?"

"Sounds like you're asking me a question. Tell me how you feel, Snow White. This is me. The man who loves you with everything he is,

I'm never going to hurt you again. Ever. You don't need to be afraid of me."

"I need to make my own decisions, Sebastian," she said, straightening in her seat. "You don't get to do that for me, not even if you say you love me. It's not okay to decide where I'll stay like I'm some helpless child. I'm not. I'm an adult. I'm ... not okay ... but I haven't given up yet. I'm scared out of my mind, but I can make my own decisions."

"There's my girl. You're right, and I'm sorry. I should have asked you and not decided for you where you'll stay. I just ... need you close right now," Rock admitted. "But that doesn't make it okay. If you don't want to stay at my place, I'll stay at yours, but I'm not going to leave you alone and vulnerable." Pulling the car over to the side of the road, he gave her the opportunity to choose where she would stay. "Where am I taking you?"

Indecision was evident in her expression. "All my stuff is at my place ..."

Although she said it, she didn't look like going to her place was what she wanted at all. "I can have anything you want brought to my place by morning."

"If I stayed at your place, where would I sleep?"

In his bed.

That was the answer he wanted to give, but he wasn't stupid enough to think that she was ready to share his bed.

"Guest room."

"Is your place big?" she asked hesitantly.

Intuition said she wasn't asking because she wanted to ensure there was enough space between the master and the guest room, but because she didn't want there to be much space. Nervous as she was, she didn't want to be alone any more than he wanted her to be alone. "Guest room is right next to the master, only the two bedrooms, both are ensuite."

Ariel turned to stare out the window, and Rock had to fight not to hold his breath. There was some possessive side to him that wanted his woman in his house. A house he'd designed and built with her in mind.

But at the very least, he owed Ariel patience while she worked to accept his presence back in her life while also dealing with her ordeal.

Because he wasn't a total control freak, he did have a bag of clothes in the back of his car, so he was prepared to stay at her place if that was what she wanted. The compound was safer by far, and obviously the smart choice, but Ariel needed to make choices she was comfortable with right now, even if they weren't the smartest from a strategic standpoint.

When she turned her head to face him, he couldn't read the answer in her eyes. All he saw was his own uncertainty reflected back at him.

"What's your decision, Snow White?"

After a long exhale, she finally said the words he wanted to hear. "I'll stay with you at your place."

~

September 18th
6:42 A.M.

Somehow, being here made everything both better and worse.

Ariel stood at the window in the bedroom, looking out at the stunning view, and knew in her heart that Sebastian had built this cabin with her in mind. Everything from the rustic exterior to the more modern interior, from the white couch in the living room to the sleigh beds in the bedroom, from the fireplace to the huge wall of glass showcasing the most amazing view.

It was all for her.

Knowing that hurt so badly because it convinced her that Sebastian had always loved her. That the words he had so cruelly and thoughtlessly flung at her fifteen years ago were his biggest regret, and that while she had done her best to forget him and their shared past, he had been constantly thinking of her.

Why hadn't he come to her sooner?

If he had, they could have already been living their lives, the life a part of her still desperately craved. Okay, not a part of her. Every single atom of her being craved this life, the one that had been her dream growing up. They would be married with kids, enjoying every moment of their time together.

As much as she wished Sebastian hadn't waited so long to come to her, tell her he was sorry, and ask for a second chance, Ariel also had to acknowledge that if he had come sooner, she wouldn't have been ready.

Would have turned him away without even listening to him, because the pain had been too great.

Ironically, it was her ordeal that had put her in a place where she could accept his apology. Being forced to endure something horrific definitely put life into perspective. Forgiveness was easy to give after living through what she had.

Not that she was ready to reach out and take the future that could have been.

Might never be.

And it wasn't even because she didn't trust Sebastian anymore. That trust was coming back, being rebuilt thread by thread with each loving word and glance he sent her way.

Jumping into anything right now just wasn't an option.

Careful.

She had to tread carefully. Right now, she didn't even know who she was. Wasn't sure she liked who she was. At the back of her mind, constantly taunting her, were the memories of willingly crawling out of her cage and submitting to a man she knew meant her harm for a bowl of cheesy pasta.

That memory haunted her. It was always there, no matter what she was doing, and it replayed in her dreams on an endless loop each night.

Would it always be there?

How could she ever hope to live her life with its constant presence?

Much as she'd like to, Ariel knew she couldn't hide out in here all day. She'd heard Sebastian get up an hour ago as she tossed and turned in bed, and while she knew he would never come knocking on her door to draw her out of her room, he was waiting for her, nonetheless.

Avoiding the bathroom like she had been every day since she'd been rescued, Ariel pulled off the old T-shirt Sebastian had given her to sleep in then grabbed the pack of wet wipes from her purse. After wiping herself down, she put on the sweatpants and T-shirt Sebastian had left out for her and headed downstairs.

It felt weird to be wearing his clothes. Intimate in a way they'd never been. Sure, they'd had sex a couple of times, but it was only that one night. It had been good, especially given they were teenagers and it was the first time for both of them. Before that, they'd had a great friendship, but again they'd only been teens, and she hadn't walked around in Sebastian's clothing.

The intimacy she felt as she breathed in Sebastian's scent was both unsettling and comforting.

Was she crazy to agree to stay here?

Sebastian loved her, she didn't doubt that. She loved him too. Pretending otherwise would be stupid. But that didn't mean she could commit to anything right now. If she decided she couldn't ever commit to anything then she was letting herself get way too attached to a man she had nothing to offer.

"Morning, sweetheart." Sebastian didn't hesitate to walk right over to her the second she reached the bottom of the stairs. His arms wrapped around her, and when his head dipped for a second, she thought he was going to kiss her.

When his lips touched her forehead instead of her lips Ariel found herself disappointed.

Great.

Now she wanted him to kiss her.

Which was insane because even just being touched made her entire body tense in preparation of the coming pain.

Conditioning was hard to overcome, and she was painfully aware it might be a task too big for her to accomplish.

"Morning," she mumbled, taking a small step back, outside the circle of his arms, not because she wanted to but because she suddenly needed a little distance. The flare of pain in Sebastian's gray eyes hurt, but she didn't have the capacity to balance anyone's feelings but her own at the moment.

"Breakfast is about ready," Sebastian told her, and she was grateful that his tone was even. He really was trying hard not to push her, and she appreciated that so much.

"White chocolate chip and mango pancakes," Arrow said, and she looked around Sebastian to see Arrow and Piper in the kitchen. "Told you I'd come to try them out when we got home."

Company was the last thing she expected this morning, and Ariel was suddenly self-conscious about being dressed in Sebastian's clothes. What would his friends think? Would they think that the two of them were a couple? If she couldn't ever commit to Sebastian, would they think she had been leading him on?

Would they think she was a whore?

As though sensing her spiraling panic, Sebastian dropped another kiss to her forehead. "Would you mind if Arrow and I popped out for a bit? We won't go far," he quickly added. "My team and I all live on this property, we have ten acres each and ten shared acres. I want to check in with the guys to see if Panther has been able to come up with anything on Arthur Gomez. We'll take some pancakes for the guys, and you and Piper can have some and hang out here."

That was a way to leave her alone with the shrink if ever she'd heard one.

Still, it was cute that he wanted to take care of her and make sure she was okay without making her feel like he thought she was one step away from falling apart.

Even if she was.

"I don't mind," she agreed. Didn't mean she was committing to this unofficial therapy session, but she liked Piper, trusted her, and knew that if anyone understood what she had gone through it was her.

"We won't be gone long," he promised.

"It's okay, Sebastian, I'll be fine." The last thing either of them needed was to develop some sort of co-dependent relationship because they were both messed up from her ordeal. There was no doubt in her mind that her ordeal had messed with Sebastian every bit as much as it had with her. But if they were going to have any chance at any sort of successful relationship, it had to stand on its own, it couldn't be born out of fear and trauma.

"Don't like having you out of my sight," he admitted.

"I'm safe here." Last night he'd told her that his place was a veritable fortress and that she would be safer here than anywhere, and she believed him.

"Doesn't mean I like being away from you."

Didn't mean she liked being away from him either.

Much too easily she'd slipped back into being used to having him around.

The guys packed up a huge stack of pancakes, and Ariel slipped into one of the chairs at the table, facing the huge wall of windows. It was beautiful here, tranquil just like Norway had been, but she was beginning to face the fact that nothing could quiet the storm inside her. Internal serenity wasn't in her near future.

"You know I'm here if you want to talk. Anytime. Your new phone has my number," Piper told her.

"It has a whole bunch of numbers of people I don't know and have never met." When Sebastian had given it to her, he'd programmed in the numbers for all the guys on his team, all the guys on Prey's other teams, all their wives, and the Oswald siblings as well. If she found herself in trouble again there were dozens of people she could call on.

Not that it made her feel any safer.

Sebastian had been standing just yards away from her when she'd been abducted, and it hadn't helped.

"I wouldn't even know where to start," she said softly. With the fact that most of the time she didn't know whether to scream or cry? Or that she felt like a whore? Or that she couldn't stand the thought of washing herself because she'd spent too long around ice?

Or her biggest fear of all, that she wasn't strong like Piper and didn't stand a chance at overcoming this.

CHAPTER Thirteen

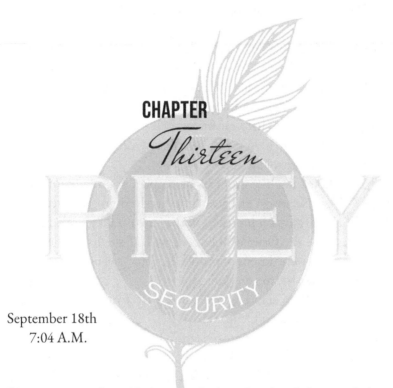

September 18th
7:04 A.M.

"How are you doing?" Arrow asked as they headed toward the main building where the rest of Bravo Team waited for them.

There was no answer to that question.

At least no answer Rock could give in a single word, or even a couple of words. Hell, an entire essay wouldn't be enough to explain the myriad of emotions he was dealing with.

Truth was, he was everything from elated to have Ariel back in his life any way he could have her, to almost paralyzed by the fear that Ariel would never be able to live a normal life because the wounds left behind were just too deep to heal. That she would slowly bleed out in front of him, dying a little more each day, until there was nothing left but the shell of the woman he had loved for a lifetime.

"I don't even know how to answer that," he said honestly.

"I feel you, man. When Piper was kidnapped ..." Arrow paused as his breathing hitched. "Still gets me right here." He pressed a hand to his chest right above his heart. "When I got her back, I still remember that blank look in her eyes. Like she was already gone even though she was right there in front of me. I'll never forget the fear that I would never be able to get her back. That it was already too late. Nothing like it. And I'd only known Piper for a few years, only just convinced her to go out with me. You've known Ariel most of your life, loved her all of that time, I can't even imagine how much this hurts."

"Worst is knowing that if I hadn't been such a coward and gone to her earlier, then this would never have happened."

"No way to know that," Arrow reminded him.

Only he did know it. If he and Ariel were together, and he knew there was someone out there who wanted to hurt his woman, he would have done whatever it took to make sure that no harm came to her.

"She seems to be doing okay, at least as well as one could hope for, but I can't shake the feeling that she's hiding a whole lot from me. From everybody. I'm hoping she might feel like Piper is a safe person to open up to. She's a woman, she's been through something similar, and she's a shrink but she's easy to talk to. It's easy to forget that she's a psychiatrist because she makes you feel like you're just talking to a friend."

"When she's ready she'll talk about it."

Problem was, by the time she was ready would she have already fallen too far into a hole of despair that she couldn't climb back out of?

"From the little she has said, I know she blames herself." How she thought any of what happened to her was her fault Rock couldn't understand. She had to do what she had to do to survive, there was no shame in that. Then again, trauma often wasn't logical, and there was a reason Ariel had fixated on blaming herself. If she could open up about it, talk it through with someone, maybe she could understand that nothing that had happened to her was in any way, shape, or form because of anything she did or didn't do.

"That's not uncommon in victims," Arrow reminded him.

He knew that, but it was cold comfort.

Right now, he didn't care about other victims. He cared about his woman, and he wanted to shake his woman until she accepted that whatever she'd done was exactly the right thing to do because it had kept her alive until he found her.

They walked the rest of the way in silence, there was nothing more to say. Rock knew the statistics, knew the psychology behind it, but none of it helped him know how to help the woman he loved.

The others were all there by the time he and Arrow walked into the large wooden building. It looked like a huge, oversized cabin, and had taken them months to build. Comprised of a huge games area with a pool table, air hockey table, foosball, and some vintage arcade games, including his personal favorite, Pac-Man. The rest of the building was a work area, a couple of large conference rooms, one that was permanently set up with all the information they had on Beth and her case, another that they'd been using these last several weeks with everything on Ariel's case, and a third that was currently sitting empty. There were a few offices, some storage rooms, and Panther's IT lab, although he had a smaller one in his cabin as well.

There was also a large living room space with a kitchen, dining table and chairs, a large screen TV and a couple of couches. This morning, the guys were hanging around the table, Tillie with them, and Beth curled up on one of the couches, keeping herself separate from the others because even though to all of them she was like a baby sister, to her they were all strangers. It might have been a few months since she'd turned back up there, but with no memory it was hard for her to connect to any of them.

Although everyone turned to face him and Arrow as they walked inside, it was Beth who stood and met them.

Catching him by surprise, she walked straight up to him and gave him a quick but fierce hug. "I'm sorry about your friend. I know I'm ... I probably can't ..." She paused, took a slow breath, puffing it out as though she were counting to ten inside her head. "If I can help, please let me know."

Without looking over her shoulder at her husband, who watched their exchange with obvious longing, because Beth went out of her way to avoid physical contact with Axe, she turned and left the room, leaving them all gaping after her. Despite not knowing who she was other than what she'd been told, Beth was still the same sweet woman with a big heart who had survived a Hell that had to be one of the worst any victim he'd ever known had gone through.

Touched by Beth's generosity, he made a mental note to ask Ariel if she'd like to meet Beth. Although their situations were different, maybe the two women could help each other. They both needed a friend, a friend who understood at least some of what they were going through. They could be good for one another.

"How's Ariel?" Tank asked immediately.

"She's holding on," Rock replied.

"Can I see her today?" Tillie asked, tears shimmering in her turquoise eyes making them look like the ocean.

"I'm sure she'd like that. I'll have her contact you," he promised. Tillie needed to hear from Ariel herself that she didn't blame Tillie for not telling her right away about the link between Tank and Rock, but his priority was and always would be his Snow White. It was up to her when she was ready to see her friend.

"Is that the pancakes?" Trick asked hopefully as he eyed the plates.

"You ever think of anything but food?" Scorpion asked with an eye roll.

"Nope," Trick agreed cheerfully. Like his name suggested, the man loved magic tricks, some of the things he could do Rock had no idea how they were physically possible, but Trick refused to give away his secrets. Other than magic tricks the only thing the man loved more was eating. They were all big guys, with big appetites, big muscles, who ran grueling PT sessions daily, but none of them had the same obsession with food as Trick did. It was a wonder the guy wasn't all flab instead of solid muscle.

Setting the plates down on the table, Rock turned his attention to Panther. There was only one thing he cared about, and it certainly wasn't food. The pancakes were just because they were Ariel's favorite, and it was an excuse to have Arrow and Piper over.

"I know we only got back yesterday, but have you had a chance to look into Arthur Gomez?" he asked the IT genius. It was a big ask given that Panther's eight-year-old son was his first priority, but he had to know if there were any leads at all because he wasn't sure how many nights like last night he could handle. Listening to Ariel's muffled cries and whimpers, knowing he couldn't go to her like he had in Norway tested his patience almost beyond what he could bear.

"I did find something. Something small," Panther cautioned. "Last night when I thanked Mrs. Pfeffer for always taking such good care of Andy, for being there for him when I'm away, I realized something. Arthur Gomez's wife died in childbirth. His daughter is seven now, old enough to remember a sister who she says was only a few years older than her. Could a lawyer with the kind of caseload Gomez works, take care of a newborn and a toddler all on his own? I don't think so. So, I wondered if he had his own Mrs. Pfeffer. I did a little research and I might have found the woman who cared for his daughters."

~

September 18th
   10:31 A.M.

"What would you like to do today?"

The question caught her by surprise and Ariel froze.

It was a simple question. One she'd been asked or asked herself a thousand times before in her life. As kids her, Sebastian, and Kayla would always ask each other what they wanted to do when they hung out together on weekends or school vacations. Usually, one of the others would come up with an idea as her younger people pleasing self hated making decisions because she didn't want to pick wrong and make someone have to do something they weren't interested in doing.

If one of them—usually Sebastian—pushed her into choosing, she usually picked going to the zoo. Or more specifically, the butterfly exhibit at the zoo. She'd always had a fascination with animals that could fly, specifically butterflies. Watching them flutter so effortlessly through the air made her long to find that same freedom. They were beautiful to watch, peaceful and quiet. She could get stuck in there for hours, completely enthralled with no idea how much time had passed.

As a single adult there wasn't anyone else to consider when she thought of how to spend her weekends or vacation days. Usually she stayed home, catching up on chores, cooking, or reading, but sometimes she went to the zoo on her own or to the park, and occasionally a museum. Most things introverts enjoyed she did, too. Anything that didn't involve too much social interaction was fine.

But for the last couple of months, choice had been eliminated from her world.

Nobody cared what she felt like doing.

Nobody cared about her at all. She was considered less than a pet would be and more of a possession. One that had no needs outside of what her possessor wished.

What did she want to do today?

She had no clue.

And having to decide was bringing on a panic attack.

How had the simplest of things become such enormous mountains she needed to traverse?

Was it always going to be like this?

Before Sebastian and Arrow had walked back in the door ten minutes ago, she'd actually thought she was doing better. Talking to Piper was as easy as it was helpful, and while she hadn't brought up all her issues, she had told Piper about the cheesy pasta and what she'd allowed to happen. The psychiatrist had told her what she'd expected, that it wasn't her fault, that she was being tortured, and that it was okay to do whatever she had to in order to survive. Those words hadn't sunk in yet, but hearing them still helped.

Now that tiny bit of progress she thought she had made had evaporated.

Gone, like a puff of smoke.

Like she wasn't on the verge of a major meltdown—although she was positive he hadn't missed the sweat that dotted her brow or the short, sharp breaths she was taking—Sebastian headed over to the kitchen. "I have a couple of things here on the compound I'd love to show you if you're up to it."

Yes.

Perfect.

Right now, making decisions wasn't something she could handle.

Forcing her breathing to slow to some semblance of normal, Ariel nodded. "I'm up to it." Anything to try to keep her mind occupied so she could avoid more potential meltdowns. Although she really was up to it. She'd been fed twice a day every day of her captivity after they'd broken her, and while her muscles had atrophied from weeks of inactivity, she had already rebuilt most of that strength back up.

"Great, because I already know you're going to love this." Sebastian's smile was so warm, so easy, that Ariel felt herself relax.

"What should I wear?" True to his word, Sebastian had had boxes of her stuff brought to his cabin. He and Arrow had taken them up to her room when they got back from their meeting. Way more than she needed, more than she would have packed herself. It was like he'd told whoever he'd sent—she assumed the rest of his team—to pack up everything that wasn't furniture and bring it over here. She had basically her entire wardrobe, all her bedding and towels, all the toiletries from her bathroom, all her books, and a whole lot of the special little things like knickknacks and throw pillows that made her house her home.

"Jeans, T-shirt, sweater in case it gets chilly, comfortable shoes," he rattled off. "I'll pack us lunch while you go change."

From the butterflies fluttering madly in her stomach, it felt almost like a first date as she hurried up the stairs to change. Of course, the two of them had never been on a date. They'd hung out hundreds of times, probably thousands, but it had always been as a threesome with Kayla.

That was why she'd never brought up her feelings for Sebastian, and why she assumed he hadn't brought up his for her. Their friendship was too special to risk damaging, and while Kayla was her very best friend in the whole world, their three-way friendship, while often called weird by the other kids at school, was just that. A friendship. It wasn't a threesome relationship, they were just friends. Kayla was too busy crushing on their class' resident genius to throw a glance Sebastian's way.

After changing into her clothes, she left the piles of boxes where they were, there would be time to unpack them later, then hurried into her bathroom. Wiping her face, neck, and hands with a wet wipe, she tossed it in the wastebasket and braided her long, dark locks. Adding a touch of lip gloss and a little mascara, she debated adding some blusher, then decided her too-pale cheeks could do with a little color.

When she was done, she gave herself a scrutinizing onceover in the mirror. The dark circles under her eyes were impossible to hide, and she was thinner than looked good on her. Still, despite the fluttering in her tummy, this wasn't actually a date, so it shouldn't matter if she didn't really look her best.

Despite her pep talk, Ariel ran her hands nervously over her jean-clad legs once she made it downstairs. "I'm ready," she said, feeling awkward as she watched Sebastian finish packing food into a picnic basket. This wasn't a date, no need to be awkward, and she'd known Sebastian most of her life.

Didn't seem to matter.

Date or not, it felt like one.

The fluttering in her stomach turned into a herd of trampling elephants when Sebastian turned to face her, and his eyes did a slow perusal of her body.

Self-conscious, Ariel fiddled with the hem of the yellow T-shirt, wondering if it was too loose hanging off her slim frame. Or maybe the jeans were a little too tight over her backside. She might have lost some weight, but she still had a slight curve to her hips and bottom.

When Sebastian's gaze finally met hers and she saw the fire burning in his gray eyes, all doubt melted away. There was obvious attraction there, and while she was not even close to being ready to do anything about it, it was nice to know that even knowing what she'd been through he still found her beautiful.

"Let's go." When Sebastian held out his hand, Ariel barely hesitated before walking over and taking it.

Together they headed out into the late summer morning. Since arriving here last night she hadn't left the cabin, and as they walked through the forest, she was too absorbed in taking in the tall trees, the gentle rush of the river, the way the sunlight fell in dappled patches through the trees, to worry about talking. Birds chattered, lazy honey-bees buzzed around the wildflowers, butterflies and dragonflies flittered about, and she felt a small piece of the heavy burden tied to her shoulders disappear.

Staying here with Sebastian had been the right choice.

"Do you get deer here?" she asked.

"Sure do. Last spring I even had a fawn just outside my cabin. We have black bears out here too."

"Bears?" Ariel cast a nervous glance around. Bears were stunning animals and all, but she didn't want to meet one in the wild.

Sebastian laughed. "Don't think one is going to jump out from behind a tree and eat you, Snow White. Besides, doesn't Snow White make friends with all the forest creatures?"

"The real one maybe, but not me." She shuddered at the thought of coming face-to-face with a bear. "The only wild animal I'm interested in getting up close to is a butterfly."

"I'm glad you said that."

Stepping out of the trees into a small clearing, Ariel spotted what looked like a greenhouse. While she enjoyed taking care of her little garden, she wouldn't say she had a green thumb, and she was curious to see why Sebastian had brought her here.

"What is it?" she asked as they crossed the clearing.

"It's your paradise."

With those cryptic words, he set the picnic basket down, opened the greenhouse door, and quickly ushered her inside.

Into paradise.

Sebastian was right, there was no other word to describe this place. Inside the greenhouse, along with an assortment of tropical plants and small ponds, were thousands of butterflies in every color of the rainbow.

With tears in her eyes, Ariel looked up at Sebastian. "Did you ...?"

"Build this for you? Yes. I always knew I was finally going to get enough courage to come to you, Ariel. I prayed, hoped, and wished that you might be able to forgive me. Give me a second chance. Guess I thought I would need all the help I could get. Even if I couldn't get you back, at least this gave me a place to come when I was missing you. I've come out here lots of times over the years, it helped me feel closer to you."

Emotion clogged her throat. She didn't know what to say to that.

At every turn this man managed to convince her that he loved her, wanted her, and was prepared to work for it.

Problem was the tables had turned, and this time—even though she didn't want to—it was probably going to be her who wound up breaking his heart.

CHAPTER

Fourteen

September 18th
2:13 P.M.

There was nothing better in the world than seeing the absolute joy and delight on Ariel's face when one of the butterflies landed on her.

A gorgeous purple one set its tiny feet down on her outstretched hand, and her eyes immediately jumped to his as she kept the rest of her body completely still.

"Sebastian, look!" she said in a muted squeal.

Some of Rock's self-loathing faded. At least he'd done something right. Ariel loved the cabin he'd built with her in mind, and she loved the greenhouse with the butterflies that he'd built because he knew how much she loved the tiny insects.

"I see, honey."

"It's so tiny and delicate. It's like it's not even there at all. I can hardly feel it on my hand, and yet I feel it. Does that make sense?"

Yeah. It did.

Kind of how he felt about her. Ariel was only a little over five feet tall and had always been thin and delicate looking. There was a fragility in her that had called out to him even as a teenager. It had made him want to be her hero. While he'd turned into her villain, lost her soft, sweet presence in his life, he'd always been able to feel it.

Ariel was a part of him. The best part. Being able to bring joy to her now, when she was dealing with so much, made him feel like he was ten feet tall. Maybe one day he could become her hero.

"It makes sense to me," he told her.

The smile she gave him was everything. It reminded him of the old Ariel, the one who wasn't weighed down with so much baggage. As a kid, he'd loved bringing that smile out of her. She could be serious, sometimes overly so, and she always tried too hard to please everyone, her parents, teachers, and other kids, that sometimes she lost her true self in the process.

In that smile he always saw the real Ariel. The one who wasn't worried about anyone else, who was relaxed and in the moment. The one who made his heart swell in his chest until he was sure his ribs would burst right open because it was just too full of love.

Love that had only grown over the last decade and a half. Every time he'd gone out to sit in there, he'd pictured Ariel at his side. In none of those imaginings, had it even come close to the real thing.

Paradise.

That's what he'd always thought of this place as being. Ariel's paradise. Turned out it was his too. Because even though he wasn't a fan of tropical climates, the muggy heat in here wasn't oppressive and he barely even noticed it, Ariel's delight eclipsed everything else.

"Do you want to leave now?" she asked as her smile dimmed. "I know you don't really like this kind of humidity."

Honestly, he could sit in there forever if it meant watching that smile on her face.

It wasn't the first time she'd offered to leave, but each time he told her they'd stay a little longer. They'd even wound up eating their lunch in there because he just couldn't bear to make her leave. She wasn't ready to yet, and he wasn't either.

"I'm not even noticing the humidity," he told her honestly.

She studied him for a moment, then relaxed and returned her gaze to the butterfly. "I think I could stay in here forever," she said with a dreamy sigh.

"Whatever happens between us, Ariel, this place is yours. I built it for you, I've tended it for you over the last three years, it's yours. Even if you don't want a future for the two of us, you can come here whenever you want. You'll have all the access codes to the gates, and we'll add your fingerprints and retina scans to the system so you can get in and out on your own."

"You'll really be okay if I say I only ever want us to be friends?"

"I won't like it because I love you and want to spend my life with you, but I'll understand, and I'll accept it. The one promise I made you was that you will always be first, I will always put your needs above my own. I won't be selfish with you again, Ariel. Ever. So yeah, I'll be okay with only being your friend. To be honest, it's more than I deserve after what I did."

Her gaze shifted from the butterfly to him. "You're making up for it."

"No way to truly do that, sweetheart, and we both know it. Those things I said to you were unforgivable. I hate myself for what I did."

Her big golden-brown eyes softened. "If I can forgive you then I think maybe it's time you work on forgiving yourself."

"Don't think so, sweetheart. I'm not as good, sweet, and pure as you are."

She gave a small laugh sending the butterfly on her hand fluttering away. "You make me sound like I really am some Disney princess."

"To me you are."

"I don't remember you being this mushy when we were in high school," she teased.

"Not a boy anymore, Snow White. I'm all grown up now."

Heat flared in her eyes, and her gaze dropped to his chest. The tip of her tongue darted out to run along her bottom lip, and a faint hint of red stained her cheeks. "Yeah, you are," she mumbled.

Desire and need arced between them. Rock felt it, knew from the way Ariel's gaze snapped up to meet his and the heat in her eyes growing into a raging inferno, that she felt it too.

Wanting to reach for her, drag her onto his lap, and kiss her until neither of them could breathe, Rock had to curl his hands into fists to stop himself. Even if she hadn't just lived through hell, it had been fifteen years since they were last together. Ariel needed to get used to him again and mauling her like a teenage boy was only going to widen the gap between them, not close it.

A butterfly chose that moment to land on the top of Ariel's head. It was one of those amazing glasswing butterflies. With its translucent wings it was simply stunning.

"Glasswing butterfly on your head, honey," he told her.

She froze, the heat fading, replaced by excitement. "Take a picture."

Carefully, moving as slowly as if he was in the field ready to take a shot, he slipped his cell phone out and snapped a couple of pictures. When he went to move slightly, a second glasswing butterfly landed on his hand.

"Ooh, two of them," Ariel giggled joyfully. "Is the one still on my head?"

"Yep."

Shifting ever so slowly, he kept his hand still and moved the rest of his body until he was behind her, then he slipped the arm with the phone over her shoulder and lowered his head so their cheeks were mere millimeters apart.

"What are you doing?" Ariel asked breathily.

"Taking a photo," he replied innocently.

As he snapped picture after picture of the two of them with the butterflies on Ariel's head and his hand, he watched with rapt attention the look on her face as she stared at the butterfly perched on the back of his hand.

Hands that ached to touch her, even just in comfort or friendship.

Anything, so long as he could feel her small body in his arms.

Subconsciously, his fingers must have twitched because the butterfly flitted off. Without thinking, Ariel lifted her head to watch and the one on her head flitted away after its friend.

"They're so beautiful," Ariel whispered. "So fragile, but so free."

"Just like you, my Snow White." Giving her plenty of time to pull away if she wanted to, Rock swept his fingertips across her cheek in a gentle caress. When all she did was suck in a breath, he spread his fingers out, palming her cheek. "You're so beautiful." His thumb brushed across her bottom lip. "So fragile, and yet so very strong." Beneath his hand, she trembled, but her eyes held his and she didn't pull away. "My Snow White."

Rock was still behind her, he still had one arm over her shoulder while his other cradled her cheek. She had made no attempt to put distance between them and he dipped his head. Her breath was warm against his face, and he felt rather than heard her sharp intake of air.

Butterflies fluttered in his stomach just as much as the real thing fluttered around them. Because he hadn't wanted to come between Ariel and Kayla, he hadn't made a move on Ariel when he should have. Just because he'd been in love with her since he was a kid, it didn't mean they'd gone out on dates, it didn't mean he'd been able to kiss her whenever he wanted or touch her in any way that wasn't just friendship.

For so long he'd dreamed about her and hoped for special moments just like this one.

Now that they were here together, and she was giving him a chance to prove to her that he could be a good friend, and maybe more, it seemed surreal.

His brain urged him to go slow, not mess things up, but his body craved her with an intensity he seemed powerless to ignore.

Feathering his lips across hers in the softest of kisses, he sighed in relief as the barbed wire that had been wrapped around his heart loosened enough that he could draw a full breath. This woman was his and yet she wasn't, but he'd taken one step closer to the future he wanted with every fiber of his being.

∼

September 19th
   9:09 A.M.

Don't be nervous.

Although Ariel had been coaching herself all morning, she was nervous as she watched Sebastian load the dishwasher.

He looked tired and she suspected he wasn't getting any more sleep than she was. Nightmares had come for her again last night, and she'd eventually given up on the idea of sleep around five.

Quiet as she'd tried to be, when she'd wiped herself down with wet wipes, run a no wash conditioner through her hair, and gotten dressed, then snuck out of her room and downstairs to watch the sunrise, he'd joined her on the porch mere minutes after she'd settled into the porch swing. As he usually did, he'd kept distance between them, choosing to sit on the steps rather than with her on the swing.

Only time he'd gotten close to her was yesterday in the butterfly greenhouse when he'd kissed her.

The kiss had been ... more than amazing, it had been special.

While the thought of sex made her cringe and nausea swell in her body, she didn't get the same visceral reaction when she thought of kissing. Maybe it was because none of the men who had trained her or the one who had bought her had ever kissed her. Kissing was an intimate thing, while sex was just that. Sex. To have power and control over someone, you didn't need to be kissing them.

Before her dreams had turned bad, they'd been filled with kisses with Sebastian, and waking up alone, shaking and sweating and not in a good way, only made her realize how much she hated the distance between them.

If she wasn't sleeping, and he wasn't sleeping, then maybe she didn't have to spend the long nights alone.

What she wanted was for him to hold her like he had in Norway.

Ariel loved that he was trying to give her space and not push himself on her because he was conscious of what she'd just been through. He was trying to show her that he respected her as well as loved her and was letting her know that she was in control of what happened between them and when.

Didn't he know she couldn't handle that pressure right now?

She needed someone to make her decisions for her. Or at least some of them.

It wasn't that she wanted to give up control over everything, in fact, she both craved control and was terrified of it in equal portions.

Right now, though, she had to be strong, say what she wanted.

What she needed.

Actually, what both of them needed.

Drawing in a deep breath, she squared her shoulders, and reminded herself for the millionth time that this was just Sebastian. He wasn't going to shove her hands in a pile of snow until they turned blue just because she told him what she'd like to do today.

"I was wondering ..." she started, hearing the obvious nerves in her voice and hating it. Her ordeal had changed her so much, reduced her to a woman who was afraid to tell her friend how she wanted to spend her day.

No.

She could do this.

"I was wondering," she started again, "if maybe we could go to the cemetery today. To visit Kayla's grave."

It would be the first visit to her childhood best friend's grave she would have made.

After the funeral, she and Sebastian had made love for the first time then the next morning he'd turned on her, telling her she was a whore who had used her friend's death to get him into bed. How could she go back there after that?

"Sure you can. I can drop you off or you could drive yourself. The guys brought your car here. If you wanted company, I'm sure Tillie would be happy to go with you. She's been dying to see you and tell you in person how sorry she is for not letting you know sooner that Tank and I were friends. I have a few errands I need to run anyway. Grocery shopping and stuff."

Ariel shook her head. She didn't want to go with Tillie—although she would make sure she assuaged her friend's fears—and she didn't want to go alone. "I was hoping you would go with me."

"Of course. I'd love to drive you. You can take as long as you want. I'm happy to hang in the car until you're ready. I can catch up on some emails."

Catch up on emails?

Like he couldn't do that any time.

It was like he was making excuses so he didn't have to go with her.

"Sebastian, I don't want to go with Tillie so you can run errands, and I don't want you to take me to the cemetery and sit in the car checking your email. I want you to come with me to the cemetery. I thought maybe since Kayla was our friend we could go together. I thought it might help. Help both of us," she added. Knowing that the words Sebastian had flung at her that morning were said out of grief and guilt, she knew that neither of them had dealt well with their friend's death.

It was time.

Life was hard enough as it was without holding onto pain. What had happened to Kayla was an accident, neither of them was to blame. Kayla was sixteen, she knew not to take off her seatbelt while driving. It had been an innocent mistake, there was no way she could have foreseen the consequences, but the only one responsible was Kayla herself. Not that Ariel blamed her friend, it was an accident, but it was time that she stopped blaming herself.

Time Sebastian stopped blaming himself too.

Pain filled Sebastian's gray eyes, and for a moment she was sure he was going to turn her down.

"Don't make excuses. Come with me. Please."

"Haven't been there since the funeral," he admitted in a rough voice. "After what I did to you, what I said, I couldn't face Kayla. I knew she'd be ashamed of me if she heard what I'd said to you."

"Exactly why I think we should go together. It's time to face our past. The future feels scary and uncertain. I can't see it right now because it's so hazy, but the past, that's something we can handle. Together."

Please say yes.

Without him by her side, Ariel wasn't so confident that she could face the past any more than she could the future. But with him ... with him almost anything felt possible.

"Together," Sebastian echoed. The pain had morphed into hope as he closed the dishwasher and walked over. His large hands spanned her waist, and he lifted her off the stool at the breakfast bar, setting her on her feet before him.

When his head dipped, Ariel felt hope flutter to life inside her with every bit as much beauty as the butterflies yesterday.

She wanted his lips on hers.

Not in a fiery, passionate kiss, just a moment of connection where she could feel his love for her in his restraint just as she'd felt it the night they gave each other the gift of their first time.

With a tenderness that made her eyes sting, Sebastian whispered a kiss to her lips, and she sighed and leaned into him, pressing her cheek to his chest right above his heart. "Together."

It was only because they were together that she was able to climb into the car and make it through the drive to the cemetery.

Neither of them spoke, both wrapped up in their own pain, their own fears, their own uncertainties. But Sebastian laid a hand on her thigh the moment he turned the engine on, and it never moved once.

Her own hand rested on top of his, and she felt something growing between them. It felt like the first few tentative shoots of trust. They were growing inside her, watered by his words and his actions. What exactly it was growing into she wasn't quite sure yet. There was a part of her that wanted to reclaim her old dreams, marry Sebastian, have a family, and grow old together. But there was another part that knew she was in no shape to be offering any sort of future to anyone.

Even before they reached Kayla's grave, tears began to trickle down Ariel's cheeks. The cemetery was quiet as they walked hand in hand through it. A few people dotted about stooped over graves as they coped with the loss of their loved ones the best way they knew how.

How badly Ariel wished she and Sebastian had coped differently than they had.

Their youth had compounded their grief and guilt and neither of them had made smart choices.

Wonderful as it had been in the moment, their first time shouldn't have been right after the funeral of their best friend. They hadn't had sex that night for the right reasons, and it had blown up in their faces.

She had been the one to make that first move.

Sebastian's words from that morning after echoed in her head.

Whore.

Used her best friend's death to have sex with him.

As they reached Kayla's grave, Ariel finally broke contact with Sebastian as she dropped to her knees before the headstone. It was a simple one, a pair of angel wings at the top, Kayla's name beneath them, and beneath that her date of birth and date of death.

Beneath that was a quote she'd heard Kayla say so many times in her short life.

Love like your life depends on it.

The trickle of tears turned into a flood. She hadn't done that. After Kayla's death and Sebastian's betrayal, she'd shut herself off from love believing she was unworthy of affection.

Sebastian had apologized for hurting her, told her he regretted the words he'd thrown at her, but had he thought they were true?

As much as it terrified her, she had to know.

Needed to know.

Looking over her shoulder, Ariel asked the question that had plagued her for fifteen years. "Do you really think I'm a whore?"

CHAPTER

Fifteen

September 19th
12:10 P.M.

There it was.

The huge elephant in the room, now out in the open.

Rock had hoped that maybe they could avoid a discussion on the specifics of what he'd said the morning after they'd made love for the first time, but it seemed Ariel needed to hear more.

Whatever she needed she got.

"Damn, baby. No. No. Not at all. Never. No!" He raked his fingers through his hair hard enough to feel the sting.

How could she think for one second he thought his beautiful, sweet Snow White was a whore?

How could she not after he threw the words so cruelly at her?

If hearing her ask him, and seeing the pain in her face, the doubt and uncertainty, was his penance, Rock would gladly fall on a hundred swords than have to go through this.

Of course, he had known that his words had caused damage, but having to see that damage firsthand hurt almost more than he could bear.

"I was the one who initiated things," Ariel said.

Those tears were killing him.

Each one rolling down Ariel's pale cheeks, leaving a silvery trail in its wake may as well have been burning a trail of fire through his heart.

Did she really believe he thought that of her?

How had she managed to go on to have such a successful life after he'd hurt her so badly?

Tears filled his own eyes. "Not the way I remember it, sweetheart," he choked out. "The way I remember it is I asked you to come up to my room after the funeral. I held you while you cried. You wouldn't stop. Tears just kept coming and coming. You were on my lap, your pain was too much, and I couldn't handle it. I kissed you first, not the other way around."

"But you said—"

"I lied. You did nothing wrong. I wanted you that night, I've wanted you every night since. The things I said to you were how I felt about myself, but I couldn't ... I couldn't face acknowledging those things about myself," he admitted, hanging his head in shame. "I was a coward, Ariel. I'm the one who used Kayla's death to finally have you. I'd wanted you for so long, but she was always between us. She didn't mean to be, and I loved her as a friend, but you ... you I loved like a soulmate. Part of me resented her. If she wasn't in the picture, you would already have been mine. Then she was gone, and I couldn't wait any longer. That night was everything. Perfection. But in the morning, in the cold light of day, I realized what I had done, and I loathed myself. Not you, sweetheart. You were everything good and perfect and I had corrupted you. I couldn't face it so I did the only thing my young, stupid, selfish self could do. I lashed out."

There weren't enough words in the world to express his regret, not enough seconds in his lifetime to apologize the number of times he needed to.

"You are not a whore, and you never were. I'm so sorry, Ariel. I hate what I said to you, and I hate that I hurt you. Baby, I wish I could take it back, but I need you to believe me that I never once, not even for a single second, thought of you as a whore."

Instead of helping, his words only seemed to make her cry harder, and she shook her head. "I am. When I was taken, I did things. Things I'm not proud of ..."

"Things you were forced to do," he reminded her.

Another shake of her head, this one so fierce he was surprised her neck didn't snap. "No. I ... it's my fault, Sebastian. I let them do it. For pasta, I let them touch me for pasta."

Rock had no idea what she was talking about, but he didn't need to. All he needed to do was see her pain to know that Ariel absolutely one hundred percent believed what she was saying.

"They kept me in a cage, there was always food sitting just outside it, just out of reach. I didn't want it, didn't want to give in but I was weak."

Unable to stand the distance between them any longer, he closed it and dropped to his knees in front of her. His hands grabbed her shoulders, squeezing a little too tightly, but he needed to know her attention was on him and not on the fears running rampant inside her head. "They broke you, honey. They were professionals, they knew what they were doing. And you're a human being. Human beings need food. They starved you knowing sooner or later you would give in. What they did to you was not your fault. If you let them touch you, then I hate them for what they did to you, but it was the right thing to do because it kept you alive. If you touched them, then again, I hate them for what they did to you, but it was the right thing to do because it kept you alive until I could find you. You are not a whore. You are a victim. A victim who was strong and survived."

"I don't feel strong," she sobbed. "I feel weak, I feel broken, I feel scared. I don't know what to do. I don't know how to feel normal. I'm so scared I won't ever be normal. I feel so dirty inside. Like I can't ever get clean again. I don't know what to do."

Her words were a clear plea, but there wasn't an answer he could give her.

Every victim was unique, which meant every victim healed in a different way on a different timeframe.

"I'm here, sweetheart. I'm not going anywhere. You are not alone. You have Tillie and Tank. You have the rest of my team, Piper and Arrow, and you have all of Prey. You have your parents, your family, so many people who love and care about you."

"I just want it to be over," she wept.

Her tears were slaying him.

Cutting him into pieces one drop at a time.

"Please, honey, don't cry anymore. I can't take it, baby."

Every time he kissed away her tears a dozen more took their place.

As much as he knew she needed to get this emotion out so it wouldn't fester and turn bad inside her, it was killing him seeing her in pain like this.

Rock felt so helpless. Angry and scared too. And guilty as hell. If he could, he would go back in time, tell Ariel how he felt about her long before Kayla's death, never hurl those cruel words at her, go reach out to her any of the hundreds of times he'd longed to over the years, wait for Tillie to talk to her first. Any one of those instances could have changed what happened.

But there was nothing he could do except pull Ariel into his arms and hold her. Rock her from side to side, stroke her hair, her back, and her arms. Touch kisses to her lips, her forehead, and each damp cheek.

Hold her and never let her go.

Pray that his love and support was enough to get her through this.

"I'm here, sweetheart. You don't have to keep anything from me, you can tell me anything and I'll make sure you know how proud I am of you, and how nothing that happened was your fault. I've let you down before. I won't ever make that mistake again. Anything you need I'll do, I'll give you. Just remember, baby, when it feels like everything is too much, you are not alone."

"Hold me tighter," she whispered through her tears as she wrapped her arms around his waist and held onto him like he was her lifeline.

Tightening his hold, Rock tucked her head under his chin and held her like she was his lifeline. Ariel might not believe it if he told her, but it was true. Sure, he knew how to swim, but without her in his life that's all there was. Swimming through an endless ocean, no dry land in sight.

She was his dry land.

His desert island.

His safe haven.

She was his everything and he was going to hold onto her and never let go.

As Ariel had said, the future was uncertain, but that didn't have to be a bad thing. It meant he hadn't lost her yet. She was still within his grasp along with the future he wanted.

A future he would fight for.

Ariel was worth fighting for, worth rolling up his sleeves, getting down in the mud, and clawing and kicking his way through it to get to the other side. Because waiting on that other side was a love that was powerful enough to do the impossible, to heal wounds and breathe new life into the dead.

True love really could conquer all.

∼

September 20th
12:19 A.M.

Ariel stirred.

Something had woken her from a deep sleep, but for once it wasn't a nightmare. On the contrary, her dreams had been sweet, and she'd woken feeling safe and protected instead of alone and terrified.

Lifting her head from a surprisingly hard pillow, she blinked open sleepy eyes to find herself staring at Sebastian's chest. No wonder it didn't feel as soft as her feather pillow.

They'd put a movie on after dinner and she must have fallen asleep on the couch. Emotionally exhausted after the visit to the cemetery, it was no wonder she'd just crashed as soon as she was sitting down.

As emotionally exhausting as it had been, it had been equally as freeing.

It wasn't like any time soon she would be able to convince her brain that she had no culpability in what had happened to her, but hearing Piper and then Sebastian tell her it wasn't her fault had helped. One day she'd be able to believe it.

Clearing the air about the past had helped too because Sebastian calling her a whore that morning, and then her giving in and allowing herself to be touched for a bowl of cheesy pasta had become tied together inside her head. The two connected, each reinforcing the other, had felt like they were pulling her down, slowly drowning her.

But now she had a life ring.

The very man who had almost destroyed her was now saving her in more ways than one.

With a smile on her face, she snuggled closer, pressing her cheek back against his chest. After she fell asleep, Sebastian must have stretched out on the couch and then draped her over him. He'd covered them both with a blanket, and with his body beneath her and his arms wrapped around her, Ariel felt safer than she had in months.

Sebastian wouldn't let anyone hurt her.

Safe in that knowledge, Ariel allowed her eyes to drift closed again. Although the threat of nightmares was always present, tonight it didn't scare her as much as it usually did.

Tonight, she wasn't alone.

Just as she was drifting off to sleep, a muted beeping had her lifting her head to see what had caused the sound.

Like a flip had been switched, Sebastian woke, gracefully moving to his feet in one smooth movement taking her with him.

Bewildered, she looked up at him. "What—?"

Her question was cut off abruptly when he pressed his hand to her mouth hard enough to startle her into silence. It wasn't so hard that she couldn't scream if she wanted to which was the only reason she didn't panic.

When he looked down at her in the dim light, she could see a hardness in his eyes that wasn't the Sebastian she knew.

Then again, she didn't really know a lot about this Sebastian.

The boy she had known growing up was from a well-off family who was likely going to follow his father into the family real estate business.

He played football, he loved music and played the guitar, he was sweet and funny, a jock but not arrogant or stuck up. He was her best friend, the boy she loved.

The man standing before her was a warrior.

Knowing that instead of going into real estate he'd gone into the military, that he'd killed people, that he'd seen evil up close and personal, that he'd even saved her life, and seeing him in warrior mode were two different things.

It scared her a little, but it also reassured her.

If something was wrong, she believed Sebastian had the skills to handle it.

Leaning down until his lips were just above her ear, he whispered in a voice that barely carried a sound, "Alarm was triggered. Need you to go upstairs to the master bedroom. There's a concealed door in the back of the master closet. Want you to get in there and stay there. Don't come out no matter what happens."

"But what about you?" she asked when he moved his hand. Even though she tried to keep her voice as quiet as his had been, it seemed much too loud in the otherwise quiet house.

"Don't worry about me. I know what I'm doing, and the alarm will have been sent to my team, they'll be here soon."

That didn't reassure her.

What if there were too many men for Sebastian to fight off on his own?

Just because this was his job, and he was obviously good at it, didn't mean he could fight off an entire army on his own. And the compound was huge, it would take the others at least ten or fifteen minutes to get here and a lot could happen in ten minutes.

"But—"

"No. No buts. Not going to let you get hurt, sweetheart. Now go. Upstairs. Hide. And don't come out. Promise me."

Her entire body rebelled at the idea of promising Sebastian that she would hide while he fought singlehandedly for both of their lives. Whoever was here had come for her. She knew it deep in her bones. Why should he have to risk his life for her?

Fear curled around her like an ice-cold noose. Tightening slowly until it felt like she couldn't breathe.

What if Sebastian was killed?

What if she was kidnapped again?

There was no way she would survive being sold again.

No way.

"Promise me," Sebastian whispered against her lips this time as he feathered a kiss to them.

"I-I p-promise," she stammered.

Pressing a harder kiss to her lips this time, he gave her a gentle shove in the direction of the stairs just as she heard the unmistakable sound of glass breaking.

Picking her up, Sebastian ran to the bottom of the stairs and set her down on a step a few up. "Go," he ordered.

His command offered no space for her to disobey, and Ariel knew that disobeying split his attention so he wasn't completely focused on protecting them. She had no skills to offer. All she would be was a hindrance if she didn't do as he told her and run upstairs and hide.

Still, it felt like a betrayal of sorts to run to safety while Sebastian put his life on the line. So far, she hadn't been into the master bedroom, there had been no need to go into Sebastian's room, but now, as she crept inside it, she realized that, like the rest of the house, it wasn't really just his bedroom, he'd decorated it with her in mind.

Tears blurred her vision as she entered the huge walk-in closet and dropped to her knees, searching for the hidden door. All these years while she had been doing her best to forget all about him, Sebastian's whole life had revolved around her.

Love for him swelled in her heart as she found the tiny door and squeezed herself into the space. It was only big enough for one person, and it was obvious that Sebastian had built it in case he ever needed to hide her in there.

Please be okay.

No sooner had she thought the words than she heard someone enter the bedroom. They weren't quiet as though they knew she was hiding somewhere close by and wanted to scare her.

It was working.

Tremors rippled through her entire body, and even though she didn't want to cry, tears trickled down her cheeks in a steady stream.

"Come out, come out wherever you are. Come on, girlie, I know you're in here."

She knew that voice.

It was thug man. Dan Johnson Sebastian had said his name was.

He was back.

Which meant these men were here for her.

They had come back for her because they knew she had been rescued. She was still a threat to Arthur Gomez, and he wanted her sold again.

If that happened, she wouldn't be found this time.

No one was that lucky.

And the only way she would be taken was if Sebastian was dead. Without him, there would be no one who would search for her with single minded focus.

"Where you hiding, girlie?" His voice was louder. Dan was right outside her hiding place, in the master closet.

As she pressed herself further back away from the little door, Ariel's fingers brushed against something that wasn't smooth wood. Running a finger along it, when she felt something cool it clicked what it was.

A knife.

Sebastian had thought of everything, even giving her a way to defend herself.

Her promise to Sebastian ran through her mind. She had agreed to hide and not come out for anything, but she could kill this man.

She wanted to kill him.

Every awful thing he'd done to her flooded through her mind, filling her with a darkness that she'd never experienced before.

Before Ariel even realized what she was doing, she had crawled out. Dan Johnson's back was to her as he was leaving the closet obviously deciding she wasn't in there.

Hide.

Promise.

Kill.

Pain.

Humiliation.

Revenge.

The words tumbled through her mind, but she had lost the ability to think clearly. All she could focus on was what this man had put her through. Like her mind snapped, focused only on one thing, she lunged, burying the blade deep in her tormentor's back.

CHAPTER

Sixteen

September 20th
12:39 A.M.

Please let her be safe.

That was all Rock cared about as he watched Ariel scurry up the stairs.

It would likely take his team at least ten minutes to get there, and he didn't have a weapon on him. There were several hidden around the house, but he wouldn't feel like he stood a chance at protecting his woman until he had one in his hand.

He'd gotten lax.

Believed the compound was impenetrable.

A stupid mistake seeing as Beth had managed to find a way onto it when she escaped her captors. Even though she knew the place and buried in her subconscious were its strengths and weaknesses, she'd still done it without knowing what she was doing.

Anyone determined enough could get in there.

Chances were, these were more men sent by Arthur Gomez for Ariel to be taken and disposed of. Likely if taken Ariel would be sold again.

There was no way he was allowing that to happen.

Ariel had barely survived her ordeal with her life and her sanity, being sold again would destroy her even if she managed to live through it.

Just as he heard footsteps and saw the outline of several shadowy figures enter his house, Rock put his hand on one of the weapons. For now, instead of shooting at the targets, taking them down one by one, he drew back into the darkness of the kitchen. While he'd turned the lights off when Ariel fell asleep minutes into the movie, with a whole wall of his house made of glass plenty of light filtered in.

All he had to do was hold them off. He had no idea how many men were there, how they'd gotten onto the property, or how they knew Ariel was even here, but none of it mattered. His team would be on their way. Keeping Ariel alive until they got there was his only goal.

Firing off a whole bunch of rounds would only serve to give away his position and engage any other men that might be waiting outside.

Better to move in as quietly as he could.

Apparently, assuming that he and Ariel had already gone to bed, the men didn't even do more than give the living area a cursory glance before heading for the stairs. There wasn't more than the two ensuite bedrooms up there, and as soon as they realized neither bed had been slept in, they would be back down here doing a more thorough search.

Thankfully, he'd turned the TV off when Ariel fell asleep. He'd done it because he didn't want anything to disturb her when it seemed she was getting good rest, but it had wound up being a lifesaver. The men were going to get a shock when they didn't find the two of them fast asleep in bed.

Following the men up the stairs, Rock moved silently behind them. They might be trained, but they weren't up to his level of training. None of the six men he counted seemed to sense his presence.

At the top of the stairs, they split off, three going further down the hall to the master bedroom, three going into the spare one.

Every protective instinct he had screamed at him to run after the men who had gone to the master bedroom since that was where Ariel was hiding. But his training told him to eliminate the men in the closer room first.

Play this smart.

Ariel is safe for now. Keep her that way.

Glad for his training that had taught him to move without making a sound, he found only one man in the bedroom, down on his knees, looking under the bed. The other two must be in the bathroom and large walk-in closet. Both bedrooms were around the same size, the other was the master only because it was at the back of the house with the amazing views.

"Come out, come out wherever you are. Come on, girlie, I know you're in here."

The voice echoed from the other room, one of the intruders taunting Ariel. Rock prayed she stayed right where she was. If they tore this place apart, then they'd find her, but as long as she remained where she was, she would be safe.

By the time the men got to tearing the place apart his team would have arrived.

Moving quickly, he killed the first man with a slice to the neck.

Just as he was dropping the body, he heard movement by the closet door.

For a second his eyes met with the other man's. Understanding passed quickly between them and the other man gave a smug smile as he lifted his weapon.

Rock threw the knife.

It hit its target, lodging in the intruder's neck and severing his carotid artery in one smooth slice.

Eyes widened as hands clawed at the handle of the knife, pulling it out. That would only hasten his death.

The man hit the carpet with a thud.

"Did you hear—" The third man came out of the bathroom gun already raised and ready to fire.

"Where you hiding, girlie?" someone asked from the other room.

Like it or not, he was going to have to use his weapon. The intruder was slower than he should have been. You didn't stop to think, when a threat presented itself you eliminated it. His hesitation was going to cost him his life.

Firing off a shot, Rock dropped the third man and then ran for the bedroom just as a blood-curdling scream filled the air.

A man's scream, not a woman's, and yet still his heart about leaped from his chest.

What had happened?

Why would one of the intruders be screaming like that?

Weapon ready, he burst into the master bedroom, firing off shots at the two men who swung around to face him.

They both dropped just as a third man fell to his knees in the doorway of the walk-in closet.

Behind the third man stood Ariel. She was breathing hard, eyes round with shock as she stared at the man who had just fallen.

Blood covered the man's back and a knife handle protruded from his left side. From the gurgling sounds emanating from the dying man —who he could have sworn was Dan Johnson—the blade had likely punctured his lung before piercing his heart.

A kill shot.

"Ariel?" he said softly as he moved toward her, stepping over the dying man.

Slowly her gaze moved to meet his. "It was him," she murmured.

"What was him, honey?" Why had she left the safety of her hiding place after promising him she'd stay hidden to attack this one man?

"He was the one. Who took me. Who sold me. Who touched me. I couldn't go back. I'm sorry, Sebastian. I was going to stay where you told me, I didn't mean to break my promise, but I couldn't go back. I couldn't go through that again. I couldn't go back." She was crying, shaking, borderline hysterical, and despite the fact they didn't have time for her to have a meltdown right now, the shots would bring in anyone else with these six men, he went to her and pulled her into his arms.

"Shh, baby. It's okay. You did what you had to do." While he wished she was still safely tucked away, he couldn't deny she deserved to avenge herself against one of the men who had hurt her.

Footsteps pounded on his stairs, and a moment later, a dozen men poured into his room.

Too many for him to shoot without risking Ariel getting hit in the crossfire. Only a couple of minutes had passed since his alarm was tripped—although it felt like a hundred lifetimes—still much too long until his team would arrive.

There was no way for him to get Ariel out of there safely.

Tucking her behind him, he faced down the intruders. If there was any chance he could take them all out before one could get a shot off at Ariel he'd do it. But there wasn't.

"Give us the girl, you don't need to die," one of the men said, stepping forward.

"You take her, you take me. I'm Prey. I'm sure you've heard of us, you can ransom me back, make a fortune."

Behind him, Ariel gasped. "Sebastian, no. Let them take me. You'll find me."

He'd try.

But chances were, he wouldn't.

"Not letting them take you without me, Ariel," he said firmly, his mind already made up. It was a small sacrifice to make, and one that didn't even come close to making up for all the pain he'd caused her. "I let you down once before, wasn't there for you while you were grieving like I should have been. I won't ever let you down again." Meeting the men's gaze squarely he lowered his weapon and set it on the floor. "You take her, then you have to take me as well. Don't care what your orders are. You take us both or you leave us both. But she doesn't go anywhere without me."

～

September 20th
   3:03 P.M.

No, no, no, no, no.

This couldn't be happening to her.

Not again.

Panic immediately clawed at her the second her mind shifted from drug induced sleep to consciousness.

Everything came back, there were no gaps in her memory, no blissful holes that let the full horror of her situation slip through.

Ariel remembered the day at the cemetery, cooking dinner side by side in Sebastian's kitchen. A place that was beginning to feel more and more like home even though she'd been there only a matter of days.

The movie. Sitting side by side on the couch. The nervous butterflies in her stomach as she wondered how close he was going to sit, if he was going to put an arm around her shoulders, if their thighs were going to touch.

If he was going to end the evening with a kiss.

Falling asleep, waking feeling content despite everything she had to deal with. Then the muted ring of the alarm. Leaving Sebastian behind to hide upstairs. Hearing the voice from her nightmares.

Finding the knife.

Stabbing him.

Sebastian shooting.

More men.

Guns everywhere.

Blood.

The realization that her nightmare wasn't over, in fact, it was beginning all over again.

Then worse than that, the knowledge that Sebastian had willingly handed himself over to the same men who would torture and sell her.

Why would he do that?

To prove to her that he loved her?

She believed that.

To prove to her that he was sorry for what he'd said and how he'd treated her the morning after they'd had sex?

She believed that too.

There was no reason for him to have come, and she wished more than anything in the world that he hadn't sacrificed himself for her. It wasn't even like it was going to help her in any way. She was still kidnapped, she would still be sold, all that it had accomplished was that now he would die too.

No, no, no, no, no.

Please let this be a dream.

Just a horrible nightmare.

Not reality.

Not real.

Please.

A sharp intake of air from the other side of the room shot to death any chances that this could just be her subconscious playing a major joke on her in her dreams.

This was all too real.

"Ariel."

It wasn't a question, but as she turned her head—still heavy with the drugs they'd been given as they were led at gunpoint out of Sebastian's cabin—to see the man she loved chained to a bed beside her, she nodded her head.

"Why?" she whispered, the sound more tortured moan than word.

His gaze was clear and steady as he looked back at her. No signs at all of the same panic and fear that ran rampant inside her. "Because I love you. Because if I couldn't protect you, I could at least stay beside you."

The tears that had been building inside her burst out in a noisy sob. "I love you, too, and I don't want you to be here. I don't want you to get hurt because of me. To die because of me."

For a long moment all she could do was cry. For herself, for Sebastian, for the past, for the future, for everything that could have been but never would.

Through it all, she heard Sebastian's soft voice murmuring words of comfort. Shockingly enough, they did offer some measure of comfort and eventually her blurry vision cleared, and she could see Sebastian grinning at her.

"Why are you smiling?" she asked totally confused. From where she was standing—lying actually—things didn't look good for them. They had been taken from his home, brought here—wherever here was—and chained to beds. While they were both still clothed, Ariel had no doubts that rape and torture were coming in the near future. For her at least. They might just kill Sebastian and be done with it. She had no idea why they hadn't already, bringing him along didn't seem like the smartest of moves.

"Because you said you love me," Sebastian said, his smile only growing wider.

That surprised a laugh out of her. Not something she would have thought possible given she already knew exactly what was coming.

But she felt Sebastian's joy at her uttering those simple words, and they brought her a measure of peace that she knew she would cling to through the worst of things. Maybe Sebastian hadn't been able to protect her physically, but his willingness to sacrifice himself for her was worth more than he could ever know.

"I do," she whispered. "I just wish you hadn't told them to bring you too. Maybe if I'd told you earlier that I still love you, that I never stopped even when I hated you in equal measure, that I didn't just forgive you but that I was ready to put the past behind us, you wouldn't be here now."

"Not your fault, Snow White, not in any way, shape, or form. I'm the one who failed you. Again. I promised you nobody would ever hurt you again, and yet here you are."

Ariel hated the recrimination in his voice. "It's not your fault," she said fiercely, willing him to believe it. "You shot and killed at least three of them, probably killed more, and there were just too many of them for you to take them all out on your own. You didn't fail me, you've proven to me over and over again these last several days that you love me, that you never stopped, and that you truly regretted the past. If this hadn't happened, I believe that one day we could have had the future that was always destined to be ours. I love you, Sebastian, and that love is all that's going to get me through this."

"Love you so much, sweetheart. Know that I will never regret what happens next. This is exactly where I want to be. Beside my Ariel, my Snow White, the other half of my heart and soul."

"Well, aren't you two cute," a mocking voice said from the doorway as three men and a woman entered.

Ariel immediately recognized both the voice and the man it belonged to. It was no shock to find that Arthur Gomez was here, she'd known he was behind her first abduction even if she had no proof. If he'd been behind her first abduction then he was behind this one too. The other two men were clearly some of his guards, they reminded her of thug man with their malicious gazes and meaty hands that loved to inflict pain.

A flicker of sympathy filled her at the sight of the woman.

She recognized the look in her eyes, saw it in the mirror when she looked at her reflection.

This woman was a slave.

"I had no idea you two were lovebirds. I thought you were just hired to protect her," Arthur said as he examined the two of them. "I must admit, when my men first called to tell me there was a man who demanded to be brought along, my initial response was to just tell them to kill you. After all, you're clearly trained, and likely part of a team. But then they told me you were Prey, and that you could be ransomed for a lot of money. So I thought that maybe there could be some good from bringing you along after all."

There was pure evil in his dark eyes, eyes that reminded her of his daughter's. Only while the little girl's eyes had been filled with fear and pain, along with a tentative hope that Ariel really could help her, her father's eyes were dark, bottomless pits of pure wickedness.

Sebastian talked about failing her, but really, she was the one who had failed.

Delilah Gomez had been counting on her, and not only had she not managed to convince anyone other than Sebastian and his team that the child had had a big sister, but she'd managed to get herself removed from the equation.

She was no help to the little girl now.

No help to anyone.

"You've been a thorn in my side for months now, Ariel Emerson. Sticking your nose where it doesn't belong and messing with what's mine. I thought I got you out of the way but you're like a bad penny, you just keep coming back. No more chances for you. This time, I'm going to sell you to someone who will never allow you to be found. Before I do that though, I have a little favor I need you to do for me."

If her situation wasn't so dire Ariel would have laughed. A favor? Why would this man think she would do anything for him?

"I need you to officially close the case on Delilah. Make sure nobody has reason to believe there was ever a sister, that my poor daughter is sick, delusional, and is a danger to herself and others. In case you're having any ideas about refusing, I'm sure your gentleman friend here will be sufficient motivation."

With a nod at the poor slave girl, she removed her clothes and headed toward Sebastian's bed. Horror at what was about to happen was enough to have her screaming at Arthur to make it stop.

CHAPTER

Seventeen

September 20th
    3:42 P.M.

This was fun.

This whole thing had been fun.

Who knew that dealing with a problem could turn out to be this entertaining. Arthur Gomez hadn't had this much fun in years.

Being wealthy was definitely fun. Throwing his money around to get whatever he wanted, to make people cater to his whims, it made him feel like a God. Knowing he was in complete control of the people in his universe, there was no feeling like it in the world.

It wasn't like he had always been the kind of man that would sell his own daughter, who would have people abducted and sold, and who would torture and abuse for his own enjoyment, but life had a way of changing people.

Today, he was the man standing in one of the bedrooms at his grand estate, with a man and a woman tied to the room's two beds. One was a man he didn't know much about other than he was some sort of hired bodyguard who worked for Prey and who lived on a remote compound in the New York State forests that was so well protected the only way in was to drop in from the sky.

The other was a woman who held the power to destroy everything he had worked so hard for.

Arthur didn't come from money. He was a self-made man. Raised in extreme poverty, they'd moved from one dilapidated apartment to another, spending time in between living out of their car, or if it got repossessed, on the streets. His mother had worked as a prostitute when she needed enough money for drugs, and his father cared only about one thing, getting so drunk he had zero idea what was going on around him.

Both his parents were mean addicts. When drunk, his father loved to take off his belt and swing it at whoever was closest, his wife, Arthur, one of his eight brothers and sisters, it didn't matter who. His mom loved psychological torture the best. Locking her children in a closet so she could hear them beg, cry, and plead to be let out was her favorite game. Even better if she could find a mouse or a spider or some cockroaches to throw in with them.

Unlike most of his siblings, Arthur had wanted out of that life.

Keeping his head down and his mouth closed, he worked hard in school. He had no friends, but then again, he had no time for friends. One goal. That was what his whole life centered around. Get out of that life, make something of himself, have enough money that he never had to go hungry, never had to sleep cold, and never had someone else with power over him.

It had worked too.

Graduating top of his class at high school, he'd gone to college on a full scholarship, and again graduated top of his class from Harvard Law School. Upon graduation, he'd been offered a job at one of the top criminal defense firms in the country.

Life was good.

With a job that paid him more than he could have hoped for, a beautiful wife who was both meek and gorgeous, everything had been perfect.

Almost.

Except a dark urge he could no longer control. It seemed you could leave your family behind, but you couldn't outrun what was inside you.

Anger.

Rage over the life he had been forced to live as a child, a life that was beneath him. Anger at the scum of the earth he was forced to interact with in his job. While he liked the money he earned and loved the fun of figuring out how to beat the system and get his clients off, he didn't appreciate associating in any way with the kind of people he had left behind.

Luckily, he had people he could release the valve and let his anger out on.

Much like his parents had used him and his siblings as their punching bags, he did the same with his wife and daughters. The younger one was a meek little mouse, but the older one, she was a spit-fire. In a way Cordelia reminded him of himself. She was strong-willed, determined, and so very smart.

But it was those same characteristics that made her so dangerous.

To the outside world the girl didn't exist. His wife was a recluse who rarely left the house, so hiding the pregnancy and the infant had been easy enough. Unfortunately, after his wife died in childbirth, he had been unable to hide the existence of daughter number two. Cordelia had thought she could beat him, go to the cops and tell them that her father beat her and passed her around to his friends. If it could be proven and he couldn't find a legal loophole to keep himself out of trouble, then he would have wound up in prison. Turned into the very people he had worked so hard to escape.

He would have been no better than his parents.

But he was better than them. He'd taken care of the problems his daughter represented by simply removing her from the equation. She was getting older anyway, less appealing to him, and he'd had his fun with her and was ready to be rid of her and move on to a more compliant victim.

Everything was perfect and then along came the social worker.

Arthur curled a lip as he looked down at her helplessly bound to the bed, watching him with terrified eyes.

How dare she think she could undo all his hard work.

Who did she think she was?

Ariel Emerson had had the kind of dream life he'd wished for as a child. Only child, wealthy, well-respected parents, smart, beautiful, a little shy but still well enough liked by her peers. She had never known what it was like to be hungry, to be cold, to be beaten, to be trapped and helpless. Her life had been a fairytale.

Until he came along anyway.

The little bubble of perfection she'd lived in had been popped. Now she knew pain, now she knew suffering, now she knew what happened when you crossed a man like him.

"P-please don't h-hurt him," Ariel stammered.

"He doesn't have to be hurt," Arthur told her. "It's all up to you. That's what you wanted wasn't it? Power over a man like me. You thought you could take me on and win."

"I-it wasn't about w-winning," Ariel said, obviously she had more backbone than he would have given her credit for. "I just wanted to protect your daughter."

"She belongs to me," he snarled. Arthur had never considered his younger daughter would wind up being such a threat. He'd believed the child to be too cowardly, especially after seeing what had happened to her sister when she tried to go against him. But the child had surprised him. He'd had a new business associate over, one who didn't yet know that what went on behind closed doors stayed there. The man had witnessed him hit his daughter, and of course CPS had been called in.

Any other case worker could have been bought off or intimidated, but not this woman. She had been relentless. She'd believed Delilah when she mentioned Cordelia and been determined to prove that there had been a daughter no one knew existed that he had sold.

Selling Ariel Emerson seemed like the easy answer. With her out of the picture, his claims that Delilah was mentally unstable and delusional would be believed, and his life could go on as it had before.

"Your lover doesn't have to suffer. That's in your hands," he told Ariel. Bringing along the man might have seemed stupid, but if he could use Ariel's lover against her and convince her to close Delilah's case, then he no longer had to worry about the life he had built crashing down around him. Once he had Ariel taken care of he could ransom the Prey man back to them for as much money as could be squeezed out of them, or he could just kill him and be done with it.

When he nodded at his personal sex slave—although according to the books, she was a maid who cooked and cleaned the mansion—she continued walking toward the bed where the man was restrained and climbed onto it, straddling the man's hips.

"You agree to close the case, put in your report that Delilah is sick, that there never was a sister, and that what was reported to CPS was misconstrued and was my daughter hurting herself, and nothing happens to your lover. I promise he'll be given a quick and painless death. You choose not to take my very generous offer, and I can assure you it won't go well for either of you. This." He waved a hand at the man's bed. "Will be just the beginning. I'll make him sorry he ever met you. I'll make him regret knowing you, regret helping you. And then when I decide he's suffered enough, I'll give him a long, slow, painful death. You on the other hand, will be sold, and you'll get to live out the rest of your life knowing that the man you loved suffered and died because of you."

CHAPTER
Eighteen

September 21st
4:15 A.M.

There were too many emotions in the room.

As a result, Rock found himself unable to concentrate as he needed to in order to get Ariel out of this alive.

It wasn't just her emotions that were clouding his mind, filling it with a fear he had never experienced before. He thought he'd known what true terror was. When Ariel had been missing, his imagination had been running on overtime, conjuring up literally thousands of horrific scenarios about what could be happening to her.

This time he didn't need to imagine.

This time he was right there beside her witnessing it.

While Ariel's terror seemed to be a tangible being, living inside this bedroom along with them, bouncing off the walls like an echo, only instead of growing softer it continued to grow louder until it drowned everything out, it wasn't the only distraction. His own fear for her added to the cacophony until it was all he could do to even keep an air of control.

If he let Ariel know how scared he was—for her not for himself—then it was only going to make things worse for her. So the energy he should be putting into escaping, or getting Ariel out at the least, was instead going into pretending he was calm and still in control so that she didn't panic more.

"I'm so sorry," she said for what had to be the hundredth time over the last few hours since they'd woken in this room.

"Baby," he said, making his tone stern, a gentle reprimand. "What did I tell you?"

"That it's not my fault. That there's no place on Earth you'd rather be. And that you should have called me Dorothy instead of Snow White, so I could just click my heels together and get myself home," she added with the smallest hint of a smile.

Rock smiled back, trying to make the smile both reassuring and teasing. He'd said the joke as an attempt to calm her down, and now it had become a kind of running joke between them. Although he absolutely meant it. More than anything he wanted—needed—Ariel to be safe.

Arthur Gomez's mind games were absolutely getting to her.

If he hadn't outright insisted that she refuse to go along with the man's plan for her to put in her report that there was no abuse in the Gomez home and that Delilah Gomez was mentally unstable and had invented a sister as an imaginary friend, then she would have done it. Whatever happened to him he could take. The woman who Arthur had threatened would rape him had done nothing more than straddle him, although Rock had no doubt that if Ariel continued to refuse to do what he wanted, Arthur would have her follow through on the act. Not that it would be the woman's fault, she was obviously as much a victim of Gomez as he and Ariel were.

But if it happened, he could take it. He could but Ariel couldn't. And sooner or later, she would snap and do anything Gomez asked of her to protect him.

That wasn't what he wanted.

Unless a miracle occurred, he wasn't walking out of here alive, but Ariel was. Arthur Gomez's plan was to kill him—or possibly ransom him—but sell her. Knowing she had caved and gone against the child she had vowed to protect would haunt her, and if he died, he needed to know Ariel was strong enough to survive until his team found her. Prey would never give up on her, that he believed with absolute certainty. But Ariel didn't know them like he did, she didn't need any other voices whispering inside her head to just give up and let go.

"Sebastian?" she whispered.

"Yeah, honey?"

"Do you really believe that?"

"What? That if you were Dorothy, you could click your heels and transport yourself back home? Sure do."

His teasing was rewarded with a small chuckle. "No, silly. That you don't blame me."

"Sweetheart, I don't blame you. Not one little bit. The only person I blame is Arthur Gomez. He didn't have to sell his daughter. He didn't have to abuse his children. He didn't have to sell you to try to get you out of the way. He didn't have to come after you again and bring us both here. He is the only person responsible for this. Let me ask you a question. What if it had been my enemies that had come after us, kidnapped us, and threatened to torture us. Would you blame me?"

"No, of course not," she answered immediately.

"Then why do you think I would feel any differently?"

For a moment she was silent. "If we had been kidnapped because of your enemies, and I was in danger, would you blame yourself?"

"Touché," he said softly. He already blamed himself for not doing more to protect Ariel, for allowing her to be kidnapped. If it was his enemies who had taken them both instead of hers, then he would absolutely be feeling the same way Ariel was right now. "Did you mean what you said earlier?"

Rock had wanted to ask her that question ever since she'd said the words he had been dreaming of hearing for fifteen very long years. But he was afraid of the answer. Afraid that it was only fear of dying, and guilt over believing his death would be her fault, that had made Ariel utter them.

"When I said I loved you?"

"Yes."

"Of course I meant it. I wouldn't say it if I didn't. I love you, Sebastian Rockman. Utterly and completely. It might take time for us to reconnect and rebuild what was damaged, but we would have done it. I believe with you by my side I could have found a way to find myself again. I could have survived the hell I lived through, and we could have been happy."

"We can still have that future, baby."

"Maybe." Doubt was obvious in her voice and in her face as she watched him.

There wasn't anything he wouldn't do to wipe away that doubt. Gomez was no amateur though. The bed frames were metal, the hand-cuffs were metal, breaking out of them wasn't impossible but it wouldn't be easy. Not even close. Even if he did get free, he had no weapons, and already knew he was wildly outnumbered. While Gomez had kept him alive this long to use as a way to try to control Ariel, Rock knew he was expendable. If he proved to be a danger to Gomez, then the man would order his guards to shoot to kill.

"How are my favorite lovebirds doing?" Arthur singsonged as he entered the room. With him was the same young woman as earlier, but two different bodyguards this time, and his seven-year-old daughter.

There were bruises on the little girl's face and exposed arms. Her head had been shorn and dark shadows sat under her red-rimmed eyes. In her tiny hands she carried a hammer, and Rock didn't even have to ask to know what was coming next.

Rage blinded him, and he shoved aside the foggy cloud of Ariel's fear for him and his fear for her and focused. Fear was going to get the woman he loved and this innocent little child tortured, abused, and eventually sold.

Not happening.

Not on his watch.

"Delilah has something she wants to say," Arthur said, prodding his daughter toward the beds where he and Ariel were chained up.

Tears shimmered in the girl's eyes, and although she gave a shake of her head, she recited what she had obviously been told to say. "I am a bad girl and I don't respect my father. I make up stories. I don't have a sister. I hurt myself, my father loves me and has never hurt me." After finishing her spiel, she looked to her father, clearly to check that she hadn't messed it up and wouldn't be punished.

"Very good, Delilah." Arthur nodded approvingly. "Now you have a recantation, Ms. Emerson, I'm sure you're ready to update your file. End this nonsense once and for all."

Ariel glanced only briefly over to him with an apology in her eyes, but also a strength he was so very proud of. "I can't—I won't—do that, Mr. Gomez. Delilah isn't a bad little girl. She didn't make up any stories, I believe she had a sister, and even if you hurt me." Ariel paused, gulped, her voice wavering as she continued, "Even if you hurt Sebastian, I won't do what you want. I can't. The case staying open is Delilah's only chance. Even if I do close the case now, it's going to look suspicious. I was sold, then I was rescued, I come back to work just to close a case and then I disappear again. That's confirmation Delilah was telling the truth."

Growling in frustration, Arthur shoved his daughter toward the bed. "I've tried being nice. I gave you a chance to do what I asked and close out the case. Instead, you've been nothing but rude and uncooperative. It didn't have to be this way, Ms. Emerson. But I warned you, and now I've run out of patience. Let's see if a little pain gives you a more amenable attitude. Delilah, do it."

The child began to cry. "No, Daddy, please, I don't want to."

"Do it," Arthur bellowed.

Still sobbing, the little girl walked the remaining distance to Ariel's bed. Ariel startled, obviously expecting that whatever was going to happen would be to him and not to her since that's what Arthur had threatened earlier.

"You're a dead man, Gomez," Rock screamed as his entire body strained against its constraints, desperate to get to Ariel to prevent her pain.

As it swung through the air, the hammer seemed to make a whooshing sound, but perhaps that was only his own pulse pounding in his ears.

Ariel's scream as the hammer made contact with her hand snapped any control Rock had, and the scream that fell from his lips was more animal than human.

~

September 21st
    4:29 A.M.

Pain exploded in her hand as the hammer made contact with surprising strength given the child's small size.

Ariel wasn't sure which was worse.

Her own howl of agony, Sebastian's growl of pained fury, or Delilah's pitiful whimpers as she looked from Ariel's smashed hand, to the hammer, to her father who beamed at her and nodded approvingly.

Or perhaps it was her own anger.

Just because she had been broken by her ordeal—an ordeal she had gone through because of the man standing at the end of the bed she was cuffed to—it didn't mean she couldn't put her pieces back together. Already, she had made some progress, admitting to both Piper and Sebastian her fears that what had happened was her fault, and allowing Sebastian back into her life.

She wasn't going to be destroyed.

Not by an evil man like Arthur Gomez who thought he was above the law and could do whatever he pleased.

Whatever happened, she would survive.

Already she had wasted so much of her life by allowing the people who hurt her to have too much control and power over her.

No more.

This was going to be the hardest thing she ever had to do, but she would survive, and she would traverse the road to healing if it killed her. And if she died here in this house, or in some small, dark basement of whoever wound up buying her, then she would at least die knowing her spirit was her own again.

The only person in charge of her life was her.

"I will kill you," Sebastian growled in a voice so full of authority that Ariel half expected to see Arthur Gomez burst into flames.

Arthur merely laughed. "I'd like to see you try. As soon as I get Ms.

Emerson to do what I want, I have no further use for you, and you will be eliminated."

Sebastian gave a scathing, mocking laugh. "Are you really that stupid, Gomez? Do you really think that Ariel closing the case will end this for you? You've only made it worse. My team know you're the one behind her abduction, and I can assure you they won't stop until they prove you not only had a daughter, but that you sold her, and that you abused Delilah, and that you had Ariel abducted and sold."

It was clear to see, even through the haze of pain encompassing her body, that Arthur had no idea just who Sebastian was.

"You think I'm afraid of your team?" Arthur asked condescendingly.

"I think you're too stupid to be, but you should be," Sebastian replied. "Still got to give you credit for your confidence, even if it is misplaced. Not many people would be so cocky when they were taking on Prey Security. You know the world-renowned private security firm that's taken down bigger fish than you without breaking a sweat?"

Arthur paled, fear sparking in his eyes as reality sunk in.

His arrogance and ego were going to wind up getting him killed or imprisoned, no matter what he wound up doing with her and Sebastian. Already she knew enough about Prey and Sebastian's team to know they would never give up on him. Or on her.

Now she finally understood why Sebastian had put all their numbers in her phone. Prey was a family, and because of her connection to Sebastian, they had welcomed her into their fold. No questions asked.

Warmth spread through her and she managed a smile despite the pain in her hand. It felt nice to belong after spending so many years on the fringes, keeping her distance because it hurt to let people in. Guilt over her belief she was responsible for Kayla's death and shame for using it to finally get Sebastian made it hard to let anyone get too close. The treatment of their classmates who had believed Sebastian's accusations without question had made it impossible.

Without even trying, she now had a huge family of warriors at her back.

Arthur's fear turned to rage. "I have connections everywhere. Prey can't touch me."

Another scathing laugh from Sebastian. "You think you have more connections than Eagle Oswald? The man who knows everyone from military generals to the President and everyone in between. The man who thinks he's right in any and all situations. Who never met a fight he didn't win. Eagle is a billionaire retired Navy SEAL who runs the most successful private security firm in the world. He will crush you like the bug you are."

"Once I dispose of your body and sell Ms. Emerson, there'll be no evidence," Arthur said, more to reassure himself, it seemed, than to convince either of them.

"You're even stupider than I gave you credit for," Sebastian mocked. "There's always evidence. You're a defense attorney you should know that. There'll be a trail and Prey will find it. When they do, they will nail you to the wall. You should know, Eagle's connections include several inmates already serving life sentences who would be only too happy to do him the favor of disposing of you."

"I'm not going to prison," Arthur roared, sounding almost manic now. "I won't. I'm not like them. Not like my parents. I won't go to prison. Prey can try to have me convicted but I'll represent myself. I've never had a client go to prison, and I'm not about to start with me."

"Whatever you say," Sebastian taunted, resting back against the pillows on his bed like he didn't have a care in the world. Like he wasn't chained up and helpless.

Fighting down her fear, Ariel did her best to trust him. He knew what he was doing. Just because this was a different Sebastian than the one she had known growing up, it didn't mean he wasn't highly trained and skilled.

If anyone could get them out of here it was him.

Arthur gave a scream of pure fury and then glared at his daughter. "Hit her again."

"No, Daddy, please," Delilah begged. The child shook violently, and tears streamed down her pale cheeks, one darkened with bruises.

"Do it, or I'll pass you around at my next dinner party as the entertainment. See if you can top your sister's performances," he sneered.

"It's okay," Ariel whispered to the girl, trying to breathe through the pain to give the little girl an encouraging smile.

Delilah might only be seven years old, but she looked so much older as resignation filled her pretty dark eyes.

Ariel braced, but there was really no way to prepare for the coming pain.

As the hammer made contact with her already broken hand, she dug her teeth into her tongue to prevent from screaming in pain.

Screaming was only going to make it worse for Sebastian and Delilah. It didn't make anything better for her, and it gave Arthur Gomez exactly what he wanted.

Still, as the hammer connected again and white-hot agony burned from her hand, engulfing the rest of her body, the smallest of whimpers escaped.

"Leave her alone!" Sebastian bellowed, and she could hear him fighting wildly against the cuffs binding him.

If there had been any doubts left about whether or not Sebastian loved her, they would have been eliminated by the sounds of his screams. She could hear his love for her in the agonized howl. He felt her pain as surely as if it was his own.

"I will kill you. I'll kill you!" Sebastian yelled over and over again.

"Shut him up," Arthur told his men.

Her heart clenched in her chest, her pain forgotten. Did Arthur mean ...?

No.

He couldn't kill Sebastian. Not here, not now, not right in front of her.

Being determined to survive was one thing, but witnessing the execution of the man she loved when she'd only just gotten him back was another.

Both the men were grinning as they approached the bed. For a moment hope jumped inside her. They hadn't pulled out their weapons, maybe they were just going to gag him or something.

The first fist slamming into Sebastian's unprotected stomach had a startled scream of surprise falling from her lips.

"No! Don't hurt him," she shrieked as another fist hit his chest, and then his jaw. While Sebastian might be calm while the two men beat on him, her blood pressure spiked, fury and terror mingling together inside her.

"It's okay, baby," Sebastian soothed.

"It's not! You're a coward!" she yelled at Arthur. "You pick on helpless little girls. You let other people do your dirty work for you and beat up on helpless people who can't fight back. You really think you're so much better than us then you uncuff him, tell your goons to back off, and take him on yourself. But you won't do that, will you? Because you're a coward and you know you won't win. You're nothing but a pathetic excuse for a man. You're nothing. Sebastian is everything. He loves me, he's man enough to acknowledge his mistakes, own up to them and try to rectify them. He's brave enough to dedicate his life to protecting others and he came with me not because he had to, but because he loves me enough to die by my side so I don't suffer alone. He's my everything, and you're just a pathetic piece of trash."

Lunging forward, Arthur snatched the hammer from his daughter's hand. "I'm not trash. I'm rich, I'm powerful, I'm the one in charge here."

The hammer slammed into her hand with much more force than a little girl could bring, and the resulting agony was too much for her mind to handle.

Blackness descended, stealing her consciousness and sending her off into a void of nothingness.

CHAPTER
Nineteen

September 21st
6:22 P.M.

Hours ticked by.

Nothing changed.

Rock's pain was a distant thrum, nothing more than an annoyance. It was Ariel and his concern for her that had that same barbed wire that had been wrapped around his heart while she was missing right back in its place again.

It was slowly draining the life out of him, and he wasn't sure how much longer he could hold it together.

Reminding himself that he was Ariel's best chance at getting out of here alive was only doing so much. This wasn't the first time he'd been caught and held captive, but that had been different. Then it was just him and his team. Not only had he had back up, but while he loved them like brothers, they weren't this woman.

Weren't the other half of his heart.

Of his soul.

They weren't his everything.

The change in her breathing was his first indication that she was awake again, even before she spoke. Ariel had been in and out of consciousness over the last several hours. Each time she passed out his heart jumped into his throat. What if she didn't wake up this time?

Knowing that a broken hand was not a life-threatening injury didn't help any.

His woman was hurting, in enough pain her brain had to keep protecting itself by knocking her out, and that was all he could think about.

"Sebastian?" Her voice trembled with fear as she bolted up as far as she could get with both her wrists cuffed. The movement jostled her injured hand and she moaned and sank back down again. Each time she woke she called out his name, her fear for him evident, and he hated that each time she regained consciousness she had to remember where she was, what had happened to her, and to him.

"Right here, baby. Didn't run out on you," he teased, even as the backs of his eyes stung with tears he wouldn't allow himself to shed.

She gave a small, half-hearted chuckle, then sighed. "Can I say it?"

"Depends on what it is."

"You know."

"If you mean can you apologize again, then the answer is absolutely not."

"Fine. But I am." Her head twisted on the pillow to look at him, and she gifted him the ghost of a smile. All too quickly it passed and her expression filled with concern. "Are you okay?"

"Not about to die on you, Snow White," he assured her, only half joking. No, he wasn't about to die, the beating the two bodyguards had inflicted hadn't left him with any serious or life-threatening injuries.

This time.

But they both knew he was living on borrowed time.

Probably the only thing that had stopped Arthur Gomez from having him killed earlier was the fact that Ariel had passed out. Rock's job here was as incentive for Ariel to do as Gomez wanted, beyond that, he was completely expendable.

Luckily for him, Ariel had been out a couple of hours, and to keep up appearances Gomez had obviously had to go off to work because they'd been left alone for most of the day. Sooner or later his luck was going to run out. Gomez would get tired of the game, accept that Ariel wouldn't do what he wanted, and with Prey breathing down his neck it was safer for him to get rid of both of them as quickly as possible.

Forcing himself to stay calm, he kept his gaze on his beautiful Ariel. "How you doing, honey?"

"Same. My hand hurts, but there's ..." Ariel trailed off, an odd look coming over her face.

"Ariel?" he asked, his anxiety spiking.

"Give me a second." Her voice was tight, strained, and he didn't like it one bit.

"Tell me what's wrong, sweetheart," he coaxed, somehow keeping his voice gentle. There wasn't much he could do for her chained to the bed as he was. He couldn't even touch her to offer comfort.

Her head turned, and her eyes were wide. There was pain in those golden depths, but there was something else as well. "I think ... I think I might be able to get my hand free."

Not what he'd been expecting her to say. Rock had expected her to tell him she was having chest pains, or she was having trouble breathing, or something equally as terrifying.

But this ...

This could be the key to getting her out of here.

"The cuff was damaged?" he asked.

"I don't think so. I think it's me. My hand, the bones are so badly broken that it kind of moves funny ... weirdly. I think if I try, I can pull it through the cuff."

Immediately his entire being rebelled at the idea of her inflicting more pain on herself even if it was for a good cause.

No.

It wasn't worth it.

Except ...

If she didn't get out of there, then she would be sold again.

His team—all of Prey—would keep looking for her, but even if they did find her it would be weeks, months, maybe even years of unimaginable suffering. If she survived that long.

Drawing in a shaky breath, it took all of his effort to remain calm. "Are you sure?"

"No. But reasonably sure." Uncertain eyes met his. "I should try to pull it through. Right?"

Forcing back the no that wanted to escape, Rock nodded slowly. "I don't like the idea of you causing yourself more pain. Okay, I absolutely loathe it. But you need to get out of here and this could be your only chance. My team will be looking for us, but we don't know where Gomez brought us or how easy it will be for them to find us. I want you safe. I need you safe. So, if you think you can get free then you should try. If you can't do it, it's okay. No pressure."

Ariel gave a shaky nod. "I wish that you could at least hold my hand —my good hand—while I do this."

"Me too, baby. Damn, me too." Straining against his bonds, Rock reached out toward her as much as the handcuffs allowed. "Imagine my fingers curled around yours, squeezing tightly. My hand stroking your hair, your back. I'm right here, baby. Right here. You can do this. I believe in you, Snow White. You are so much stronger than you know. You survive. Whatever happens you keep moving forward. You got this."

Her gaze never left his, even as he saw her body brace for the coming pain.

His body did too.

Every one of his muscles was pulled tight as Ariel maneuvered her broken hand through the handcuff. Her guttural moan of pain had his entire body wincing as nausea churned in his stomach.

"You okay, honey?" he asked as Ariel panted and trembled and tried to get herself back under control.

"I ... could lie ... but no ... not even close to being okay. That ... hurt. Why isn't there a word strong enough to describe pain like that?" Her eyes were dull and shadowed with agony, but he saw her inner strength still shining through.

"I don't know, baby, but you did amazing. You are amazing."

Lifting her head, she looked over at her cuffed hand. "But I'm still stuck. I have one hand free but that's it."

"You have pins in your hair right? You always do because you hate those wispy little bits underneath that always manage to escape your ponytail."

Her gaze brightened. "I do. Unless they fell out."

When she lifted her broken hand Rock got his first good look at it. It was bruised and bloody, obviously misshapen, and it shook badly as she moved it.

But his girl didn't give up.

Somehow, she managed to maneuver the broken hand under her head and came away with a black bobby pin.

"Now what?"

"Now you pick the lock on the handcuffs."

Brow furrowed she looked at him like he was crazy. "Do you think I graduated from spy school some time in the last few hours?"

Surprising him, Rock barked out a laugh. "I'll talk you through it. Trust me, if you can pull a broken hand through a metal cuff, then you can pick a lock easy-peasy."

Ariel didn't look convinced, and he could see the weight of the last few hours weighing down on her. She was exhausted, she was in pain, she was dirty, and hungry, and thirsty. Her hair was a mess, her clothes —like his—were soaked with urine. They'd had no sleep, been chained to beds for hours, and drugged, but she was still standing, still fighting, and that was all he could ask of her.

"I believe in you, baby. You can do this," he said softly.

It took several tries. Using a broken hand to do anything was agony, especially something as small and intricate as picking a lock. By the end tears were streaming down Ariel's cheeks, her whole body trembled, and she was breathing hard, but she was free.

Not safe yet, but one giant step closer.

As she carefully swung her legs over the side of the bed, she looked over at him. "Now what?"

"Now you go out the window and get the hell out of here."

~

September 21st
6:57 P.M.

. . .

"Go out the window?" she squeaked. Surely Sebastian couldn't be serious.

"Dead serious," he said as though he'd just read her mind.

It wasn't so much his expression as the word dead that had a fine tremor rippling through her body. After hours of being chained to the bed her limbs felt dead, add to that the excruciating pain in her hand, and all Ariel wanted to do was find a quiet, dark place to curl up and sleep for a week.

Or a month.

Or a year would be better.

But hiding, burying her head on the sand wasn't going to improve her situation. Or Sebastian's situation. Because right now, she was the one who was free not him.

Not yet at least. But she'd managed to get herself free so she could pick the locks on his cuffs too. Then they could both get out of here.

As exciting as it was to think of getting far, far away from this house of horrors, it was exhausting as well. Already her body trembled, the pain in her hand meant it wasn't going to be of much use to her for much longer.

Better get on it.

Forcing her shaking legs to hold her, she pushed to her feet.

Big mistake.

The entire room seemed to do one long, slow revolution around her, and she very nearly toppled right over.

Somehow, she managed to stay standing and quickly squeezed her eyes closed in an attempt to stop the dizziness.

"Ariel? You okay?"

It was only the concern in Sebastian's voice that stopped her from falling apart. If she lost it now, Sebastian would be the one to pay the price.

"Sorry, just a little lightheaded," she said as she crossed the room to the bed.

"This is the opposite direction from the window," Sebastian said.

"Need to get you free first, and I don't think I can handle a window right now." Honestly, she wasn't sure she could handle much more of anything that didn't include clean clothes, painkillers, and a soft, snuggly blanket. Not that it mattered. None of those things were in her immediate future. For now, she just needed to keep putting one foot in front of the other.

"Wasn't a request, babe. You'll give me the bobby pin, and you'll get yourself out the window."

There was a harshness to his voice that at any other time would have made her flinch in fear, but she knew that harshness wasn't directed at her, it was toward Arthur Gomez. Sebastian was in full on warrior mode now, she could see it in the way his eyes were slightly unfocused as though he were running through a dozen scenarios in his head, and in the tightness of his body as though he were preparing it for a fight.

"I'm not leaving without you," she said in a small voice. Was he crazy?

"Yeah, Ariel, you are. If Gomez isn't home already, he will be any minute. If he finds you here, that's it, you won't get another chance to escape."

"But you can still come with me."

"No. I'm staying to buy you as much time as I can."

He sounded so certain, so sure of himself, but to her it was simple. All she had to do was unpick one of his locks then he could do the rest way quicker than she could. Then they could both get out of here. "But—"

"No buts. Go. Now."

His command made her waver, she was wasting time. Time neither of them had. Sebastian was a protector. He was going to do whatever was needed to try to up her odds. His mind was already made up and arguing wasn't going to change it.

"I love you," she whispered as she pressed the pin into the palm of his right hand and then stooped and pressed her lips to his. "Please don't die. I need you."

The admission was easier to make than she would have thought it would be. Putting her trust in the man who had already shattered her heart once would have seemed insane to her a couple of months ago.

A lot had changed in that time.

With her, with him, with them.

Knowing how much Sebastian had suffered over hurting her helped to heal those wounds, and now she knew she needed him by her side to traverse the harrowing road of healing that lay ahead.

Assuming they both survived.

"Don't plan on dying, sweetheart. Just got you back. Love you more than anything in this world. Go. Please."

Leaving him behind was one of the hardest things she would ever have to do. The only reason she did it was because there were no other choices.

Shaky legs took her to the window, and when she looked out, she spotted something below her that could get her out of there alive. "There's a delivery van down there, unloading groceries."

"Get in there. Hide. If the man has loyalty to Gomez when he stops, try to run. If you can't, scream, chances are he'll be at another house, and there will be people to hear you. You can do this, Ariel. I believe in you. You have survived so much you can absolutely do this."

It was probably only the fact that Sebastian believed in her that she was able to swing open the window and tentatively climb out. Like it had been planned all along, beneath the window was a porch, the drop wasn't far, and even injured and afraid of heights, she could make it.

"Love you, my beautiful Snow White."

Those were the last words Ariel heard as she used her good hand for balance and lowered herself down.

The drop felt so much longer than the couple of feet it actually was.

The landing sounded loud to her ears, and for a moment, she just sat there, frozen, sure someone had heard and would be coming to drag her back into the house.

What if they killed Sebastian as her punishment?

What if they killed him when they realized she was gone?

Too late to do anything about it now, when she sat for several seconds and nobody came running, Ariel carefully slid over the side of the porch and down onto the ground. Although the drop had been no more than a couple of feet, the landing seemed to jar through her, sending pain screaming through her hand.

She hadn't been able to look at it, not properly anyway. It made her too queasy. Blood had always made her feel a little sick, but the sight of her own made her want to throw up.

Now was not the time for throwing up.

Clutching the injured hand to her chest, Ariel snuck toward the van. Her heart pounded so hard in her chest it physically hurt, and her pulse raced so fast it added to the dizziness, bringing her dangerously close to passing out.

Someone was going to spot her.

She was sure of it.

Yet there were no shouts as she climbed into the back of the truck and hid herself behind a stack of boxes.

There was nothing.

Just her and her fear.

Fear for herself she had learned how to handle during her ordeal, but there was no way to train to control your fear for somebody else.

Sebastian was putting everything on the line for her. Ariel knew some of it was because of him hurting her in the past and his need to make up for it, but the rest was just because he was the kind of man who put his life on the line on a daily basis, usually for people he didn't even know.

He was a hero.

Her hero.

Footsteps sounded and she went completely still, hardly daring to even breathe. This could be it. If she was discovered now, it would be all over.

When the door closed without incident, enclosing her in darkness, Ariel let out a shaky sob.

Just one before she reigned it in.

No time for sobbing, she was hardly out of the woods yet. There were still a dozen things that could go wrong. What if the driver didn't stop at someone's house? What if he stopped somewhere isolated? If he was loyal to or sympathetic to or even afraid of Arthur, he would take her right back to him.

Seconds ticked by with excruciating slowness, and with each one that passed her anxiety grew. The throbbing in her hand was hard to ignore and almost impossible to bear. The one thing she wanted the most—Sebastian's arms wrapped snuggly around her—wasn't an option, and she was so afraid of what happened next.

Injured as she was, she couldn't fight. She felt helpless all over again just like she had when she had been kidnapped the first time. If she survived this, she was going to learn how to shoot, learn how to defend herself, and never ever take for granted the simple pleasure of not having danger dancing around her.

Eventually, the van pulled to a stop.

There was no more waiting.

Whatever was going to happen would happen.

With Sebastian relying on her to send in his team she had to survive, had to make sure she did whatever she needed to get him help.

The engine turned off.

The muted thump of a door closing told her the driver had gotten out.

A moment later, light flooded the back of the van.

Ariel opened her mouth and screamed with everything she had.

CHAPTER

Twenty

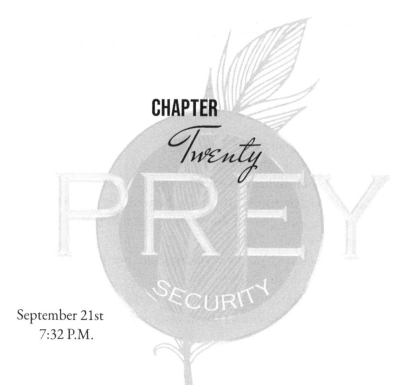

September 21st
7:32 P.M.

Did she make it?

That was the only thought running through Rock's head. The only thing he cared about.

Lying in the dark, under the bed he had been chained to, there was nothing to do but wait and see. Wait and prepare to attack.

One goal.

One purpose.

Buy as much time as possible for Ariel.

So long as she got away that was all that mattered. While he had no intention of dying and missing out on the amazing gift Ariel had given him of a second chance at happiness, if he didn't make it out of this alive, he knew she would be well taken care of. Her parents might be self-centered and preoccupied with their own needs, but they did love their daughter. And she had the whole of Prey to rally around her.

She would survive.

More than that, she would thrive.

Like the butterflies she loved so much, she would go through her own metamorphosis. There was no way she could still be the same Ariel she had been before her ordeal, too much had happened to her, she had suffered too greatly. But she could become a newer version of herself.

One he prayed he got the chance to spend his life with.

His hands flexed, pulling the makeshift chain tight. While he would have loved to have a real weapon, especially since any time the guards came into the room with Gomez they were armed, he'd had to make do with what he had. The four handcuffs had been all cuffed together to make one long chain. His plan was to pounce as soon as they realized where he was hiding and take out as many of the guards as he could before they overpowered him.

Unless he could get his hands on a gun, then he might be able to take them all out. It all depended on how many men Gomez had there. If the number he'd sent to the compound was anything to go by, Rock didn't like his chances of not being ridiculously outmanned.

After getting himself free, he'd left the window open, assuming that the first thing the men would think when they came in and saw the empty beds was that the two of them would have gone out it. This wasn't like a typical mission, he wasn't trying to take out as many tangoes as possible, all he was doing was buying as much time as he could for Ariel.

If they didn't find his hiding place and instead all headed outside to search, then he would go in search of a real weapon, otherwise it was just him and the chain.

At least he had one thing on his side. These men would assume that sooner or later his self-preservation instinct would kick in and he would do whatever he could to protect himself rather than Ariel.

They would be wrong.

There was nothing he cared about more than her life, her safety, and her happiness.

Nothing he could do about her happiness right now, but he could absolutely do something to make sure she was alive and safe.

Rock registered the sound of approaching footsteps before the door opened.

"What the—?" Arthur Gomez's shocked exclamation brought a smile to his lips.

Not so smug now, are you?

"How did they ...? Where did they ...?" Gomez stuttered as Rock watched two pairs of boots run across the room toward the window.

"Looks like they went out here," one of the bodyguards said.

"Not much of a jump with the porch right beneath," the other added.

Thank goodness for that. While he knew she hated heights, Ariel had gone right out that window like a trooper. Since he hadn't heard the sounds of anyone falling, or screams of pain, he'd assumed she had made it safely into the back of the delivery van and away. Hearing that there had been a porch so her descent down was easier made him feel a whole lot better about deciding to stay behind.

Just because he believed it to be her best chance didn't mean it was easy.

Especially when she'd all but begged him to come with her.

Knowing she was alone out there, that he wasn't at her back, that she was injured and might have to defend herself, it ate at him. But this was the only way to ensure she got as far away as she could.

Using himself as a distraction had to work because if it didn't, he had just missed out on spending the last minutes of his life with the woman he loved.

"They could be anywhere by now," the first man said.

"No," Arthur said slowly, thoughtfully. "The guard at the gate didn't mention seeing anyone leave. And we haven't had any reports of people on the grounds. I think they're still here."

"Big house. Plenty of places to hide," the second guard said.

At least they hadn't seemed to think of the possibility that Ariel—or the two of them—had escaped in the back of the delivery van. If they thought that they were both hiding somewhere in the house it would take them a long time to search it all and realize they were wrong.

Long enough for Ariel to get far away and make contact with his team.

Thank goodness for rich monsters and their mansions.

"No," Arthur said again. "I don't think they went that far. They're trying to throw us off, make us look in all the wrong places."

A moment later the bedframe hiding him was flung sideways at the same time as the bedframe of the bed Ariel had been cuffed to was also thrown sideways.

The smug look on Arthur Gomez's face quickly faded when he realized that only one person had been hiding in the room and not the two he had been expecting.

Not wanting to waste a second, Rock sprung to his feet. While the beating he had been given earlier had left him with some aches and pains, it was nothing that was going to hinder him in a hand-to-hand combat fight.

Before either of the bodyguards could react, he had the chain wrapped around the closest one's neck. Squeezing tightly enough that the man was incapacitated for the moment, he trusted his instincts when they told him to move, and turned, angling his body so his human shield was between him and the threat he detected.

His instincts proved to be correct, and instead of taking the bullet fired at him, it went into the other bodyguard. The man howled in pain, his hands moving from where they had been clawing at the chain, to press to the wound gushing blood in his abdomen.

Too bad the man had dropped his weapon when Rock lunged at him. Showed what kind of lackluster men Gomez was hiring. A solider was supposed to know to never let go of his weapon, it was the difference between life and death.

Needing to do everything he could to give himself some sort of advantage, Rock threw the man's body, which was quickly becoming dead weight, at the remaining bodyguard.

Not expecting that the man startled, the shot he'd been about to fire went wide, hitting the ceiling as his hands moved to catch the two-hundred-pound body coming directly for him.

The two men landed in a tangle of limbs as Gomez turned and fled the room.

"Coward," Rock yelled as he went after him. There was no need to attempt to be quiet, the gunshots would have alerted everyone in the building that something was going on even if Arthur hadn't somehow signaled them already by setting off an alarm.

Running after him, he caught up to Gomez in the hall. Grabbing him around the neck he slammed the man up against the nearest wall, enjoying the flare of fear in the other man's eyes.

"You're nothing but a coward, Arthur Gomez. Remember what I said to you?" His hand tightened around the man's neck, cutting off his air supply. While his goal was to keep the action centered here in the house to let Ariel get away, he wasn't going to pass up an opportunity to kill the man who had inflicted so much pain and suffering on the woman he loved.

Eyes bulging, face turning red, Arthur clawed at Rock's hands much as the bodyguard had moments ago.

"I said I'd kill you. Remember that?"

"Not happening today," a new voice announced, and in his peripheral vision Rock noted several men moving in to form a circle around him.

Reluctantly, he loosened his hold on Gomez, watching with a smile as the other man slumped sideways.

Apparently believing he had once again achieved the upper hand, Arthur's expression quickly morphed into arrogant. But Arthur Gomez didn't have the upper hand because Ariel wasn't hiding in the house somewhere, she was already long gone.

"Tell me where she's hiding. I know you love her, but it's over for both of you. Save yourself some pain and give up her hiding place," Arthur commanded.

"Not a chance in hell that's happening," Rock said calmly like there weren't a dozen weapons aimed at him.

"Then we better start putting some bullet holes in you to see if that loosens your tongue."

~

September 21st
     9:08 P.M.

. . .

Where were they?

Ariel was sure they would have come by now.

How long had it been?

Felt like both seconds and hours since the delivery driver had opened the back of his truck.

She wasn't sure who was more shocked when she started screaming, but she was pretty sure it was him. The man was nice, had taken one look at her, dirty, disheveled appearance, with her broken hand cradled against her chest, and immediately paled.

Even though he had offered to call the cops for her, Ariel had been afraid that Arthur Gomez would have at least one on his payroll who might just deliver her right back to him, so she'd asked if she could borrow his phone instead.

There was only one number she wanted to call.

If she couldn't have Sebastian by her side, then she wanted his team. They were the people he trusted so they were the people she trusted.

Shivering, she huddled into the blanket the delivery driver—Jeffrey Dale—had given her. While he had insisted that he needed to call an ambulance, she had managed to talk him out of it. Right now, she didn't want to go anywhere alone. At least here at the back of the grocery store she felt marginally safe. It was just her and Jeffrey and the man didn't scare her.

Didn't scare her, but didn't make her feel safe either.

Not the way Sebastian would.

Not even the way his team would.

Please, hurry up and get here.

Other than getting the address so she could pass it along to Sebastian's team, she hadn't done more than beg Jeffrey to let her use his phone and to not call anyone else and tell them she was there. Ariel absolutely wouldn't put it past Arthur Gomez to have called all his contacts to let them know she had escaped, and she couldn't risk being recaptured. Not before she talked to Sebastian's team. He was counting on her, and she wasn't going to let him down.

The sound of an engine caught her attention, and she stood on wobbly legs as headlights came around the corner. A moment later, two big, black SUVs were pulling up in the loading area of the supermarket where she and Jeffrey had been waiting.

Tension immediately filled her limbs.

What if it wasn't Bravo Team?

Her good hand clenched around the wrist of her bad hand almost to the point of pain. She knew it had to be Sebastian's team even as fear that it wasn't, that it was some of Arthur Gomez's men, had nausea churning in her stomach.

Then the car doors opened, and she saw Tank. Then Panther, Trick, and Scorpion also filed out, and relief literally took the wind out of her sails, and the next thing she knew she was falling.

Expecting to land on the concrete, she was surprised when instead a pair of arms caught her. Somehow Tank had closed the distance between them before she hit the ground, scooping her up into his arms.

"Who's he?" Trick asked in a menacing voice.

Looking to see who he was pointing at, she saw it was Jeffrey. "He's the delivery van driver." On the phone earlier, all she'd said was that Sebastian needed them and told them where she was.

"Where's Rock?" Panther asked.

Cracks in her composure had everything around her going blurry as tears filled her eyes. "He's not here."

"What happened, sweetheart?" Tank asked as he carried her over to the back of one of the SUVs and set her down on the back seat.

What happened?

Such a simple question and yet the answer seemed much too big to give in any kind of concise way, and they didn't have time to waste.

Gripping Tank's wrist, she used it as leverage to pull herself forward a bit then reach for the seatbelt. "We have to go. Sebastian needs you."

Instead of jumping right into the driver's seat and taking off like she had expected him to, Tank gently took the seatbelt from her hand before she could buckle it. Not letting her go, he kept his hand on hers, offering her strength she so badly needed right now.

"We can't just go running off without knowing what we're running into. I know you're scared, I know you're worried, but I need you to hold it together a little longer. Can you do that for me?" Tank asked.

Drawing in a deep breath, she willed herself to calm. If she could handle everything else she had been through, she could hold it together for a little longer.

Anything for Sebastian.

Blinking away the tears, she nodded.

"You're hurt." Tank nodded at the arm still cradled to her chest. "Can I take a look?"

Pain throbbed in her hand at just the thought of letting anyone touch it. Protectively, she tucked it closer and shook her head. "It's broken, but I'm safe. Sebastian isn't." Leaving him behind hurt so badly, and the desperation to get to him before it was too late smothered her.

"It was Arthur Gomez?" Panther asked, standing behind Tank, Scorpion and Trick were there too, forming a protective little circle around her, and Ariel felt the noose of fear locked around her neck loosen a little.

She wasn't alone anymore.

Sebastian's team would do whatever it took to rescue him.

It was almost over.

"Yes. He wants me to close Delilah's case. Thought that he could use threatening Sebastian to make me do it. But ..." her voice wavered, "Sebastian was only there because he wouldn't leave me behind. He ... he insisted they bring him too."

"Course he did," Tank said like anything else wouldn't have been an option. "He loves you more than anything else in the entire world. We always knew that the woman he was pining over was his soulmate, the only woman he wanted. Not anything he wouldn't do for you."

"I know, but ... I don't want him to die because of me." She had barely survived Kayla's death and stopped letting anyone in because it hurt too much to lose the people you loved, either to death or them pushing you away. It had come at the worst time of her life, when she had more on her plate than she could handle, and yet Sebastian's reappearance had come when she needed it the most.

Without him she would be lost.

"We're not going to let him die." Scorpion said it with such complete and utter confidence like it was already a foregone conclusion.

A little of his confidence rubbed off on her. "Mr. Dale knows where we were. I think it must have been one of Arthur's houses, but it wasn't where he lived before because I did a home visit to talk to Delilah. I don't know how he got onto your compound, or how he even knew I was there. Sebastian hadn't been part of my life in fifteen years."

"They parachuted in," Panther told her. "And they must have tagged you."

"Tagged me?"

"With a tracking chip. They must tag their merchandise so they can keep track of it. That's how he knew where you were, he simply followed the GPS coordinates," Panther explained. "We were trying to hack into the system, get a lock on your tag, so we could find where you were, but so far I hadn't been able to do it."

Ariel felt sick. It was like she was an animal, or a cell phone, not a human being. "I have a GPS tracking device in me?"

"We'll get it removed at the hospital when you get your hand attended to," Tank assured her.

"Hospital? No!" There was no way she was being sent off to the hospital while Sebastian was putting his life on the line for her.

"Need to get that hand attended to, Ariel," Tank reminded her like she wasn't in constant agony from the shattered hand. "It's going to need surgery. You're weak and shaky. I'm guessing you haven't eaten or had anything to drink since you were taken." As if to emphasize his point, he pulled out a bottle of water, uncapped it, but instead of handing it to her he held it to her lips.

Refusing on principle since she did have one working hand crossed her mind, but she was too thirsty to care and took several long gulps.

"I know you love Rock, and I know you want him safe, but we'll get him back to you. I promise," Tank said gently.

She appreciated the promise since there was no way they could possibly know whether Sebastian was even still alive.

"You did great. Amazing. Got out, got help, called us. You did your part, now let us do ours." Tank spoke to her with a brotherly tone, and it warmed her even as it irritated her. Ariel had always wanted siblings, a big brother in particular, and now she had four of them standing around her, ready and willing to go and do whatever it took to get the man she loved back.

But it didn't change her mind.

"I'm going," she said firmly.

"Rock'll kill us if we let anything happen to you," Trick said.

"Then don't let anything happen to me."

"We're going to have to bandage your hand first, and we don't have the good drugs the hospital will have," Scorpion warned her.

She merely huffed a laugh. "I can take it. I pulled the damn thing through a handcuff to get free." All four guys winced in sympathy, and she beamed in pride. She had been a victim long enough. No more. She'd killed thug man at Sebastian's cabin, and she'd gotten herself free and out of the house. She was no weak woman who had to be tucked away safely. "What else have you got? Because the more time you waste trying to convince me not to do what I've already made up my mind to do is time the man I love might not have."

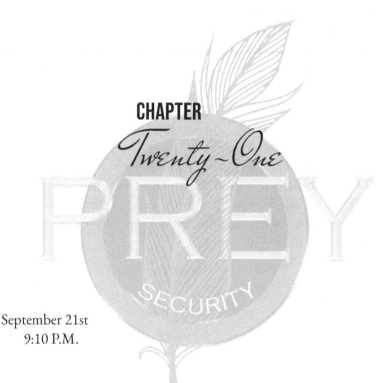

CHAPTER
Twenty~One

September 21st
   9:10 P.M.

This wasn't so much fun anymore.

Arthur was getting annoyed.

Actually, he was well past annoyed. Definitely had left that emotion behind a long time ago, and was well and truly in the utterly furious, rage-filled zone now.

Who did this man think he was?

Just because you worked for Prey, it didn't mean you were better than everybody else. Although his experience with the firm had showed him that they did in fact seem to think they were in a class of their own.

From time to time, he'd had to work with the firm. Usually, it was because they had somehow been involved with helping the victim or on the odd occasion had been the ones to bring into custody the man he was defending. Taking their statements was easy enough, they gave detailed reports, were calm and collected, and never wavered in their stories. But that was half the problem when you put them on the stand.

They were painted as these virtuous, valiant warriors of justice, who only did good and saved the innocent. While Arthur didn't argue with the fact they did do good, and did save the innocent, it was hell trying to tear them apart on the stand to get his clients off.

Thankfully, Prey didn't work often within the traditional justice system so he hadn't had too many encounters with them.

Not that it mattered.

The man currently standing before him had become a scapegoat for everything a young Arthur had been jealous of, had wanted for himself, and everything that he had worked hard to become as an adult.

This man had the power to ruin everything, and there was no way he was going to let that happen.

Only he was starting to doubt his abilities to get the job done.

For years now he had been the one in control. His wife had been a petite and timid little thing who wouldn't say boo to a mouse. His daughters were young and his to do with as he wished. Punishments had been dealt out any time they disobeyed. His clients depended on him to keep them out of prison, so they were only too willing to do whatever he told them to. His bodyguards—which he surreptitiously had to protect himself should any vigilante family member of the victims decide to take their anger out on him—were his employees, they followed his orders without question.

But this man didn't seem to care about anything.

Not his own pain, not his own life. Bribing him with money hadn't worked, threatening him with bodily harm hadn't worked, offering him a trade—his life for the woman's—hadn't worked.

Nothing was working.

And it made him furious.

Stomping his foot, he glowered at the man standing calmly before him. Amusement sparked in the man's gray eyes and it only added fuel to the fire of rage burning brightly inside him.

How dare he.

Who did he think he was?

There was no man in Ariel Emerson's life. Arthur knew that because when the woman had first been assigned the case and spoken with his daughter, he had used his resources to dig into her life and find something that could be used against her, something he could threaten her with to get her to back off.

Only there had been nothing.

Nothing and no one.

No one he could threaten to acquire her cooperation, nothing he could use to blackmail her. She had parents, but they didn't appear to be close, she had no friends, except this one woman who she worked with, but it seemed they had only grown close in the weeks before he had Ariel taken care of.

"I don't know who you are or where you came from, but this great love story you and Ms. Emerson are selling, I'm not buying," he growled.

The man merely shrugged.

Hissing in an annoyed breath, he tried to rein in his temper. He wasn't his parents, he was better than them. He was smart and logical. Everybody had a weakness, all he had to do was find this man's and then exploit it.

"You two aren't really lovebirds, you were just playing me, trying to throw me off my game. If you were really in love with her, I would have found you when I had my people check her out."

Another shrug.

Looking closely at the man, Arthur's eyes narrowed. There was something vaguely familiar about him. The dive into Ariel Emerson's life he had ordered had been a deep one, going all the way back to her teenage years. He knew about the car crash that had killed her friend, but the investigation had been thorough, there had been no way to try to pin it on her. There had been a boy involved in the crash and in some apparent bullying of teenage Ariel after the accident.

This man looked like ...

Arthur laughed. "I know who you are. You're Sebastian Rockman. You and Ariel were friends in school. You aren't in love with her, you haven't had anything to do with her since graduating. You're here now out of guilt because of some accusations you threw at her after the death of Kayla Morrow."

If he'd been expecting a rise out of Sebastian, he didn't get one. Just steady gray eyes watching his every move.

Guilt could be a powerful motivator. Perhaps he'd been going about this all wrong. If this man felt guilty for tormenting a girl who had once been a friend, he really might be prepared to do whatever it took—including giving his own life—to protect Ariel. She was somewhere in this house, and while he had men searching, they were yet to find her. Time was running out. There was every chance he could be considered a suspect in her disappearance, he had been questioned last time, but he'd dotted all his Is and crossed all his Ts.

He needed this over. Needed Sebastian Rockman dead, his body disposed of. Needed Ariel Emerson sold and out of this house.

A faster way to get Sebastian to give up Ariel's location was to use something against him. Since bribery, blackmail, and threats of pain were out as useful tools maybe he could use something else.

Someone else.

Prey operatives were nothing if not defenders of the innocent. What was more innocent than a small child?

"Get Delilah," he ordered.

For the first time a flicker of something other than control lit in the gray eyes that had been watching him so steadily.

Perfect.

A crack.

One crack was all you needed. It was all it took to bring an entire building crumbling down.

Only it wasn't going to be his life that crumbled. He had worked too hard, too carefully, to let that happen. The life of addiction and poverty was behind him. He had everything he had ever wanted. Money, power, and prestige, no one was going to take that from him.

"Maybe you're willing to accept pain to protect your old friend, but are you willing to watch me inflict pain on a child to keep Ariel's location secret?"

There was clear conflict in the man's eyes now. He didn't want to give up where Ariel had squirreled herself away, but neither did he want to watch a little girl be harmed because he kept silent.

Everybody had a weakness, and he'd just found Sebastian Rockman's.

Unlike him, not everybody exploited weaknesses. He had to, it was a huge part of how he was so successful at getting his clients off for crimes it was more than obvious they had committed. But all it took was one person to see a victim as something other than a victim, to see a so-called expert as not quite the expert they promoted themselves to be.

One crack changed everything.

And tonight, it was going to change it to his favor.

"Delilah, on your knees," he ordered as one of his men marched his daughter into the room. There were no paternal feelings as he looked at the trembling child. All he saw was a girl who had tried to destroy him, that made her an enemy. Whatever happened to her she had brought it upon herself.

Tears streaming down dirty cheeks, the little girl knew better than to disobey. Although she wasn't as fiery as her sister had been, the child had enough spunk that it needed to be dealt with, and promptly. There was no way he could make this girl disappear like he had Cordelia. Which meant he was going to have to make sure she never presented herself as a threat again.

"Lie down," he prompted once the girl was on her knees before him. With barely a hesitation, the child stretched out on her stomach. Lifting a foot, he held it above the child's left arm. "She's a tiny little thing, isn't she? Wouldn't take much to snap those young bones of hers. There's plenty of them. Fingers, hands, wrists, arms, legs, knees, ankles, feet. You prepared to stand there, listening to her screams of pain, and keep quiet? Is that really what that do-gooder social worker would want?"

The sigh of defeat Sebastian Rockman gave was everything.

He'd done it.

He'd won.

Cracked the man, found and exploited his weakness, and now he was going to get Ariel's location. Arthur knew it before Sebastian even parted his lips.

"It's too late. Ariel is gone. She went out the window and into the back of the delivery van. By now I hope and pray she's a long way from here and somewhere safe."

The words stopped him short, froze him, and turned the rage inside him into something that didn't even have a name. It was too strong, too all-consuming.

Everything he had worked so hard for had just come crashing down around him.

A howl of rage fell from his lips.

CHAPTER
Twenty-Two

September 21st
9:24 P.M.

Rock prayed he had done the right thing.

It had been almost two hours since Ariel had gone out the window and into the delivery van. The van wouldn't be traveling all that far from its home base, so there was every chance she had gotten herself to safety and called his team. If the driver had been loyal to Arthur, then the man would have turned her in already, and Gomez wouldn't be standing before him threatening to hurt his own daughter just to find out where Ariel was hiding.

Sooner or later, Gomez would have learned Ariel wasn't here anyway, so he didn't think he had put his woman in any extra danger.

Whatever happened to him, he was at peace with.

So long as Ariel was safe that was all he cared about.

By now, she should be safely tucked up in a hospital bed. There was no way her hand wasn't going to need surgery, and while he wished he could be there with her while she waited, he knew that Tank would have called in Tillie to sit with her while his team came looking for him.

Of course, he hoped they made it in time.

Being at peace with whatever happened wasn't the same thing as wanting to die to protect Ariel.

On the contrary, he wanted to live and have the life they would have shared if he hadn't ruined things all those years ago.

Knowing Ariel was warm, likely out of pain now, and somewhere Arthur Gomez couldn't get to her made it easy to keep his cool while Arthur threatened, bribed, and stomped his feet like a tantrum-throwing toddler. It was quite amusing and definitely pathetic to see a grown man—a respected defense attorney—behave like a spoiled brat.

The howl that fell from Gomez's lips when he learned that his search of the house had been in vain and Ariel was no longer on the grounds was well worth whatever was coming next.

Bullets.

That was what was coming next.

While Arthur had initially backed away from his plan, likely the logistics of cleaning blood and DNA evidence off his floors had been quite the deterrent, Rock had no doubts the man was more than ready to follow through now.

"How dare you," Arthur raged, turning his back on Delilah, who remained where she was, to storm toward Rock. "You've ruined everything. Do you know how hard I had to work to build this life? I came from nothing. Nothing! Mean alcoholic father, nasty drug-addicted mother, poverty, abuse, hunger, cold, that's how I grew up. But I got out of the life. I made something of myself. And now you've taken it all away!"

If Arthur expected to get some sympathy, he wasn't going to find any.

While there was definite sympathy for the child Arthur Gomez had been back then, there was none for the man who stood before him now. It took guts to work your way out of nothing, and on the surface, Gomez had done a good job. It took a lot of hard work and dedication to become a lawyer, and he worked for one of the biggest defense firms in the city. He had money, a nice house, and a lavish lifestyle, and yet, underneath it all, he was no better than the parents he had left behind.

A bully, an angry man who used whatever power he had to hurt those smaller and weaker than himself.

The position Arthur found himself in now was of his own making.

It could have been enough to have a good job, a nice house, plenty of money, a pretty wife, and two beautiful children. But while you could leave your past behind, you couldn't really ever outrun it. It was inside you, part of you, and while Arthur's plan had probably been to escape so he never became his parents, he had in fact turned into them. Abusing his own children to cater to his own needs and desires, using them, hurting them, and putting himself above them.

Now it was over.

Ariel would tell the world who had abducted her, sold her, and come after her a second time, and there was no defense lawyer in the world who could get Arthur Gomez off on the charges that would be coming his way.

"Kill him," Arthur snarled, his face contorted into an expression of fury. "Make sure it's painful. And slow. Kill the girl, too, it's too much effort to bring her along with us. I have to go and pack, if the woman got away then it won't be long before the cops get here. I need to be gone before they do." Gomez paused, his fury turning into a smug smile. "You think you've won but you haven't. I'll be long gone before the cops get here. Out of the country, heading to one that doesn't have an extradition treaty. I have plenty of money in accounts no one will ever find. More than enough to pay to have your girlfriend taken care of. I might have lost this life that I built, but I haven't lost everything."

Just as Arthur was turning away they all heard it.

Gunshots.

Rock grinned.

Back up had finally arrived.

Unable to resist their natural instincts to turn toward a sound, Rock used the momentary distraction of the guards holding their weapons on him and dropped to his knees, rolling away from them and out of the immediate line of fire.

It was Arthur who noticed him first. "Get him. I want him dead. Even if it has to be fast."

Before anyone could fire at him, Rock kicked out, overbalanced, and knocked down the closest guard.

The man fell hard, and as soon as he hit the ground, Rock was on him, wrenching the weapon from his hand, the crack as he broke the man's wrist audible to everyone within a couple of feet radius.

More shots were fired downstairs, and once again Rock took advantage of the distraction to fire off a few rounds of his own. The men around him dropped. All dead with a single wound between their eyes.

"What's wrong with you?" Arthur yelled at the couple still left standing. "There's only one of him. I want him dead. I want them all dead."

The shrieked words were evidence of the man quickly devolving. No longer was he the cocky, arrogant lawyer who thought he was the one with all the power and control that had been standing here in the hall just moments ago. Now he was just another panicked criminal ready to lash out and do whatever it took to get away.

But there would be no getting away.

Figures were moving up the stairs, and Rock recognized each and every one of them.

His team was here.

It was over, or at least as good as over.

"Don't make this any harder on yourself, Gomez," he said as he stood slowly, his weapon pointed squarely at the man who had caused so much pain and devastation to the woman he loved. Rock wanted nothing more than to fill the lawyer with bullet holes as though by the shedding of blood some of Ariel's pain could be erased.

"He's not worth it, Sebastian."

The softly spoken words caught him by surprise. She shouldn't be here. She was supposed to be safe in the hospital.

What had his team been thinking, letting Ariel come with them?

An evil grin spread over Arthur's face, and he lunged for one of the weapons that had been dropped by one of his guards when the man fell dead.

"Kill them all!" Arthur yelled at the remaining bodyguards.

All hell broke loose. The remaining men began to fire, his team returned it. Everybody was moving. Ariel sprinted across the hall toward

Delilah who was still lying right where she had been when her father threatened to hurt her.

Arthur noticed her, and immediately lifted his weapon, aiming squarely at Ariel's distracted form.

There was no hesitation on Rock's part.

He couldn't get off a clear shot that didn't risk hitting Ariel because she was now between him and Arthur Gomez.

Flinging his body toward them he prayed he got there in time.

Like in a movie, everything seemed to slow down. It was only in his imagination, but he could have sworn he heard the bullet whiz through the air as he collided with Ariel, knocking her down and pinning both her and Delilah Gomez beneath him.

Pain burned through his leg, but he had only one concern.

"Ariel? Are you hit?" he demanded.

"Only by you," came the muffled reply from beneath him.

"Gomez is down," Scorpion called out.

"All tangoes eliminated," Trick added.

Easing himself off Ariel, he grabbed her shoulders, yanked her up against him, and kissed her hard on the mouth, then began to run his hands all over her body in search of a wound. Although she yelped in pain when he jostled her broken hand, there were no injuries that he could find.

She was okay.

"You're not hit," he said. Relief overcame him and he suddenly felt lightheaded, the room spinning around him.

"But you are!" Ariel's panicked exclamation reminded him of the searing pain in his left thigh and he looked down to see blood spilling everywhere.

Exhaustion made everything fuzzy, and despite his best efforts not to, he swayed sideways, almost knocking Ariel over in the process.

"Help him, Sebastian is shot," she yelled, he assumed to his team, who were suddenly all around him.

"Take care of my girl," he mumbled. It was suddenly very hard to hold his head up, too much effort to keep his eyes open.

Rock slumped over. The last thing he remembered were Ariel's gentle hands on his face, the murmuring of her voice. It was soothing even though he couldn't make out the words.

They didn't matter.

Ariel was alive, Arthur Gomez was dead, and the woman he loved was no longer in danger.

Letting go, he allowed the darkness to claim him.

September 22nd
   12:18 A.M.

"What's going on?" she asked as a doctor came out of the room they'd rushed Sebastian into the second the ambulance arrived at the hospital.

Thankfully, they had allowed her to ride in the ambulance along with Sebastian. Ariel suspected it wasn't so much to be nice to her and more the fact that between her shattered hand and the exhaustion etched into her every feature, she probably didn't look a whole lot better than Sebastian did.

She knew he'd been shot.

Knew it wasn't good.

Had inferred from the flurry of activity after Sebastian passed out, first from his team and then from the EMTs when they showed up, that his condition was serious, but nobody would give her any details.

Bravo Team had followed in their vehicles and arrived at the hospital the same time the ambulance had. Although doctors had tried to usher her into her own room to be attended to, Ariel had refused. She wasn't doing anything until she knew that Sebastian was going to be all right.

He had to be all right.

There was no other option as far as she was concerned.

What would she do without him?

How would she cope, knowing that he had literally given his life for hers?

"You're Sebastian Rockman's family?" the doctor asked, looking mildly suspicious.

"She's his fiancée," Tank supplied.

While Ariel didn't feel good about the lie, she wasn't going to argue. Besides, she and Sebastian did love one another, and while they weren't ready to get engaged and married right this second, it was in their future.

Assuming they had a future.

"Is he okay?" she asked. In her limited medical knowledge, it hadn't looked like he was okay. There had been so much blood, it kept soaking through the bandages the paramedic kept wrapping around the wound. He'd been so pale, and after passing out he'd never woken up again. Before loading him into the ambulance, the EMTs had intubated him, they'd said it was just as a precaution, but she wasn't sure she believed them.

Was he dying?

Already dead?

"Bullet nicked an artery," the doctor said in that slow and patient voice people used when they had bad news to give and knew it wasn't going to be well received.

Ariel swayed.

She had enough medical knowledge to know that was bad.

The kind of bad you died from.

An arm wrapped around her waist, and she was steadied against a solid chest. Tank was at her back and the rest of his team stood around her. She might not be alone, but without Sebastian, she would always feel like she was.

Living these last fifteen years without him by her side had felt like living with a part of herself missing. How was she supposed to go on without it—without him—for the rest of her life?

"Wh-what does that m-mean?" she stammered, her voice wobbling right along with the rest of her body.

"It means we need to rush him right into surgery. If we can repair the damage to the artery then he should make a full recovery," the doctor said it like it was that simple. But repairing an artery had to be dangerous. There were no guarantees they would be successful.

"What are his chances?" Scorpion asked.

The doctor hesitated for a moment. "He's lost a lot of blood. We've already given him a couple of units. But the doctor that will be performing the surgery is top notch. One of the best anywhere in the world. They say she has magic fingers. If anyone can save Mr. Rockman's leg and his life it's Dr. Clover Ellis. Now, ma'am, I'd like to take a look at your hand."

It took a moment for Ariel to register that he was talking to her. His words kept running through her mind on a loop. Save his life and his leg. That's what the doctor had said.

Of course, it had occurred to her that Sebastian might die but she'd never thought of the possibility that he might lose his leg.

What if he lived but the limb couldn't be saved?

It would end his career at Prey. If that happened, he would lose a huge piece of himself. Would he resent her for that? Blame her? It seemed like something completely different to have to give up what you loved because of someone versus giving your life for them.

Sure, in the big picture dying was of course worse, but it was final. Living every day knowing she was responsible for costing him the job he obviously loved and was good at seemed worse somehow.

How could he not wind up resenting her for that?

"Ariel, honey, let the doctor look at your hand," Tank prompted when she didn't say anything.

Shaking her head, she pulled out of his hold and backed away.

No.

She couldn't handle strangers touching her right now. More than that, she didn't want anything to help her with her hand right now.

She needed the pain.

Deserved it.

Sebastian was lying on a hospital bed, about to have surgery, all because of her.

"No. I ... no ... just no," she said, shaking her head wildly. Space. She needed them to give her space.

The doctor's brow furrowed, but Trick stepped close and whispered a few words. Ariel couldn't hear what they were, nor did she care because she saw the door to the room where Sebastian was open, and a gurney was hurried out.

She rushed over to it, halting their path. "Can I just say goodbye?" she asked, afraid they were going to tell her no and to get out of their way. It wasn't that she wanted to slow them down, she knew he needed that surgery if he was going to survive, but this might be the last time she got to see him alive. Even though he was unconscious she needed him to know how much she loved him and how grateful she was to him for saving her life in so many ways.

Sympathetic blue eyes gave her a small onceover, and the woman she assumed was Dr. Ellis gave her an encouraging smile as she smoothed a stray lock of blonde hair that had escaped the pile on top of the doctor's head. "Course you can. I always say my patients heal quicker and better when they have a reminder of exactly what they're fighting for. You go ahead and remind your man why he needs to come back to you, sweetie."

Ariel nodded, then turned her attention to Sebastian. She wasn't used to seeing him like this, all still and helpless looking. Tears blurred her vision, but she leaned in and touched her lips to his forehead. "Thank you," she whispered. "For everything you've done for me. For never giving up on me. For loving me even when I didn't know it. I love you. Don't leave me. Please. I need you."

When she took a shaky step backward, Dr. Ellis gave her another encouraging smile, and squeezed her hand. "I've got your man. You take care of you, okay?"

With that, the woman walked off, rattling off instructions to the team with her and Ariel allowed herself a small amount of hope. Dr. Ellis seemed competent and caring, and the other doctor had said she was the best.

Sebastian needed the best.

Life couldn't be so cruel that after everything they had been through, both together and apart, that it would end like this.

So many shadows seemed to dance around her. Kayla's death, the words that Sebastian had thrown at her so cruelly that morning, fifteen years of separation, hatred and anger on her part, longing on his. Her abduction, the tortures she had endured, her fears, and the blame she had placed on herself. Those hours spent tied up in Arthur Gomez's house, knowing Sebastian had taken a bullet for her.

Fear, pain, and uncertainty.

It was all so overwhelming. It weighed down on her so heavily that her knees buckled. Again though, the guys seemed to know what was about to happen, and she was once again pressed up against a solid chest.

Only this time it was the chest of a stranger.

Looking over her shoulder, Ariel saw that the hospital hall was filled with people. Bravo Team of course, Piper and Arrow, a few people she recognized as being the Oswald siblings, and a whole bunch of people she had never seen before in her life.

Dazed, she looked up at the man behind her.

"Brick," he said by way of introduction. "I'm on Alpha Team with Arrow. Almost a year ago I was in your shoes. The woman I loved was fighting for her life, and I was so afraid I was going to lose her." His brown eyes shifted to a pretty woman standing at his side. "Skye lived, I never gave up hope, never gave up on her. We're all here for you, for Rock, to make sure you don't give up hope. He needs you."

Hope.

Sebastian had never given up hope that someway, someday he would find his way back to her and they would be together again. All these years he had been thinking of her, fitting her into his life even as she didn't know it. Building a house with her in mind, furnishing it the way she would have. The tattoos, the greenhouse with the butterflies, the way he had tried so hard to become a man he thought was worthy of her.

Never once had he given up on her.

Not when she had been snatched off the street in front of him, not when he'd spent weeks searching for her, found her, and never left her side since.

Ariel knew she owed it to him to never give up on him either.

No longer able to hold back her tears, she pressed her face to Brick's chest and sobbed. Surrounded by so many people who had pledged to be there for her despite not even knowing her, and yet feeling so very lost and alone.

CHAPTER
Twenty~Three

September 23rd
12:44 A.M.

Rock wished someone would stop the damn beeping.

Enough already.

The sound was going to drive him insane.

"Sebastian?" The tentative voice spoke his name with an uncertainty that struck deep into his heart, causing him pain, and rousing him from the state of semi-slumber he seemed to be stuck in.

Ariel's voice.

His woman needed him.

Opening his eyes seemed like a much harder task than it usually was, but somehow, he managed it. No surprise he found himself in a hospital room. The white walls were depressing in their bleakness whereas the white walls in his cabin at home offered a soothing sort of peace. There was the smell of antiseptic he hated, and the muffled sounds of a busy hospital in the background.

But it was the pale face hovering over him that he zeroed in on.

Red rimmed eyes looked down at him, glowing with a hope that seemed to be growing by the second.

"Are you awake? Really awake I mean?" she asked.

"I'm awake, Snow White," he croaked. Damn, he hated that fresh from surgery croak and the dry throat that accompanied it.

As though knowing exactly what he was thinking, Ariel leaned over, and a moment later a cup appeared. She held the straw to his lips, and he sucked down a couple of mouthfuls, already feeling stronger.

"You didn't get hit by the bullet, did you?" he asked. Although he could remember what had happened. Remembered throwing himself at Ariel and Delilah, the pain of the bullet plowing through his leg, and his frantically scanning Ariel for injuries after his team had confirmed there were no more active threats, he needed the reassurance of hearing her say that she was okay, unharmed.

"I didn't get hit. You took the bullet Arthur meant for me. Delilah is okay as well. In the hospital being treated for shock and in the care of social services. You didn't just save me, you saved her as well." The awe and admiration in her voice warmed him. For so long he had been working hard to become a man that she could be proud of, who would be worthy of her, and for the first time Rock felt like he was that man.

"Love you, sweetheart." There was a tiny hint of uncertainty in his words that he couldn't quite seem to hide—damn drugs. When Ariel had told him she loved him before it had been while they were both being held prisoner. She'd told him that it wasn't fear that had motivated her to say it, and that she meant those words, but he needed to hear them again now that the danger had passed.

"Oh, Sebastian, I love you too. So much." Like a damn had burst, Ariel began to sob. "I was so scared I was going to lose you. They said the bullet nicked an artery, they had to give you blood, and I think if anyone else but Dr. Ellis had performed the surgery you might not have made it. But you did. And Dr. Ellis said your leg is going to be just fine after some physical therapy. I almost cost you your leg and your life. You could have died. You could have lost your leg. Brick said I needed to keep hope, that you needed me to be strong for you. And Dr. Ellis said that when patients hear that someone needs them they do better, so I told you I needed you, told you I loved you, and asked you not to leave me and you didn't."

Tears filled his own eyes. Hearing how afraid for him Ariel had been hurt. How had he even thought he needed to be reassured that she loved him?

He could see her love, feel it.

It was in the anguish of her tone, the tears she shed, the dark circles of exhaustion under her eyes.

"Never going to leave you again, Ariel," he said seriously. He had waited too long for this second chance, there was no way he was going to mess it up.

"Good, because I don't want you to." Although she was still crying, a small smile curled up the corners of her lips. "Besides, you're going to need some help getting around for a while until your leg heals."

"Look who's talking. You're going to need help while your hand ..." He trailed off when he looked at her hand and saw it was in the same simple bandage he'd noted when he was desperately searching her body for gunshot wounds.

Reality sunk in slowly thanks to the meds dripping into the back of his hand.

She hadn't had it treated.

She'd been sitting by his bedside for who knows how long with an untreated broken hand that absolutely would require surgery to fix.

The magnitude of the sacrifice she had made to be there for him stole his breath.

"You didn't have your hand treated," he said, voice strained.

Red stained her cheeks. "I told them I couldn't leave you. I couldn't bear it if the worst happened and you died while I wasn't here. I know your team would have been here, but it's not the same, you would have been alone. Without me. I ... couldn't."

"Ariel." The word felt torn from his soul, and he wasn't sure if he was thanking her for her sacrifice, telling her he loved her, or reprimanding her for putting herself in pain for his benefit.

"I love you and I'm not sorry I waited," she said defiantly, and she looked so much like the stubborn old Ariel he used to know that he barked out a laugh.

"Love you, too, but don't you ever do something so stupid again."

"It's not stupid to stay with the person you love while they're fighting for their life." When he arched a brow, her expression turned guilty. "Dr. Ellis did tell me I was being crazy. And all the guys, and their wives, did kind of agree with her."

"They're not wrong, sweetheart."

"I don't care. I'm glad I stayed with you. I wanted to be here when you woke up."

"Have you at least had something to eat?" She was wearing scrubs, so he at least knew someone had forced her to change her clothes, but from the knotty ponytail he knew she hadn't gone so far as having a shower.

"Yeah, Tillie and all the wives made sure I ate. I didn't want to but they bullied me into it." From her expression she didn't seem to mind being bullied into eating in the least.

"Wives?" he asked.

"Yeah, Alpha Team and all their wives are out there. Eagle and Olivia and their family too. I think Eagle said Charlie Team were out on a mission so they couldn't be here, and Delta team are working something, so they've been in and out. Plus, there were some West Coast teams that kept calling to check on you. You have a whole big family of people out there who love you so much."

"And a woman in here who loves me more than I deserve." There would never be enough words or actions to make up for how he had hurt Ariel in the past, but he was going to treasure the love she had gifted him because it was more precious than he could ever hope to convey.

"No more talk of deserving, okay? You've proved to me that you are sincerely remorseful for those things you said to me, and that you love me and never stopped. This road we have ahead of us is going to be hard enough to walk as it is. I don't think we need to be picking up extra baggage and carrying it with us. Okay? Let's just leave the past where it is and do our best to make this second chance work out the way we both want it to."

"When did my girl get to be so wise?" he teased, amazed by her ability not only to forgive but to set aside old hurts and look forward instead of backward.

"I was always wise, you're just not as arrogant as you used to be," she teased back, and he got another glimpse of the old Ariel. The one who was still inside even if she was buried beneath pain and trauma. "And I like when you call me your girl." Her cheeks blushed the prettiest shade of pink.

"Good. Because you know what being my girl means, don't you?"

"Umm ... no," she said hesitantly.

"It means you are in big trouble for not getting your hand attended to right away. Not only have you been in pain, but you've likely caused yourself more damage because the bones in your hand are going to be starting to heal in all the wrong places, making it that much more work for the surgeon, and your recovery that much harder."

"I don't care, Sebastian. There is no worse pain in the world than fearing the other half of your heart is going to die."

"Damn, you know how to take the wind out of my sails, honey. You're off the hook. They," he said, gesturing at the door, on the other side of which he knew was his Prey family, "on the other hand, are not. You guys get in here," he yelled, "and you better have a hell of an excuse as to why you didn't force my woman to go and get the surgery she needs."

∾

November 12th
5:23 P.M.

"Hhmmff," Ariel huffed out an irritated breath when she reached for the brush on the dresser with her bad hand and missed. The amount of care she had taken, and the concentration it required, just to pick up a brush was crazy.

It had been two months since Sebastian and his team first rescued her from the man who had bought her, seven weeks since she'd had the first surgery on her hand, and it had been a long and bumpy road. While

Sebastian had healed quickly, jumped right into his PT, and now walked without a noticeable limp unless he'd really overdone it that day, her recovery hadn't gone quite as smoothly.

As predicted, the delay in surgery first because she'd still been chained up, and then because she had refused treatment until she knew Sebastian was going to be all right, had compounded the problem. There had been over a dozen broken bones, and they had started to heal in odd places. They had to be rebroken and screwed into place, and by the time the first three surgeries were complete, she'd spent two weeks in the hospital, well over a week longer than Sebastian who had been the one to almost die.

Like she'd told him that day, she didn't regret her decision, and still didn't. She'd been where she needed to be, and the truth was, her hand had been so badly broken it was never going to heal completely and be back to what it had been before whether she had surgery immediately following the injury or a couple of days later.

Sebastian had stayed by her side, sleeping in a chair beside her bed with no care for his healing leg. Sometimes, she would convince him to sleep on the hospital bed with her, easier to do when nightmares came for her in her sleep.

There had been a lot of nightmares on both their sides, a lot of trauma to be unpacked. The time in the hospital turned out to be a good thing because it gave her and Sebastian a lot of time together to talk and get to know each other again. Also gave her plenty of time to spend with Piper unpacking her ordeal and talking it through a bit at a time.

There was still one thing she had yet to tell anyone.

Although since they had been living together for the last five weeks, she was surprised Sebastian hadn't already figured it out and asked her about it.

"You okay?" Sebastian asked, coming up behind her and scooping up the brush.

"Yeah, just annoying that this stupid hand doesn't seem to want to cooperate with my brain the way it's supposed to." Time. Ariel knew it would take time, and lots of physical therapy, but not regretting her decision and getting annoyed at the slow progress were two different things.

"I'd say I told you so, but given your decision was to stay by my side that would seem mean of me," he teased as he pulled her hair from its tie and began to run the brush through it.

How could he not notice?

He was touching her hair, it had to be obvious that she hadn't washed it in months. There was no way to wash hair with wet wipes and Ariel still hadn't managed to crack her fear of water.

Every day she ached to tell someone, but every time she tried to get up the courage to tell Sebastian or Piper, she ended up backing out. It all sounded so stupid. So the man who had bought her had an obsession with ice, so what? Didn't meant that she should be so terrified of getting wet that it paralyzed her.

"Sebastian?"

"Yeah, baby?"

"I'm afraid to get wet," she blurted out.

Instead of the shock she had been expecting, or the reassurances that she had nothing to be afraid of, Sebastian merely set the brush down, turned her to face him, and engulfed her in a hug. "Thank you for telling me," he said and then touched a kiss to her temple.

"You knew?"

"Figured out something was going on a while back, although I'll admit I should have put it together sooner. Can you articulate exactly what it is that scares you?"

A weight off her chest now that she'd finally said it out loud, Ariel shook her head. "I've tried. But every time I go to turn the tap on, I freeze. It's like I'm back in that cold little room, lying on a block of ice, completely aware, prepared, and yet unprepared for what he's going to do to me."

"Will you let me face this fear together with you?"

His eyes were so serious, and she knew that if she said this was something she had to tackle on her own that he wouldn't push or hold it against her.

But she wasn't on her own.

Prey had gone out of their way to show her that these last several weeks. Someone was always dropping off meals, driving her or Sebastian to appointments, making sure the cabin was cleaned and stocked with food.

And this man holding her so tenderly had been there through all of it, never wavering in his support.

"Together," she said softly.

After dropping a quick kiss to her lips, he took her hand and guided her into the bathroom. "Bath or shower?"

In the bath the water would surround her, at least in the shower it would only be bouncing off her and then going right down the drain. "Shower."

Leaving her only long enough to turn on the faucet in the huge glass and tile walk-in shower, Sebastian then helped her ease her arm through the sleeve of her hoodie, and remove her leggings. There was no embarrassment being naked before him, he loved her, he would never hurt her or take advantage of her. She was safe here.

Having graduated out of a cast, nothing stopped her getting in the shower except her own fears.

They almost won out.

If a fully clothed Sebastian hadn't stepped under the spray first, she very well might have.

But his presence coaxed her in, and the next thing she knew, water drummed down upon her from the large rainwater showerhead.

Her body tensed, but instead of panic, when Sebastian poured some of her shampoo into the palm of his hand and turned her so his big body was behind her, close enough she could feel him, all she felt was his love.

It was too big, too powerful, too strong to let anything else in.

Big hands began to work the shampoo into her dirty locks, and she moaned in delight as they massaged her scalp.

This wasn't the hell she had been expecting, instead, thanks to the presence of this wonderful man, it was heaven.

Sebastian worked two more rounds of shampoo through her hair, rinsing it out carefully each time, making sure not to get the soapy suds in her eyes. Then he moved onto the conditioner. Using a generous amount, he covered every inch of her long locks.

Moving her slightly so she was mostly out of the spray, he picked up a comb and began the arduous task of working out the dozens of knots. He was so very gentle, so careful not to tug on her hair and make her scalp sting, that it was her eyes instead that stung with tears.

How very glad she was that he hadn't given up on her. That he was here now, showing her with every touch, every word, every ounce of restraint she knew he used as they slept in the same bed together every night, that he loved and respected her.

When her long hair was knot-free, he moved her back under the spray and washed the conditioner out. Then he grabbed a loofah and the bodywash and proceeded to clean her body. He started at the top, touching kisses to her forehead, her cheeks, and the tip of her nose as he followed the kisses with the loofah. Her neck was next, and then her arms. When he washed her broken hand, his touch was featherlight, and instead of bringing pain it just brought more warmth.

His touch shook a little when he moved onto her chest, and while she couldn't say it was clinical when he washed her breasts, she knew he was doing everything in his power not to make her feel like he expected something from her.

It was that exact attitude that had the warmth inside her turning into heat and pooling low in her stomach and between her legs.

Piper had told her in one of their many talks that there was no time-line in recovering from rape. That there was no too soon and no too long, that she and she alone would know when she was ready to take that step.

Sebastian knelt before her, and picked up one foot. Placing her good hand on his shoulder for balance, he rested her foot on his thigh and began to wash her leg.

That was when she knew.

She was ready.

She wanted him to touch her, wanted to feel normal, and wanted to share this with the man she loved who she knew loved her more than anything in return.

His fingers trailed lightly up her leg, brushing across her center as he ran the loofah up her inner thigh. Each caress of his fingers as they cleaned her skin, stoked the fire inside her, and she knew he wasn't even trying to turn her on. He was just taking care of her and that was the hottest thing of all.

Finished with one leg, he moved on to the other, but when he was done and moved to stand, Ariel pressed on his shoulders.

"Please," she whimpered.

Sebastian went completely still. "Going to have to be extremely explicit with me, sweetheart. Tell me exactly what you're asking for."

"You."

"Need more than that."

"I want you. I want to feel you inside me. I want to know that we're joined together forever."

His large hands moved until they curled around her backside. Ariel waited for panic to hit as she remembered the last time someone had touched her there, but it didn't come. All she felt was a throbbing inside her, a desperation for Sebastian's touch.

"You tell me to stop and I'll stop," he said as he stayed right where he was on his knees, showing her without saying anything that he was giving her the power, keeping himself beneath her.

"Okay," she said breathily as he nudged her legs apart and buried his head between them.

Water poured down upon them, and Ariel didn't think there was a sexier sight in the world than the dark head of the man she loved buried between her spread legs.

That first touch of his tongue was pure heaven.

The fingers on her bottom kneaded gently as he ate at her with a desperation that echoed what was inside her. His tongue seemed to be everywhere at once, flicking against her needy little bud, swiping along her center, spearing inside her.

Dizziness—the good kind—assailed her as sensations built, crescendoing until they were almost more than she could bear before exploding inside her with a ferocity that had her shaking and crying.

"I love you, I love you, I love you," she murmured over and over again as he kissed his way up her stomach, touching the lightest of kisses to her erect little nipples.

"Thank you for trusting me, sweetheart," Sebastian said when he was standing before her.

"Thank you for loving me."

His lips quirked up. "Not a hardship."

He hadn't pressed for more. He hadn't asked her to attend to the bulge in his jeans or even removed his clothing. Again, she was reminded how absolutely and completely safe with him she was.

That was why it was easy to unbutton his shirt, not exactly an easy task one-handed. "You sure?" he asked.

Her eyes landed on the tattoos of their birthdates and the butterfly that sat beneath. It was this tattoo that had clued Tillie in on the fact that Sebastian was the man Ariel had told her about. Standing on tiptoes, she pressed a kiss to the butterfly tattoo.

"Positive."

Brushing away her hand, Sebastian took over the job of unbuttoning, so she unzipped his jeans instead and shoved them down his legs along with his boxers.

His erection sprung free. Since they were standing close it touched her belly, as though reaching out for her, and again she waited for a moment of panic but it didn't come.

Instead, there was more heat pooling inside her, and when he lifted her and wrapped her legs around his waist, his length sliding inside her as though that were absolutely where it was meant to be, it was peace that filled her.

Sebastian's thrusts were slow, and while he took her weight with one hand his other found her bundle of nerves, working it as he moved in and out of her.

Pleasure built slowly this time, but when it reached its peak, the orgasm was more powerful because Sebastian came a moment after she did, filling her with his love and his essence. Birth control meant she wasn't getting pregnant today, but already the thought of Sebastian's baby growing inside her made her feel all giddy with excitement.

Just as slowly as it had built the pleasure began to ebb, leaving her all tingly and sated. Happy. Loved and protected. Safe and secure.

"Thank you for never giving up on me," she whispered against his lips.

"Never have to thank me for that. I'm yours, always have been."

"And I'm yours." That meant she could never be possessed by the ordeal she had lived through because Sebastian owned her heart, and he wouldn't let anyone else take it. "Love you so much it almost hurts."

"True love always does. That's why it's the stuff of fairytales. Love you more than you will ever know, my sweet, beautiful, brave, strong Snow White."

CHAPTER

Twenty~Four

November 12th
7:07 P.M.

Life couldn't get any better than this.

Rock was certain of it as he sat with Ariel curled up on his lap. They were sitting on the white couch that looked even better with her collection of throw pillows scattered across it. The TV was on although both of them were looking out the window at the view rather than at the screen. Dinner was done and the dishwasher loaded, there was nothing else to do for the day but enjoy one another.

Even though he was sure life couldn't get better, each day surprised him with another new and special moment.

Today was no exception.

Two wonderful gifts had been given to him today.

The first was Ariel finally trusting him enough to share one of her fears with him. He had suspected for a while now that Ariel had some hang up with water. Since they were living together, it was a bit of a giveaway that they were going through wet wipes at an ever-increasing pace and that her hair never got any cleaner.

As much as he'd wanted to know what her issue was, he hadn't wanted to push, knowing it would feel so much better when she came to him herself rather than him pushing her into it. He'd talked through his decision with Piper and given Ariel's lack of control over her own life when she'd been kidnapped and sold, they had both decided to give her space. She knew he was there for her—Piper too—and once he'd earned her trust enough she would open up.

Finally, today she had.

The pressure to respond the way she needed him to had been immense. If he messed it up, she wouldn't open up again for a while. Trusting his instincts had worked, and not only had he given her what she needed, but she'd also given him another gift.

It wasn't just sex. It was knowing that even after being raped she trusted him with her body, knew he would never betray that gift, and he wasn't ashamed to say he'd shed a few tears in the shower after he'd come inside her.

Now as he cradled her in the protective bubble of his arms, one hand absently stroking her now clean and shiny hair, he needed to be sure.

"You don't regret what happened earlier, do you?"

Ariel lifted her head from his shoulder. "You mean what we did in the shower?"

He nodded. Over the last several weeks they had both gotten used to embarrassing conversations. She'd told him some of the things that had been done to her while she was being trained and after she'd been bought. He had talked about some of the things he'd seen and done, and that had been done to him, while he'd been serving in the military and with Prey.

But this took embarrassing conversation to another level.

"No, not at all." Ariel paled. "Why? Do you?"

Instead of answering with words, he framed her face with his hands and kissed her, pouring everything he felt for her into the kiss. "Seem like I regretted it?"

Her color returned. "No. Why did you ask? Do you feel like you pressured me?"

"Not exactly. It was just amazing and ..."

"You want to know if it was as amazing for me too?"

"Kind of," he said sheepishly, knowing it sounded like he wanted his ego stroked, but that wasn't it. He just had to know that she was okay with it. Whether it was a one-off and it would be a while before she was ready again or it became part of their day to day routines, it didn't matter, all that mattered to him was Ariel's trust, and he worried constantly that he was going to do something to break it.

Her expression turned serious. "Sebastian, I think we need to talk."

That was never good. "Okay," he said slowly.

"Nothing bad," she added. "I think you need to stop seeing me as Ariel the girl you hurt and Ariel the victim. I'm more than that. I'm more than the girl you threw thoughtless words at when we were in high school, and I'm more than just a victim of sex trafficking. You've gotten to know me over the past few weeks, you know who I am, please see me as that person. Not saying that what happened to me isn't a big part of my life right now, I still have a lot of healing to do, and a long way to go to be the person I was, but I don't want it to define me. I was able to get some of my power back when I killed the thug man right upstairs, and when I ran to protect Delilah. It reminded me that I can be me again, that I don't always have to be victim Ariel. I want you to see me like that too."

There was a pleading look in her eyes, and Rock knew it was important to her that he not always think of her as the woman he'd found tied up in ropes in that cold dungeon. Because if she was only ever a victim to him, then their relationship would forever be lopsided because he would always be trying to fix her.

Framing her face again he kissed her harder, more passionately than he had moments ago. "You are always going to be just Ariel to me. So many parts to you. Part of you will always be the gangly little kid I first met, part of you will always be the girl I hurt, part of you will always be the woman I pined over for a decade and a half. You'll also be the amazing social worker you became, the woman who survived hell, who killed one of her tormentors, who got herself free, and who was willing to protect a little girl with her life. And you'll be the woman who hogs all the covers when we sleep, who has to start her day with a cup of peppermint tea no matter the season, who loves sitting here watching the moonlight over the forest, and who will want me to build a fire on a hot summer's day as much as she wants one in the winter."

Shifting her so that she straddled his legs, he smoothed a lock of hair off her cheek and tucked it behind her ear, letting his knuckles linger. She was finally his and he had no intention of letting her think he didn't love every single part of her.

"You're the woman I'm going to marry, the mother of my children whether we have biological kids, or adopt, or foster, or just have fur babies. You're the woman who is going to celebrate Christmases and Easters and birthdays with me, and who's going to grow old by my side. You're the only woman I've ever wanted and the only woman I will ever want."

Tear drenched eyes looked at him, a watery smile beneath. "What you just said right now, that's exactly what I want you to say for our vows."

"Ariel," he groaned. "I don't remember what I just said."

"Sure you do."

Rock laughed and it felt good to relax with his woman and just chill. She still had a long way to go, and a lot to work through, but she was making progress every day and he couldn't wait to see how life got even better tomorrow.

Before he could ask her if she wanted to go upstairs so he could have dessert, the code for the alarm went off.

Ariel stiffened, looking around in fright, ready to see men in black break in like they had the night they'd both been kidnapped.

"Only us," Tank yelled out before Rock could reassure Ariel.

She sagged in relief.

"First thing when these guys go, I'll show you what the different alarms mean," he promised.

"Aww, aren't you two cute," Trick teased as the guys walked into the living room.

"Don't you want to show us your disappearing trick?" Rock grumbled.

"See, cute," Trick said, his grin only growing.

"What do you guys want?" Since Ariel got out of the hospital and moved in here the guys had been giving them space, while also making sure they visited enough that Ariel knew they were thinking of her. They hadn't made plans for all the guys to come by at once, so he assumed this wasn't just a social call.

Immediately all the guys sobered.

"We got a lead," Axe informed him. "A sighting of Leonid Baranov's second in command on a boat a little way off the coast."

"The doctor cleared you to go back to work, but if you're not ready to leave yet, we understand," Tank added, casting a glance at Ariel.

"You should go," Ariel said immediately.

"Are you sure?" Leaving her was the last thing he wanted to do, but Beth was family, too, and they needed to get the target off her head.

"Remember that talk we just had about you not just seeing me as victim Ariel? I can do this, your team need you, and I'll be fine here. 'I'm safe, protected, and maybe Tillie can come over and we can have like a sleepover?" She cast a glance at Tank who immediately nodded.

"She'd love to," Tank said.

"Then I guess 'I'm in," Rock said. They'd taken down Arthur Gomez—along with a well-known trafficking ring—taking the target off Ariel's head. It was time to do the same for Beth.

Scorpion will risk everything to save the spoiled sister of an old friend in the third book in the action packed and emotionally charged Prey Security: Bravo Team series!

Brutal Scars (Prey Security: Bravo Team #3)

Also by Jane Blythe

Detective Parker Bell Series

A SECRET TO THE GRAVE

WINTER WONDERLAND

DEAD OR ALIVE

LITTLE GIRL LOST

FORGOTTEN

Count to Ten Series

ONE

TWO

THREE

FOUR

FIVE

SIX

BURNING SECRETS

SEVEN

EIGHT

NINE

TEN

Broken Gems Series

CRACKED SAPPHIRE

CRUSHED RUBY

FRACTURED DIAMOND

SHATTERED AMETHYST

SPLINTERED EMERALD

SALVAGING MARIGOLD

River's End Rescues Series

COCKY SAVIOR

SOME REGRETS ARE FOREVER

SOME FEARS CAN CONTROL YOU

SOME LIES WILL HAUNT YOU

SOME QUESTIONS HAVE NO ANSWERS

SOME TRUTH CAN BE DISTORTED

SOME TRUST CAN BE REBUILT

SOME MISTAKES ARE UNFORGIVABLE

Candella Sisters' Heroes Series

LITTLE DOLLS

LITTLE HEARTS

LITTLE BALLERINA

Storybook Murders Series

NURSERY RHYME KILLER

FAIRYTALE KILLER

FABLE KILLER

Saving SEALs Series

Prey Security Series

Prey Security: Alpha Team Series

Prey Security: Artemis Team Series

IVORY'S FIGHT

PEARL'S FIGHT

LACEY'S FIGHT

OPAL'S FIGHT

Prey Security: Bravo Team Series

VICIOUS SCARS

RUTHLESS SCARS

Christmas Romantic Suspense Series

CHRISTMAS HOSTAGE

CHRISTMAS CAPTIVE

CHRISTMAS VICTIM

YULETIDE PROTECTOR

YULETIDE GUARD

YULETIDE HERO

HOLIDAY GRIEF

Conquering Fear Series (Co-written with Amanda Siegrist)

DROWNING IN YOU

OUT OF THE DARKNESS

CLOSING IN

About the Author

USA Today bestselling author Jane Blythe writes action-packed romantic suspense and military romance featuring protective heroes and heroines who are survivors. One of Jane's most popular series includes Prey Security, part of Susan Stoker's OPERATION ALPHA world! Writing in that world alongside authors such as Janie Crouch and Riley Edwards has been a blast, and she looks forward to bringing more books to this genre, both within and outside of Stoker's world. When Jane isn't binge-reading she's counting down to Christmas and adding to her 200+ teddy bear collection!

To connect and keep up to date please visit any of the following

Made in the USA
Monee, IL
17 March 2024